AN AMISH SPRING

OTHER NOVELS BY THE AUTHORS

AMY CLIPSTON

THE AMISH HOMESTEAD SERIES
A Place at Our Table
Room on the Porch Swing Coming May 2018

THE AMISH HEIRLOOM SERIES
The Forgotten Recipe
The Courtship Basket
The Cherished Quilt
The Beloved Hope Chest

THE HEARTS OF THE LANCASTER GRAND HOTEL SERIES
A Hopeful Heart
A Mother's Secret
A Dream of Home
A Simple Prayer

THE KAUFFMAN AMISH BAKERY SERIES
A Gift of Grace
A Promise of Hope
A Place of Peace
A Life of Joy
A Season of Love

YOUNG ADULT
Roadside Assistance
Reckless Heart
Destination Unknown
Miles from Nowhere

OTHER NOVELS
Amish Sweethearts

NOVELLAS
A Plain and Simple Christmas
Naomi's Gift included in *An Amish Christmas Gift*
A Spoonful of Love included in *An Amish Kitchen*
Love Birds included in *An Amish Market*
Love and Buggy Rides included in *An Amish Harvest*
Summer Storms included in *An Amish Summer*
The Christmas Cat included in *An Amish Christmas Love*

NONFICTION
A Gift of Love

BETH WISEMAN

THE AMISH SECRETS NOVELS
Her Brother's Keeper
Love Bears All Things
Home All Along

THE DAUGHTERS OF THE PROMISE NOVELS
Plain Perfect
Plain Pursuit
Plain Promise
Plain Paradise
Plain Proposal
Plain Peace

THE LAND OF CANAAN NOVELS
Seek Me with All Your Heart
The Wonder of Your Love
His Love Endures Forever

OTHER NOVELS
Need You Now
The House that Love Built
The Promise
An Amish Year

NOVELLAS
A Change of Heart included in *An Amish Gathering*
A Miracle for Miriam included in *An Amish Christmas*
Healing Hearts included in *An Amish Love*
A Perfect Plan included in *An Amish Wedding*
A Recipe for Hope included in *An Amish Kitchen*
Always Beautiful included in *An Amish Miracle*
When Christmas Comes Again included
in *An Amish Second Christmas*
Rooted in Love included in *An Amish Garden*
In His Father's Arms included in *An Amish Cradle*
Under the Harvest Moon included in *An Amish Harvest*
A Cup Half Full included in *An Amish Home*
Winter Kisses included in *An Amish Christmas Love*

Vannetta Chapman

The Amish Village Mystery Series
Murder Simply Brewed
Murder Tightly Knit
Murder Freshly Baked

The Shipshewana Amish Mystery Series
Falling to Pieces
A Perfect Square
Material Witness

Other Novellas
An Unexpected Blessing included in *An Amish Cradle*
Love in Store included in *An Amish Market*
Mischief in the Autumn Air included in *An Amish Harvest*

An Amish Spring

Three Novellas

Amy Clipston, Beth Wiseman,
and Vannetta Chapman

ZONDERVAN®

ZONDERVAN

A Son for Always
Copyright © 2016 by Amy Clipston

A Love for Irma Rose
Copyright © 2015 by Elizabeth Mackey

Where Healing Blooms
Copyright © 2009 by Vannetta Chapman

This title is also available as a Zondervan e-book.

Requests for information should be addressed to:
Zondervan, *3900 Sparks Dr. SE, Grand Rapids, Michigan 49546*

Mass Market ISBN: 978-0-7852-1723-7

Library of Congress Cataloging-in-Publication
CIP data is available upon request.

Printed in the United States of America

18 19 20 21 22 / QG / 5 4 3 2 1

CONTENTS

A Son for Always by Amy Clipston 1

A Love for Irma Rose by Beth Wiseman 105

Where Healing Blooms by Vannetta Chapman 205

A Son for Always

Amy Clipston

To my husband, Joe, with love

GLOSSARY

ach—oh
aenti—aunt
appeditlich—delicious
Ausbund—Amish hymnal
bedauerlich—sad
boppli—baby
brot—bread
bruder—brother
bruderskinner—nieces/nephews
bu—boy
buwe—boys
daadi—granddad
daed—dad
danki—thank you
dat—dad
Dietsch—Pennsylvania Dutch, the Amish language (a German dialect)
dochder—daughter
dochdern—daughters
Dummle!—hurry!
Englisher—a non-Amish person
fraa—wife
freind—friend

freinden—friends
froh—happy
gegisch—silly
gern gschehne—you're welcome
grossdaadi—grandfather
grossdochder—granddaughter
grossdochdern—granddaughters
grossmammi—grandmother
Gude mariye—Good morning
gut—good
Gut nacht—Good night
haus—house
Ich liebe dich—I love you
kapp—prayer covering or cap
kichli—cookie
kichlin—cookies
kind—child
kinner—children
kumm—come
liewe—love, a term of endearment
maed—young women, girls
maedel—young woman
mamm—mom
mammi—grandma
mei—my
mutter—mother
naerfich—nervous
narrisch—crazy
onkel—uncle
Ordnung—The oral tradition of practices required and forbidden in the Amish faith.

schee—pretty

schmaert—smart

schtupp—family room

schweschder—sister

Was iss letz?—What's wrong?

Willkumm—welcome

Wie geht's—How do you do? or Good day!

wunderbaar—wonderful

ya—yes

CHAPTER 1

Carolyn Glick hefted her tote bag onto her weary shoulder as she climbed the porch steps and headed toward the back door of her farmhouse. The bag felt as if it weighed a hundred pounds while the warm afternoon sun kissed the back of her neck. She opened the door, stepped into the mudroom, and walked through the kitchen to the family room, where she dropped the bag onto the floor.

She sank onto the sofa and moved her fingers across her protruding belly. Her legs were achy, and her swollen feet throbbed as if she'd walked her back pasture two hundred times. With her elbow propped up on the arm of the sofa, she rested her chin on her palm. Her head felt heavier than usual, and she was certain every muscle in her body was sore after spending the morning working at the Lancaster Grand Hotel. She still had two more months before her baby was born, but it felt as if she'd been pregnant for years. The exhaustion gripped her, nearly stealing her breath.

Would she always feel this tired? Would this level of exhaustion continue after her baby was born?

Before long, the back door creaked open and then

closed, and footsteps sounded like they were coming from the mudroom.

"Carolyn?" Joshua appeared in the family room doorway. *"Wie geht's?"* Her husband's handsome face clouded with concern. He must have noticed the pained look on her own face. "Are you all right?"

Carolyn nodded. *"Ya.* It was a long day at the hotel. Linda called in sick, and I had to help finish her rooms along with mine." She tried to smile, but it felt more like a grimace.

"You look worn out." He sat close to her on the sofa and pulled her legs up and toward him, placing her feet on his lap. Gently, he massaged her feet, his fingers carefully working through the pain and soreness that she'd felt building all day long.

"I'm fine. It was just a long day." It was a sin to lie, but she didn't want to worry Joshua. Lately he seemed to become concerned every time she complained that she felt a twinge of soreness. "How are the boys doing?" she asked. Her son, Ben, and Joshua's assistant, Danny, both worked on the horse farm with Joshua.

"They're fine. I was out in the pasture, and I didn't see you get home. But when I stopped in at the stables, Ben said he heard your van pull up." He continued to move his fingers over her feet, softly relieving the stress. "How does this feel?"

She nodded. *"Danki.* That definitely helps."

"How are your shoulders?" he asked.

She reached up and felt her right shoulder. "They are hard as rocks."

"Would you let me try to help you?" He gently moved

her legs to the floor and patted the sofa beside him. "Spin around, and I'll see if I can give you some relief."

She gingerly moved her achy body, turning her back to him. She closed her eyes and relished the feel of his strong fingers soothing her tight shoulders. The tension in her muscles slowly dissipated, and she blew out a deep sigh. Joshua always seemed to know what she needed, and sometimes he knew before even she realized it. Her shoulders drooped slightly as she looked back toward him.

"*Danki.* My shoulders don't feel like boulders anymore." She leaned back against the sofa.

"*Gern gschehne.*" He took her hand in his and his blue eyes sparkled. "I'm glad I could help you a little bit."

"How has your day been?" she asked.

"*Gut.*" He fingered his dark brown beard. "Two customers came by this morning and another customer called and asked to come out tomorrow to see a couple of horses. It's getting busy now that spring is here. Sales are definitely picking up." His expression clouded with concern. "You still look tense. Is the *boppli* okay? Are you feeling sick?"

"I'm certain the *boppli* is fine," she insisted. "I'm feeling better. Being home always helps. You don't need to worry. I'll start supper after I sit for a little bit." The truth was that she needed a nap, but she couldn't admit it out loud. After he went back out to the stables, she'd sneak into the bedroom and lie down. Just thirty minutes would do her and the baby a world of good. After she awoke, she would figure out what to cook for Joshua and Benjamin for supper.

"Okay." He pointed toward the pile of books on the coffee table. "Since you need to sit, I wonder if you would look at the books for the farm. Some bills arrived today, and I haven't had a chance to look at them because we've been so busy with customers."

Carolyn's lower lip began to quiver as she stared at the pile of books. How could she possibly find the brainpower to balance the books when she felt as if she might fall asleep just sitting at the table? All she wanted was a nap. Just one short, little nap.

"I can't." Her voice cracked as tears splattered her hot cheeks. "I'm too tired to possibly do any more work today. My legs hurt, my feet feel like they're swollen two sizes bigger than usual, and my body is completely worn out. I'll have to do the books tomorrow. I'm sorry." She stared down at the table to avoid his gaze.

"*Ach, mei liewe.*" He moved her into his arms, and his voice was warm and soothing in her ear. "Maybe you should quit the hotel. The *boppli* will be here in only two months. Now is the time for you to slow down."

Carolyn shook her head while clearing her throat. "I can't quit." Her voice was still weak, but she willed herself to stop crying. She had to pull herself together. She was too strong to act like this.

"Why not?" He dipped his chin and his eyes searched hers.

"I just can't." She scooted forward on the sofa and pointed toward the stack of books. "I'll do them right now." She reached for the top book.

"They can wait until tomorrow." Joshua touched her arm. "You need a *gut* night's sleep."

"I'll be fine." She opened the book and swiped her hand over her wet cheeks. "I can do it now."

"Carolyn," he began. "You're pushing yourself too hard. It's not *gut* for you or the *boppli*. Why won't you slow down? You just told me how exhausted you are."

"I just can't." She studied the record book and hoped he'd go back outside. She didn't want to have this conversation now. She wasn't strong enough to admit the truth.

She could feel him studying her while she began opening the stack of bills on the table.

"I'm going back out to the field," he said as he stood. "Call me if you need me."

"Danki." She forced a smile as she looked up at him. "I'll get these done and then start supper."

"Fine." He kissed her forehead and headed through the kitchen toward the mudroom and back door.

Carolyn waited until she heard the door close and then heaved herself up from the sofa, gathered the pile of books and bills in her arms, and walked into the kitchen. After placing everything on the table, she moved to the sink where she filled a glass with water and sipped it. She looked out the window to where Benjamin, her sixteen-year-old son, walked from the stables to the pasture alongside Daniel King, Joshua's assistant. Benjamin grinned as he spoke to Daniel.

Benjamin was the spitting image of Carolyn with his sandy blond hair and brown eyes, and he'd been born when Carolyn was only sixteen. She had given in to the pressures of her then boyfriend and found herself pregnant and alone. Her boyfriend had abruptly left the community before she found out she was going to be a teen mother.

Carolyn had been convinced she'd always live with her parents and never find love, until she met Joshua Glick. They quickly fell in love and married last fall.

She turned back toward the kitchen table and blew out a puff of air. She had to find the strength to do the books for Joshua. The task was daunting when she was this tired, but she was strong and had faced adversity in her life before. She could do this for him.

As Carolyn sank into a chair, she felt the baby kick, and she smiled. She'd get through this exhausting time with God's help. And she couldn't wait to meet her new baby.

Mustering all the will she could find in her body and spirit, Carolyn set out to balance the books. She was determined to keep her promise to her husband and also to her son.

CHAPTER 2

Carolyn hummed to herself while hanging out the laundry the following morning. She'd finished the books after supper last night and was thankful to have that task completed. This morning she'd made breakfast for Joshua and Benjamin before starting on the laundry.

Although she was moving slowly, she was making progress. She pinned up a pair of Joshua's trousers as she watched Benjamin help Joshua work with a horse in the pasture. She was thankful for the joy that Joshua had brought into her son's life. Thanks to Joshua, Benjamin found a love for horses and training.

She only wished she could feel secure in Benjamin's future. Would he have the same support most Amish children with two biological parents had? Most prosperous Amish parents helped their sons buy land and build a home. They would also help furnish their daughters' homes. Would she be able to help Benjamin build a home when he was ready to go out into the world?

She pushed the thoughts away and finished hanging out the wash before returning to the kitchen to make lunch. She was pouring four glasses of water when Joshua, Benjamin, and Daniel walked into the kitchen.

"*Danki* for lunch," Daniel said to Carolyn as he washed his hands at the sink.

"*Gern gschehne.*"

Joshua surveyed the table. "It smells *appeditlich, mei liewe.*"

"I thought you might like potato salad along with your sandwiches." Carolyn filled the last glass and set the pitcher on the table. "Everything is ready."

Joshua and Benjamin washed their hands before they all sat down at the table. Carolyn sat across from Joshua and, like the men, bowed her head in silent prayer before they all began reaching for the platters. Carolyn took a roll and then a slice of cheese and two slices of turkey from a platter before passing it to Benjamin. Utensils scraped the dishes, and the kitchen filled with noise.

"Your potato salad is amazing, Carolyn," Daniel said between bites. "I'd love to give your recipe to *mei mamm.*"

"*Danki*, Danny. I'll write it down for you." Carolyn glanced at Joshua, who was smiling at her. "How is your day going?"

"*Gut.*" Joshua wiped his mouth with a napkin. "Some customers are coming out this afternoon to look at two horses. We're all ready for them to arrive." He turned to Ben and Danny. "The horses are brushed and ready to be seen, right?"

"Oh, *ya.*" Benjamin nodded as he added mayonnaise and mustard to his sandwich. "We're all set."

"We had more messages this morning from people interested in seeing horses," Joshua added. "Business is booming."

"It's a blessing." Carolyn lifted her glass of water. "God is *gut*."

"*Ya*, He is," Joshua agreed with a nod.

When the meal was over, Benjamin and Daniel thanked her again for lunch and headed back outside. Carolyn carried a stack of dishes to the counter and began to fill the sink with hot, frothy water.

"It's nice having you home today." Joshua came up behind her and set the empty platters on the counter before leaning his lanky body against it. He reached over and touched her arm.

"I'm always off from work on Tuesdays." She glanced up at him and then set the dishes in the hot water. "I've been working the same schedule for a long time."

"I know that, but I'm just saying I like having you here at the farm." He gently squeezed her arm. "I enjoy having lunch with you. I'd love to have you home every day so we can work together and enjoy all our meals together."

Carolyn averted her eyes by focusing on the dish she was washing. She knew what was coming next. Joshua was going to ask her to quit her job at the hotel, but she had to hold fast to her commitment to Benjamin's future.

"You seem happier when you are at home during the day," he continued. "You're much more relaxed today than you were yesterday when you got back from the hotel. And you always smile when you're working in the garden. I think you long to be here, too, but for some reason you just won't admit it."

She placed a clean dish on the drain board. The baby suddenly kicked, and she gasped while gripping her abdomen with a wet hand.

"Carolyn?" Joshua asked. "Are you all right?"

"*Ya.*" She smiled up at him. "The *boppli* kicked. I'm certain the *boppli* recognizes your voice."

Joshua's eyes were warm and tender as he smiled in return. He reached out, touched her belly, and bent down closer to his child. "Hi, little one. Do you know your *dat's* voice?"

The baby kicked again, and Carolyn couldn't stop smiling at Joshua. "I'd take that as a yes."

Carolyn's heart warmed as Joshua's face lit up again. He held his hand to her abdomen and seemed fascinated as the baby continued to kick. She relished the moment between her husband and her unborn child.

"I can't wait to meet our *boppli*," Joshua finally said as he let his hand drop from her belly. "I hope he has your milk-chocolate eyes."

"Well, I hope *she* has *your* blue eyes instead." Carolyn wagged a finger at him. "But we don't know if we'll have a he or a she. We won't know until our baby enters the world."

"It won't matter if it's a *bu* or a *maedel*." He cupped his hand to her cheek and smiled. "We'll be *froh* either way." He turned, retrieved the glasses from the table, and brought them to the counter.

"You don't have to help me, Josh. I can do the dishes."

"I don't mind." He set the glasses next to the platters

before reaching for their utensils. "I enjoy helping you." He brought the rest of the dishes and the condiments to the counter, too, and then kissed her. "I'll be outside. The customers should be here soon."

Joshua went through the mudroom to the back door, and Carolyn smiled. She was thankful for her kind, thoughtful husband. God had certainly blessed her and Benjamin the day Joshua Glick came into their lives.

. . .

Joshua playfully slapped Benjamin's arm while the customers loaded the two geldings onto their trailer. "*Danki* for your work today. We have two *froh* customers, and you are part of the reason those horses are trained so well."

"*Danki, Dat*." Benjamin smiled.

Joshua's heart warmed at the word *Dat*. He enjoyed being someone's father, and soon he'd have two children to call him dad. He could hardly wait to meet his new child.

"I appreciate all you've taught me," Benjamin added.

"You do fantastic work. I'm proud of you."

The customers closed and locked their horse trailer before turning back toward Joshua. "Thanks again!"

"You're welcome!" Joshua waved as the men hopped into the pickup truck and drove away, the trailer bumping and rattling down the rock driveway toward the road.

Joshua and Benjamin started toward the barn. Joshua had been hoping to get Benjamin alone at some point today so he could talk to him. Now seemed to be the perfect time.

"I was wondering if I could ask you a question," Joshua began. "It's about your *mamm*."

"Oh?" Benjamin raised an eyebrow. "What did you want to ask me?"

"I'm worried about her." Joshua stopped a few feet from the barn to keep their conversation private. While he trusted Daniel, he wanted to keep family matters within the family. "She was exhausted when she got home yesterday, and she burst into tears when I asked her to do the books for the farm. She's really overexerting herself."

Benjamin folded his arms over his slight frame. Although he was close to seventeen, he looked more like thirteen with his skinny arms and legs and short stature. "Well, she didn't seem like herself at supper last night. I asked her if she was okay, and she insisted she was fine. I could tell something was wrong, but she's not *gut* at expressing herself when something is wrong. She tends to shut down."

"I've noticed that." Joshua sighed. "It's apparent to me that she's overdoing it, but I don't know how to get her to admit it. Why do you think she's determined to keep working at the hotel when it's obvious that she's tired? The *boppli* is sapping her energy, and she really doesn't need to work there anymore. Business here at the farm is booming. We need her at home more than we need any income she brings in from working at the hotel."

Benjamin gnawed his lower lip before responding. "You know *mei mamm* is stubborn."

"*Ya*, I know that. Her tenacity was one of the qualities I admired about her when I first met her. I'd never met a *maedel* who was so determined to stand up for what she believed in. She was very outspoken when you first came to work for me, and she wasn't afraid to tell me when she thought I wasn't treating you right."

"Exactly," Benjamin agreed. "*Mamm* was always determined to contribute. She once told me she didn't want to take handouts from her family even though she had me when she was so young. She felt she had to work and help pay for groceries and everything I needed."

"I understand how that made sense when you were little, but she's not living with her folks anymore." Joshua looked back toward the house and considered Benjamin's response. "Why would she still feel like she had to contribute when we're a team now?"

Benjamin shrugged. "I don't know. Maybe old habits and feelings are hard to break."

"Maybe," Joshua muttered as he stared at the house.

"I'm going to go see what Danny's doing." Benjamin continued toward the barn.

"All right." Joshua lifted his hat and raked his hand through his thick hair. Why did Carolyn feel she still had to bring in extra income even though they were married now and working the farm together? Was there something he wasn't giving her that she felt she needed? Why would she want to work at the hotel when she said she loved the farm so much?

None of it made sense. Was she stuck in the mindset she'd been used to while living with her parents on her brother's farm? If so, then he needed to show her that she didn't have to keep living in the past. He was determined to find a way to show her that he would support her now.

CHAPTER 3

Carolyn moved her gardening stool over to another patch of weeds and then sank back down onto it. Determined to keep her garden pristine despite her protruding belly, she swiped her hand over her brow as the late-April sun warmed her skin, then leaned down and pulled more weeds before dropping them into a bucket.

She was still working that same patch when she noticed a shadow had dropped over her.

Glancing up, Carolyn found her mother-in-law staring at her, gripping a casserole dish in her pudgy hands.

"Carolyn," Barbie began. "What are you doing?"

"Hi, *Mamm*." Carolyn wiped her hands on her apron. She wondered why it wasn't perfectly obvious to Barbie what she was doing, but she decided to give the obvious answer. "I'm weeding."

"But why are you weeding in your condition?" Barbie asked. "You should be resting since you're close to your time."

"I still have two months before the *boppli* will come, and I need to get ready to plant tomatoes." She thought about Joshua's comment about her garden earlier. "And

I enjoy working in my garden. It helps me relax. What brings you over here today?" she asked, hoping to move the focus of their conversation away from her.

"I brought supper for Josh and Ben. I made chicken and dumplings, which is one of Josh's favorites." Barbie held up the casserole dish and frowned. "With all of the hours you work at that hotel, I worry that they might starve if I don't bring them food. I'm certain my son will appreciate a nice, warm meal after working so hard all day long."

Carolyn's lips formed a thin line as she pushed to her feet. "You know I only work part-time. I always make sure my family is fed, and I always make sure my husband gets to eat his favorite, warm meals."

"I'm sure you think you do, but you should be home with your family." Barbie pointed toward Carolyn's middle. "Especially with the *boppli* coming. You have things to do to get prepared, but you already know that. This isn't your first *boppli*."

"No, this isn't my first, and I will be ready." Carolyn ran her fingers over her belly and studied her mother-in-law's steel-blue eyes. Why had Barbie felt the need to point out that this wasn't Carolyn's first child? Was she making a derogatory comment about her teen pregnancy? Everyone else in their families and most, if not all, in their community had forgiven her years ago for her transgression, and Benjamin was a special young man.

"I hope you're not considering going back to that job after the *boppli* is born."

"I probably will go back." Carolyn felt herself grow

weary while the sun beat on her face. She didn't want to have this conversation with Barbie. After all, this was something she had to decide, not her husband's meddling mother.

"You shouldn't even consider going back to that hotel. That's no place for you or any other Plain woman."

"I enjoy working there," Carolyn said while massaging her abdomen.

"I will never understand why you would want to work there and be around those *Englischers* all day long when you belong here taking care of your family. Besides, there is plenty to do here on my son's farm." Barbie turned to where the men were working with horses in the pasture. She tented her free hand over her eyes, and her frown creased her chubby face as she abruptly changed the subject.

"Josh may have adopted Ben, but with Ben's blond hair, brown eyes, and slight frame, he'll never be mistaken for Josh's biological son."

Carolyn gritted her teeth and bit back the sharp retort that bubbled up from her throat. *And that is precisely why I won't quit my job at the hotel.*

Barbie turned toward Carolyn and held up the casserole dish once again. "I'll put the chicken and dumplings in the refrigerator for you. Do you need me to do the dishes or anything else inside? I have some time, so I can clean or start the laundry if you'd like."

"*Danki*, but everything is done. I finished the laundry earlier, and the *haus* is already clean."

"*Gut.*" Barbie started toward the porch, and Carolyn closed her eyes while trying to will her heart to stop beating so fast. Joshua's mother had a way of saying things that cut Carolyn to her bone, but her comment about Benjamin had sliced straight to her heart.

Carolyn had always assumed that Barbie wouldn't really accept Benjamin into the family, but she never imagined Barbie would express her unkind thoughts aloud and so offhandedly.

. . .

Carolyn propped herself up in bed with two pillows while she brushed her long, blond hair that was falling in waves to her waist. She loved this time of night when the work was done and she had some quiet time alone with her husband. She could feel the soreness in her muscles begin to release while she moved the brush through her hair. The tension in her neck and ache in her feet also subsided slightly.

Why had Barbie's words hurt her so deeply? She should be used to dealing with Barbie by now. It was because of Ben. If only she could let go of her worries about his future.

Joshua stepped into the room clad in his blue pajamas, his dark hair wet from the shower. "You've been quiet this evening. Are you all right?" He sank onto the edge of the bed beside her and began to stroke her feet. "Are your feet bothering you?"

"No, tonight it's not my feet really, although I do love when you massage them." She continued to move the brush through her thick hair, carefully choosing her words. "I've been wondering something."

"What is it?"

"Do you love Ben?" she asked. "Do you really love him as if he were your own son?" She held her breath as she waited for his response.

Joshua stopped massaging her feet and his eyes searched hers. "Of course I do. That's why I adopted him and gave him my name."

She could see the truth glistening in his eyes, but she had to press on to the question that had been echoing through her mind ever since Barbie's visit. Carolyn looked down at her baby bump. "Will you still love him after our *boppli* is born?" Her voice vibrated as her eyes filled with tears.

"Carolyn, look at me." Joshua quickly moved closer to her, placed his fingers under her chin, and tilted her head so that she was looking into his confused eyes. "Of course I'll still love Ben. He's my son, and he even calls me *Dat*." He paused. "Why would you ask that? Have I ever done anything to make you doubt my feelings for Ben?"

"No, you haven't." She shrugged and wiped her eyes. "I suppose my crazy hormones have my feelings all jumbled up as if I ran them through the wringer washer."

He didn't smile despite her lame attempt at a joke.

An uncomfortable silence stretched between them, and she felt the need to flee his pained expression.

"I'm really tired. I better go to sleep." She placed the brush on her nightstand. *"Gut nacht."* She tucked her legs under her quilt and pulled it around her as if to shield her heart from the doubt assaulting her mind.

With her eyes closed, she felt the bed shift as Joshua

stood and then heard his footsteps as he made his way around to his side of the bed. The frame creaked as he climbed in next to her. He reached over and drew circles with the light brush of his fingers over her cotton nightgown.

"Carolyn?" His voice was soft and gentle next to her ear. "I have something I want to ask you."

"*Ya?*" she asked, keeping her face toward the wall.

"Do you feel like you have to work at the hotel to contribute income toward the household?"

Carolyn shrugged. "*Ya*, I do. I've always worked to contribute toward the household and also to save money for Ben. I have an account where I put a little bit of money away for Ben every paycheck."

"You don't need to worry about that, Carolyn. You're not living with your parents on your *bruder's* farm anymore. We're a team, and I can support all of us."

Carolyn nodded. "I know. You're a *gut* provider." She said the words out loud, but her worries still echoed in her mind, and she didn't want to confess them to Josh. He said he loved Ben, and she believed him. But still, Ben was not his biological child like the baby she was carrying.

"You have nothing to worry about. We're fine financially. *Gut nacht, mei liewe.*" His voice was soft and tentative. "I hope you believe me when I say that I love you and Ben, and I always will." His fingers brushed across her shoulders.

"*Danki*," Carolyn whispered. She held her breath as more tears threatened to give away her doubts.

CHAPTER 4

Joshua guided his horse down the main road toward his farm, and his parents' house came into view. All morning he had longed to talk to his father, who always gave Joshua the best advice. Today he needed to bend his father's ear and ask him for some of that coveted guidance.

He brought his horse and buggy to a stop in the driveway and hopped out of the driver seat. He made his way behind the house and found his father brushing a horse in the barn, just where he suspected he would be.

"Josh." *Dat* set the brush on the top of the stall. "*Wie geht's?*"

"Hi, *Dat.* How are you?" Josh leaned against the stall. "I was on my way home from the feed store, and I thought I'd stop by." He stroked the horse's neck. "How are you, Fred?" The horse nodded his head as if to respond.

"Would you like to come inside for a snack?"

"Oh, no, *danki.* I really need to get back to the farm. We have customers coming this afternoon."

"Is there something on your mind?"

Joshua sighed and nodded his head. It was time

to get to the true reason for his visit. "Carolyn hasn't been herself lately. Last night she asked me if I really love Ben and if I'll still love him after the *boppli* is born."

Dat's brow furrowed. "Why would she ask you that?"

"I don't know," Joshua said, throwing his hands up as if to surrender. "That's what I've been trying to figure out. I keep telling her I love Ben like my own son and I will always love both her and him. I'm not sure what else I can do to make her believe that's never going to change. I feel like I'm doing something wrong. I do my best to compliment Ben's work, and I'm teaching him everything I can about the business. I don't know what else I'm supposed to do to show her I'm a *gut dat*. Do you have any advice?"

Dat fingered his graying beard. "From what I've seen, you are a *gut dat*. In fact, you remind me a lot of your *bruder* and how he was with his *kinner*."

Joshua's heart tightened as he thought of his older brother, Gideon, who had passed way from a heart attack nearly a decade ago. "*Danki*. I can't think of a higher compliment. Gideon was a *wunderbaar dat*."

"*Ya*," *Dat* said. "He was a *gut dat*, and you are too. That's why I don't think Carolyn's worries are your fault."

"What do you mean?"

"I think Carolyn is just going through a lot with getting ready to have the *boppli*. Women tend to change during this time." His father smiled. "Your *mamm* went through a lot. She changed a bit."

Joshua raised an eyebrow. "Was she more uptight?"

Dat nodded. "She was worried and nervous. Everything had to be perfect, and I tended to get things wrong." He paused and grinned. "I got them wrong often."

Joshua chuckled. "So *Mamm* was a handful while she was pregnant."

"*Ya.*" *Dat* shrugged. "But it was worth it. I had two *wunderbaar* sons." He patted Joshua's arm. "Have patience and faith. I know things are changing quickly, and it's a scary but exciting time for both of you. Your lives are going to change completely, but it will be for the better. Everything will be fine."

"I hope so." Joshua could hear the uncertainty in his voice.

"I'm certain Carolyn is worried that something will go wrong, but God is *gut*. Keep telling her how much you love her and Ben. She'll eventually realize she has nothing to worry about."

Joshua adjusted the hat on his head and longed for his father's wise words to settle his worry. "I'll try."

Dat crossed his arms over his chest and tilted his head. "You don't seem convinced."

"It's not that I don't believe you." Joshua struggled to put his thoughts into words. "I can't really put my finger on it, but it's almost like there's something she's not telling me. Something more than whether I'll still love Ben after the *boppli* is born."

His father's face clouded with a frown. "What do you mean?"

"She tells me she loves the farm, and I know she's telling me the truth. She seems happier and more relaxed on the days she's home instead of at the hotel." Joshua ran his fingers over the stall wall. "But she still seems stressed out much of the time. I think it's because she's overdoing it, but she won't admit it. Why can't I convince her to quit that job? I just don't understand it. She seems to think she needs to contribute income to our household, but that's not true. I can support all of us."

"Hmm." *Dat* shook his head. "I don't know about that, but I imagine Carolyn is still adjusting to being married after being a single mother for so long. Give her love and support, and she will get through this."

"That sounds like a *gut* plan." Joshua nodded toward the barn door. "I better get back to the farm. It was *gut* seeing you."

During the ride back to his house, Joshua contemplated his father's words and prayed Carolyn would believe that he would always love Ben and that the farm would support them all.

. . .

Carolyn wiped her hands on a dish towel as the aroma of freshly baked apple pie wafted up from the oven beside her. She turned to her mother, who was pouring hot water from the percolator into coffee cups. "*Danki* for bringing the apples over. I think the *buwe* will enjoy the snack this afternoon."

"*Gern gschehne*," *Mamm* said. "I saw those apples at the market and thought of you." She dropped tea bags into the cups and held them up. "You look like you could use this cup of tea. Let's sit and talk."

Carolyn tossed the dish towel onto the counter and

then sat across from her mother at the table. She sipped the tea and curled her fingers around the warm cup.

"You look positively exhausted, *mei liewe.*" *Mamm* reached across the table and touched Carolyn's hand. "Are you sleeping well?"

Carolyn shrugged and cleared her throat where a lump swelled. "*Ya*, I guess I'm sleeping okay."

"Are you certain?" *Mamm* studied her. "I had a difficult time in my last trimester when I was pregnant with your *bruder.* My back hurt so badly that some days it was all I could do not to break down in tears. Does your back hurt?"

Carolyn tried to smile as a tear trickled down her cheek. "Today I think everything hurts."

"Oh, Carolyn." *Mamm* scooted her chair around the table and pulled Carolyn into her arms.

Carolyn rested her cheek on her mother's shoulder as tears flowed from her eyes. She felt like a child who had fallen and scraped her knee. Why was she acting so childish today? It was so unlike her!

"*Was iss letz?*" *Mamm* moved her hand over Carolyn's back. "Talk to me."

"I'm just so tired." Carolyn wiped her eyes with a paper napkin. "I wake up during the night when the *boppli* kicks, and I worry about everything."

Mamm's brow knitted above her brown eyes. "What are you worried about?"

"Everything." Carolyn sniffed and wiped her nose. "Will the *boppli* be healthy? Will I be a *gut mamm*? Where will Ben fit into our family?"

Mamm smiled and pushed a lock of Carolyn's hair

under her prayer covering. "*Ach*, Carolyn. You worry too much. The *boppli* will be fine, and you already are a *gut mamm*. Ben will always fit into your family. He'll be a *wunderbaar* big *bruder*. What is there to worry about?"

Carolyn shook her head. "When I close my eyes at night, I feel stuck in a well of worries. I know I need to give my worry over to God, but I struggle daily."

"The Lord has control, and He will take care of you and your family, Carolyn." *Mamm's* eyes glistened as she squeezed Carolyn's hand. "You're blessed beyond measure. You have a wonderful family already, and soon it will blossom. Give thanks for all you have, and don't let doubt ruin these last few weeks of your pregnancy. You remember how much life changed when Ben was born. You'll need your rest now."

"*Ya*, I do, but I was a *kind*. It will be different this time."

"True, but it will still be overwhelming." *Mamm* tapped the table for emphasis. "You should listen to your body. If you're that tired, then Sarah Ann and I can come over and help you more. Do you want us to come and clean for you next week?"

"No." Carolyn shook her head. "I can handle it, but *danki*."

"I think it's time you quit working at the hotel. You need your strength for the *boppli*."

Carolyn bit her lower lip. "I'm not sure." Her mother would never understand why she wanted to earn money. She hadn't made the same mistakes Carolyn had made when she was a teenager.

"Well, you need to think about quitting soon. You look like you could use more time preparing for the *boppli*." *Mamm's* expression brightened. "Is Josh working on the cradle?"

"*Ya*, he is, and it's going well." Carolyn lifted her cup. "Ben loved the idea of fixing up his old cradle. They've been working together on it."

"That's so nice. I'm certain Ben loves the time he spends with Josh."

"*Ya*." Carolyn sipped her tea. "I just pray that doesn't change, that Josh will still have time for Ben when the baby comes."

"Oh, I'm certain it won't." *Mamm* patted her hand. "Everything will be fine. Stop putting so much pressure on yourself. God is in control."

"*Ya*, He is." Carolyn nodded and prayed that she could share her mother's confidence that everything would be okay.

CHAPTER 5

Six weeks later Carolyn took a deep breath and sank into a chair in the hotel room she'd been cleaning. She hadn't felt right all day. Not only did her feet and legs ache, but her lower back also felt as if someone had been kicking it with steel-toed boots since she'd awoken early that morning. The discomfort began intermittently and increased as the day wore on.

When a sharp pain radiated through her lower back, Carolyn sucked in a breath.

"Carolyn?" Linda Zook, a petite brunette in her early thirties, appeared in the doorway. "I was coming up to check on you since you said you didn't feel well earlier." Her eyes rounded. "*Ach*, no. Are you all right?"

Carolyn looked at her coworker and shook her head. "No, I'm not feeling well. I'm actually feeling worse. I didn't feel right when I woke up this morning, but the pain in my back was bearable. I told Josh I didn't feel like myself, and he suggested I go back to bed. I guess I should've listened to him and called in sick today. He said I was pushing myself too hard, but I thought I would feel better once I got moving."

Another pang hit her, and she took deep breaths until the pain stopped. "I just need a minute to rest."

Linda grimaced. "You don't look well."

Carolyn swiped her hand over her sweaty forehead. "I'll be fine. I just need a moment."

"*Ya*, we need to get you home. I think you should rest there." She lifted the receiver on the hotel room phone. "Hi, Stacey. This is Linda. Carolyn isn't feeling well, and I think we need to get her home. Would you please tell Gregg? We need to get her a ride right away."

Carolyn gripped the arms of the chair as more pain drenched her like a wave. "Maybe you're right," she gasped. She gritted her teeth through the wave of pressure radiating from her lower back through her abdomen.

"Oh no. It's getting worse."

Linda was still listening to Stacey on the phone. "Thank you. I'll bring her right down." She hung up and frowned at Carolyn. "You look terrible. Let's get you home. We'll need to call your midwife so she can take a look at you too."

"Okay." Carolyn balanced her weight on the chair arms and slowly hefted herself up. As she stood, she felt liquid trickle down her legs, and she gasped again.

"Carolyn?" Linda's eyes widened. "*Was iss letz?*"

"My water just broke." She blinked. "*Ach*, no. Why is this happening now? It's too early."

"No, apparently it's the right time." Linda grasped Carolyn's hand. "We have to get downstairs. I'll call Josh so he can alert the midwife, and we'll get you home."

"But it's not time yet." Carolyn stood frozen to the carpet while the liquid continued to seep down her legs. "I still have two weeks."

"No, you don't have two weeks. Apparently God has chosen this day for your *boppli* to be born, so we have to get you home as soon as possible." Linda gently nudged Carolyn to the door. "Let's go. Stacey said Gregg will take us to your house. Everything will be just fine."

Carolyn continued to hold Linda's hand as they made their way down to the lobby where their supervisor, Gregg, was waiting for them.

Stacey, who worked at the front desk, rushed over to them. "What can I do?"

"Please call Carolyn's husband—they have a phone in their barn—and tell him that he needs to call Carolyn's midwife," Linda said. "Tell him we're on our way to his house, and they need to get ready to have this baby."

"I will." Stacey gave Carolyn a concerned expression. "Everything will be just fine. I'll call him right away."

Carolyn nodded as another contraction rose up, and she tried to breathe.

Linda guided Carolyn to Gregg's sedan, which he'd already moved to just outside the front door. As Gregg drove to the farm, Carolyn sat in his backseat, gripping Linda's hand as the contractions came like fire shooting through her lower back to her abdomen.

"It will be okay," Linda whispered in Carolyn's ear. "Stacey is going to call Josh, and I'm certain your midwife will be waiting for you at the *haus*. It will be fine."

Carolyn swiped her hands across her hot cheeks and stared at her apron while trying to control her breathing. The pain was almost too much to bear. Everyone kept telling her everything would be fine. Would it?

Gregg stopped his car in front of the farmhouse, and

Linda helped Carolyn climb out. Carolyn leaned on Linda's arm for support as she headed toward the porch steps.

"Carolyn!" Joshua's handsome face emerged as he stepped out through the back door. "How are you?" His eyes flickered.

She shook her head, unable to speak through the pain.

"Let's get you inside." Joshua took her arm and gently led her up the steps. "You're going to be just fine. Everything's fine. Just breathe through the pain."

Carolyn gasped as another contraction gripped her. She opened her eyes and found Joshua studying her. He smiled, and Carolyn's stress eased slightly. If Josh thought everything would be fine, then maybe it would be.

"We're going to bring our *boppli* into the world," she whispered. "It's time."

"*Ya*, it is time, and I love you," he said as he squeezed her hand.

. . .

Joshua's eyes filled with tears as he held his newborn baby in his arms. He smiled over at Carolyn, who was propped up on the bed while studying him. She was breathtakingly beautiful with her blond hair peeking out from under her prayer covering and her coffee-brown eyes glistening in the low light of the propane lamp on the bedside table. He thought his heart might burst with love for both her and their new baby.

"She's perfect," he whispered, his voice quaking.

Carolyn reached over and squeezed his arm. "*Ya*, she is. God has blessed us."

He stared down into the baby's face. "She looks like you."

Carolyn chuckled. "I think it's too early to tell."

"No, she's too *schee* to look like me." He grinned over at her. "*Danki*."

Carolyn tilted her head. "Why are you thanking me?"

"*Danki* for making me the happiest man on the planet."

"*Gern gschehne*." She paused for a moment. "What do you think of the name Sadie Liz after our two favorite aunts?"

"Sadie Liz?" Joshua smiled. "Sadie Liz Glick. *Ya*, I like it." He tilted his head in question. "Why did you change your mind? I thought we had agreed on Rachel Elizabeth."

She shrugged. "I can't explain it, really. I just looked on her *schee* face and thought of Sadie Liz. We can stick with Rachel Elizabeth if you'd like."

"No." He studied the baby's face. "I agree that Sadie Liz fits her."

"*Gut*." Her eyes slowly closed. "Sadie Liz is her name."

"You should rest." He caressed her arm with his free hand. "I'll take care of things from here."

"Okay." Carolyn yawned and closed her eyes.

As he held his baby girl, memorizing her tiny nose and pink skin, Josh was certain he must be dreaming. Here he stood in their bedroom with his beautiful wife and his healthy baby girl. It wasn't too long ago that Joshua was convinced he'd spend his life alone running

Glick's Belgian and Dutch Harness Horses, the horse farm he had built with his brother so many years ago. Now he had everything he'd always wanted—a family, a real family. He had Carolyn and a daughter and a son he could call his own.

He settled into the rocking chair, and Sadie Liz nuzzled against his arm. Soon she was asleep. She was like a tiny doll, so content and fragile, wrapped in a blanket and wearing a tiny pink crocheted hat. Time seemed to pass slowly while Carolyn slept in their bed and he held Sadie Liz. The midwife came to check on him twice, and each time he told her they were just fine.

After a while, a soft knock sounded on the bedroom door. Joshua opened the door and found his in-laws, Titus and Miriam Lapp, standing in the hallway with Benjamin.

"May we come in?" Miriam asked, craning her neck to look into the room. "Is Carolyn okay with having visitors?"

"*Ya*, of course," Joshua said. "Please come in."

"We got here as soon as we could," Titus said. "I'm so glad you called and left a message."

"I knew you'd want to be here. This is Sadie Liz." Joshua tipped the baby slightly so his in-laws and Benjamin could see her little face peeking out from beneath the light-blue-and-pink blanket Carolyn had made for the baby. "Sadie, this is your *mammi*, *daadi*, and *bruder*."

"Oh!" Miriam took Sadie Liz's tiny hand. "Look at her, Titus! She's so *schee*."

Titus smiled and nodded. "*Ya.* Just like our little Carolyn was when she was born."

"Come in." Joshua nodded toward the inside of the room. "Don't be shy."

Carolyn opened her eyes. "*Mamm. Dat.* I'm glad you're here."

Miriam and Titus stepped into the bedroom, but Benjamin lingered in the doorway. He looked at the baby with his eyebrows knitted together.

"Can I hold her?" he finally asked.

"Of course you can." Joshua turned toward the rocking chair. "Would you like to sit first?"

"*Ya,*" Benjamin said. "That's a *gut* idea." He sank into the chair by Carolyn's bed, and Joshua placed Sadie Liz into his arms.

"Just hold her like this. Support her head with your arm." Joshua squatted beside the chair as the baby squirmed and then settled down again. "Are you okay?"

Benjamin looked at his little sister still swaddled in the blanket, and his brow remained furrowed. "*Ya,* I'm *gut.*" He looked up at Joshua, and his serious expression melted into a wide smile. "I like this."

"That's *gut.*" Joshua grinned.

Joshua stood and walked over to the side of the bed where Carolyn's parents spoke to their daughter. As he placed his hand on his wife's shoulder, he silently thanked God for giving him his precious family. At that very moment, he had everything he'd ever dreamt of, and his heart overflowed with joy.

CHAPTER 6

Carolyn settled into the rocking chair in her bedroom and hummed while Sadie Liz suckled on a bottle. She both nursed her baby and supplemented with formula. It was difficult to believe her newborn was already three days old. A peace had immediately settled over Carolyn when Sadie Liz was born, and she still felt that peace. After waiting and planning, her baby was here. She couldn't be more thankful for the blessings in her life.

Although Sadie Liz had her days and nights mixed up, she was eating well. She seemed to be as healthy and perfect as she could be, but a worry still reverberated at the back of Carolyn's mind: Why had her baby been born two weeks early?

Carolyn had spent most of last night staring into the basinet and watching Sadie Liz as she snuggled under a blanket. She watched her newborn move and tried to ignore the questions that buzzed around in her mind. Was Sadie Liz breathing right? Were her little lungs fully formed? Was she truly ready to be born, or had Carolyn been working too hard, which caused her precious baby to come early?

Sadie Liz grunted and groaned while her little lips smacked against the bottle's nipple. Maybe the worries were just part of the hormones that were still surging through her. From what Carolyn could remember, she'd been emotional after Benjamin had entered the world as well. Perhaps this was just a part of giving birth.

"Carolyn?" Her mother's voice sounded from the hallway.

"I'm in the bedroom, *Mamm*." Carolyn balanced Sadie Liz on her shoulder and patted her back.

Mamm and Carolyn's sister-in-law, Sarah Ann, appeared in the doorway.

"Oh, there she is!" Sarah Ann rushed over with her arms stretched out. "May I hold her?"

"Of course." Carolyn stood and handed Sadie Liz to Sarah Ann. "I was just trying to burp her. Maybe you'll have more success than I did. She doesn't seem to want to burp this morning."

"Oh, hello there." Sarah Ann kissed Sadie Liz's pink, bald head. "Aren't you the sweetest thing? I'm your *aenti* Sarah Ann." She sat in the rocker, hoisted Sadie Liz onto her shoulder, and continued to whisper to the baby while trying to coax a burp.

"How are you feeling?" *Mamm* asked Carolyn.

"I'm sore, but I'm fine."

Mamm touched Carolyn's hand. "Let's go into the kitchen. I want to show you what we brought for you."

"You didn't need to bring anything." Carolyn followed her mother into the kitchen.

"Sarah Ann and I want to help you." *Mamm* moved to the refrigerator and pulled out two casserole dishes.

"I made macaroni and cheese, and Sarah Ann sliced up some roast beef with gravy."

"Oh, *Mamm*." Carolyn inhaled the sweet aroma of the meal. "This is wonderful. *Danki*. The *buwe* will love it."

"We're *froh* to help." *Mamm* placed the dishes back in the refrigerator. "What else can I do to help?" She peered toward the sink. "Why don't you sit, and I'll do the dishes."

"Oh, no. You don't need to do that. I was going to take care of them later." Carolyn waved off the offer.

"Don't be *gegisch*." *Mamm* turned on the faucet and squirted in the dishwashing liquid. "Sarah Ann and I came here to help. You sit down and get some rest. You look exhausted."

Carolyn lowered herself gingerly into a kitchen chair.

"Would you like a cup of tea?" *Mamm* began to fill the teakettle with water.

"*Ya*, that would be perfect." With one elbow on the table, Carolyn rested her head on her palm. Like Josh, her mother always seemed to know exactly what she needed, and Carolyn hoped she was just as intuitive with her own children.

"How is everything going?" *Mamm* asked as she prepared to wash the breakfast dishes. "Josh seems to be positively glowing."

"*Ya*, he's *froh*." Carolyn smiled. "I really enjoyed watching Joshua talk to Sadie Liz while I dressed her this morning. The little moments between the *boppli* and Josh warm my heart. I was a little concerned when Joshua kept calling Sadie Liz a *bu* instead of a *maedel* before she was born. I was hoping he wouldn't be disappointed when we had a *maedel*, but he's not disappointed at all. I can see it in his eyes every time he looks at her. Josh is definitely in love with his *dochder*."

"Of course he is." *Mamm* glanced over her shoulder at Carolyn. "Did you really think he wouldn't be in love with his child?"

Carolyn shrugged. "No, not really. I just didn't want him to be disappointed in me if I didn't give him a son."

"Even if you had any control over that, I don't think Josh could ever be disappointed in you, Carolyn. He's a *gut* man, and he loves you. Besides, Ben is his son now, so he has a *bu*." *Mamm* placed a dish in the drain board. "How is Ben doing with Sadie Liz?"

"He's fine." Carolyn nodded, putting aside her fears for Ben. "He fed her last night, and he seemed to enjoy it. I caught him whispering to her and telling her all about his favorite horses. It was really sweet."

"I knew he'd be good with a younger sibling." *Mamm* rinsed off a glass. "Your *dat* is outside talking to Josh and Ben. He wanted to come by to visit too."

"Oh, that's nice. I like it when Josh spends time with *Dat*."

"I do too." *Mamm* talked about Carolyn's niece and nephews while she continued washing the dishes. When the water in the teakettle was ready, she brought mugs, tea bags, and creamer to the table and sat down. Carolyn sipped the tea and closed her eyes, enjoying the sweet taste of her favorite drink. "I always enjoy my cup of tea."

"You should go take a nap after you finish it." *Mamm* cradled her mug in her hands. "Sarah Ann and I will take care of things here."

"Are you certain?" Carolyn asked. "I imagine Sarah Ann has things to do at the dairy farm."

"Neither of us has a certain time we have to be home. Sarah Ann told Amos that she planned to help you today, and he said he understood. He sent his love. We're here to do whatever you need. We can bring the bassinet out to the kitchen and take care of Sadie Liz while you sleep. You need your rest." *Mamm* glanced around the kitchen. "Just let me know what you want us to do. We can sweep or even start on the laundry for you."

Carolyn cupped her hand over her mouth to stifle a yawn. "I think I might take you up on your offer. I want to keep Sadie Liz up this evening, so she might sleep for longer periods tonight. I know she's very young, but I'd like to try to help her get her days and nights straight as soon as possible." Carolyn didn't want to admit that the sooner she could get her rest at night, the sooner she could go back to work at the hotel. Thoughts about her job were already trying to disturb the peace she'd been feeling since Sadie Liz was born.

"If that's the case, then you definitely need a nap." *Mamm* drank more tea. "I remember when you had your days and nights mixed up. I worried I'd never sleep again, but babies do make that change eventually."

"How long did it take me?"

"I think it was a few weeks. Maybe even a couple of months."

Carolyn grimaced. "Oh dear." She was certain she might pass out from lack of sleep, and there was no way she could return to work at the hotel without more sleep.

"It will be fine. You did a great job with Ben. You'll survive."

Carolyn drank more tea while thinking about the worries that had gripped her last night as she fed Sadie Liz. "*Mamm*, why do you think Sadie Liz came two weeks early?"

Her mother raised her eyebrows. "What do you mean?"

"Sadie didn't make it to my due date, but Ben went a little past his." Carolyn ran her fingers over the warm mug. "Why do you think she was early?"

Mamm shrugged. "I don't know. Some babies are early. Don't you remember your friend Mary's baby? He was nearly a month early."

Carolyn nodded. "*Ya*, baby Jake was so tiny. He looked like a doll."

"That's true, but he was just fine." *Mamm's* gaze remained on her. "Why are you asking about that? Is something wrong with Sadie Liz?"

"No, nothing is wrong. She seems just as healthy as can be. I was just wondering if there was a reason she came so unexpectedly. It's a *gut* thing Josh had finished the cradle and gotten the bassinet together for me."

"The Lord has His own timing. It's not our place to question that."

"I know." Carolyn cupped her hand to her mouth as another yawn overtook her.

"You need some sleep. I'll help Sarah Ann bring Sadie Liz and her supplies out here." Her mother stood. "Let's get you to bed."

As Carolyn followed her mother to her bedroom, she

wondered again if the stress from working at the hotel and also at home had caused her baby to come into the world early. Her eyes widened and her heart pounded. Had she caused her baby to come too soon? Was it all due to her stubbornness? She prayed she hadn't caused her baby any undue stress.

. . .

Carolyn's eyes flew open, and her vision focused on a thin line of early-morning sunlight reflecting off the white ceiling. She yawned and stretched as the fog of sleep lifted from her mind. When she rolled to her side and saw that the bassinet was missing, she sat up with a start. Glancing around the room, she didn't see it anywhere. Her heart thumped in her chest and its beat accelerated.

Where's Sadie Liz?

Carolyn leapt from the bed, pulled on her robe and slippers, and rushed out of the bedroom.

"Josh?" She hurried through the family room to the kitchen where she found Joshua leaning against the counter and giving Sadie Liz a bottle. She stood in the doorway as he leaned down and nuzzled his nose against the baby's cheek.

Carolyn hugged her arms to her middle as her heart-beat gradually returned to a normal pace. Joshua looked so handsome as he gazed down at his baby girl. She could feel the love shining in his powder-blue eyes, and she was thankful for her wonderful husband.

Joshua looked toward the doorway and smiled. "*Gude mariye.* Did we wake you?"

"No, which is why I'm confused." She crossed the kitchen. "I never heard you get up."

"*Gut.* That was the plan." He lifted the baby onto his shoulder and patted her back. "Sadie Liz and I decided to let you sleep this morning." He looked down at the little body on his shoulder. "Right, Sadie?"

"You did?" Carolyn shook her head and looked at the clock on the wall. She couldn't remember a time when she'd slept past nine. "But it's so late, Josh. Why didn't you wake me up so you could go out to work while I took care of the *boppli*?"

"Sadie and I talked about it, and we both agreed that you needed your rest today. You've been working so hard, and we wanted to do our best to help you. Right, Sadie?" The baby responded with a soft belch and Josh grinned. "She already sounds like her *bruder.*" He cradled Sadie Liz in his arms and returned the bottle's nipple to her little mouth.

Carolyn touched Sadie Liz's cheek. "But you have work to do today. Didn't you tell me that you had more customers coming to visit this afternoon?"

"Ben and Danny have it under control. Ben made breakfast while I held Sadie Liz, and we took turns eating. We did really well this morning. You'd be proud."

"Oh." Carolyn tried to imagine Joshua and Benjamin caring for the baby while she slept. She was thankful for their efforts, but she had to do her part. What self-respecting woman would sleep all day while her husband cared for their children? "*Danki* for letting me sleep, but I'm certain you want to get outside now. Just give me a minute to get dressed. I'll hurry."

Joshua met her gaze. "You can take all the time you need. I'm enjoying my *dochder*." He nodded toward the doorway. "You go ahead and get dressed, and Sadie and I will put on your eggs for breakfast."

Carolyn studied him. "How are you going to do that?"

He pointed to the seat on the floor. "Remember the baby seat your *mamm* brought over for you?"

"Oh, right." Carolyn smiled. "I had forgotten about that." She kissed his cheek and touched his shoulder. *"Danki."* She didn't know what she'd done to deserve such a wonderful husband and family.

CHAPTER 7

Carolyn was sitting on the porch and holding Sadie Liz when she spotted a horse and buggy making its way up the rock driveway past the Glick's Belgian and Dutch Harness Horses sign and toward her house. The horse came to a stop near the barn, and her mother and her eighteen-year-old niece, Rosemary, climbed out. They waved to Benjamin in the pasture before making their way to the house.

"*Aenti* Carolyn!" Rosemary rushed to the porch and sat beside her. "Hello, Sadie Liz. How are you?"

"She's doing fine. It's so *gut* to see you." Carolyn handed the baby over to her. "Sadie Liz, do you remember your cousin Rosemary?"

The baby grunted as Rosemary took her in her arms.

Mamm climbed the porch steps. "How are you feeling, Carolyn?"

"I'm fine." Carolyn tented her hand over her eyes. "I didn't expect to see you today."

"I told you we would come and help you as much as we could." *Mamm* sat down beside her. "What can we do today? We're ready to do whatever you need—housework or laundry. We can also do your grocery shopping if you need us to. I can call a driver and head out to the market if that will help you. We're at your disposal."

"I think Sadie Liz needs a change. May I do it for you?" Rosemary lifted the baby to her shoulder. "You can trust me. I've been babysitting since I was twelve."

Carolyn smiled. "I know you can handle it. Everything is set up in my bedroom."

"I'll take care of it. Sadie Liz and I will be inside if you need us." Rosemary stood and headed into the house.

"So, how are you sleeping?" *Mamm* asked.

"I'm sleeping a little bit better. I'm trying to keep Sadie Liz up as late as I can so she sleeps longer periods during the night. She slept for a few hours in one stretch last night, which was a big improvement." Carolyn looked toward the garden. "I've been sitting here staring at the weeds and thinking about those tomato seeds I really need to plant. I'm just not certain I have the strength to do it on only a few hours of sleep."

"How about we work in the garden together?" *Mamm* offered. "I can get the seeds and help you plant. I'll do the heavy bending, and you can sit on a stool to do the rest."

Carolyn smiled. "That sounds fun." She retrieved the seeds from the kitchen while her mother headed to the barn for the gardening tools.

Carolyn met her mother in the garden and took her place on her favorite stool. She was so thankful when Joshua bought her the stool as a surprise last year. Sitting helped relieve some of the pain when the baby began to put pressure on her back.

Carolyn began pulling weeds and dropping them into a bucket while her mother tilled the ground and planted the seeds. The warm May sun caressed Carolyn's cheeks as they worked together, and she smiled. Her eyes moved toward the pasture where she found Joshua, Benjamin, and Daniel training horses, and her smile deepened. She felt as if she were truly home. This was where she belonged.

"It's so *gut* to see you so *froh*," *Mamm* said while planting the seeds at the far end of the garden.

"What do you mean?" Carolyn stopped weeding and looked at her mother.

"You've been smiling so much lately." *Mamm* wiped her hands on her apron. "I can't remember a time when I've seen you this *froh*. You positively glow when you hold Sadie Liz, and I've been watching you work in the garden today. You smile without realizing it. I'm so thankful you've found this much happiness. I know you had a hard time when you were younger, but God had the perfect plan for you. You've found your joy."

Carolyn's lip quivered. "*Danki, Mamm.*"

"God is *gut.*" *Mamm* went back to her planting.

Carolyn looked toward the pasture as a tear trickled down her cheek. She was thankful for all the blessings in her life, especially her family. Her mother was right that she'd never been happier, but a dark, ominous cloud lurked at the back of her mind—she'd have to return to work at the hotel in a little over a month since her boss expected her to take only six weeks of maternity leave.

"Carolyn?" Rosemary called from the porch. "I put Sadie Liz down for a nap. Is it okay if I make lunch?"

Carolyn looked toward the porch. "*Ya*, that would be *wunderbaar. Danki*, Ro."

She turned back toward the pasture to where the men worked. She enjoyed being home to have lunch with her children and husband every day. Oh, how she wanted to stay home with her family, but she knew she had to go back to work, for Benjamin. She was his mother, and she had to make sure his future was secure. He was her responsibility, not Joshua's. She would do what was right for him.

After all, her parents supported her when she went astray and became a teen mother. She would give her children all the support she could, but especially Ben. It was the right thing to do. She felt sure no one else would understand, but she couldn't risk being unprepared if Joshua did not invest in Ben's future the way she knew he would for his own flesh and blood.

. . .

"Supper was *appeditlich*," Benjamin said as he brought his dish to the counter. "*Danki, Mamm.*"

"*Gern gschehne.*" Carolyn dropped the dish into the soapy water in her sink.

Sadie Liz began to fuss in her seat by the table, and Carolyn wiped her hands on a towel before starting to reach for her.

"Would it be all right if I got her?" Benjamin asked. "I haven't had a chance to hold her today. Ro hogged her most of the day."

Carolyn raised her eyebrows. "You want to hold her?"

"Of course I do." Benjamin shrugged. "Why not? She is my baby *schweschder*. We're going to be stuck with each other, so I might as well get to know her." He grinned, and Carolyn knew he was joking.

"All right," she said. "But she needs to be changed and fed."

"I can do that. Ro showed me earlier. She gave me a lesson on everything I wanted to know so I could help you."

"She gave you a lesson?" Carolyn asked as she lifted the baby and handed her to Benjamin.

"*Ya*, I asked her to show me. I told her I wanted to learn so I could take my turn too."

"Oh." Carolyn watched him, surprised that he wanted to learn how to care for a baby.

"I'll go change her and then warm up a bottle. I'll feed her in the *schtupp*."

Carolyn's heart warmed as she heard Benjamin whispering to Sadie Liz on their way out of the kitchen.

"Are you all right?" Joshua appeared behind her and placed a stack of books on the end of the table. He gently massaged her neck, and she felt tension release in response to his tender touch.

"*Ya*." She looked back at him. "I was just surprised that Ben wanted to take care of Sadie Liz."

"Why are you surprised? You once told me Ben was a very sensitive *bu*. You were right." He stopped stroking her neck and began retrieving dishes and utensils from the table. He brought them to the sink and dropped them in the water. Carolyn never had to worry about scraping food off their dishes before washing them. The men never left a trace on their plates—unless there were bones to contend with.

Josh started washing the dishes without a word.

"What are you doing?" Carolyn tried to take the dish-cloth from him, and he moved it away from her.

"What does it look like I'm doing?"

"I can do the dishes, Josh." She reached again, but he took a step to the side, blocking her move. "Why are you being so stubborn?"

He nodded toward the stack of books on a chair next to the table. "I'd rather you look at the books. You told me earlier that you'd look at them."

"Oh." Carolyn looked at the books and at the sink, where he was now scrubbing a pot. "I can do the dishes and then look at the books."

"I can do the dishes before I go check on the ani-mals." He peered over at her. "Why won't you ever let me help you? You let your *mamm* help you in the gar-den earlier, and you let Ro and now Ben take care of Sadie Liz. Why can't I do the dishes for you?"

He had a point. She had let other members of the family help her. There was no use in arguing with Joshua. Instead, she settled in a seat at the end of the table and began looking over the books. She was rec-onciling the bills for the farm when Joshua sat down beside her.

"I've told you this before, but I love having you home," he said. "The *haus* is complete when everyone is here, especially you."

Carolyn looked up at his warm smile, and her heart thumped in her chest. "*Danki.*"

"This is how it should be. We have our meals together every day, and our *kinner* are here with us too. Before you know it, Sadie Liz will be helping you in the kitchen while Ben and I are working with the horses." He leaned over and brushed his lips against her cheek. "I'm going to go check on the animals. I'll be in soon."

He headed out through the mudroom, and Carolyn sighed. If everything was as it should be, then why did she feel the need to return to work at the hotel? Josh just wouldn't understand.

CHAPTER 8

Joshua pushed the rocking chair back and forth on the back porch the following morning and smiled down at his newborn baby girl in his arms as she suckled on the bottle he held for her. She was even more beautiful than he remembered from the day before. Her little nose and dark eyes reminded him of Carolyn. He thought his heart might explode with all the love he felt for the tiny child. Even though he loved Ben very much, he had no idea parental love could be such a consuming emotion with an infant. His love seemed to grow each day, with each gaze into her eyes.

"Did you see the horses?" he asked her while she stared up at him. "Your *bruder* and I raise and sell horses. When you're bigger, we'll show you how to train them, and you can help us if you'd like."

As Sadie Liz continued to stare, he thought about how blessed he was to have this perfect little being in his arms. He was so thankful for all the blessings in his life.

"So many people in our community love you," Joshua continued. "I'm eager for you to come to church and meet all of your cousins and friends. They will be so *froh* to see you, Sadie Liz." He moved his finger over her tiny hand, examining her perfect little fingernails. "They will say that you're so *schee*. They will all want to hold you and talk to you."

"Why aren't you working?"

Joshua looked up to where his mother stood staring at him from the porch steps.

"*Mamm?*" he asked. "I didn't hear your buggy." He looked past her to where her horse and buggy sat by the barn. He'd been so distracted by his daughter that he hadn't noticed a visitor approaching the farmhouse.

"I've been standing here for nearly two minutes." She smiled toward the baby in his arms. "May I hold her?"

"Of course." He stood and handed Sadie Liz and the bottle over to her. "What are you doing here so early on a Thursday?"

"I wanted to come by and check on you. I thought Carolyn might need some help today, and I wanted to see my newest *grosskind*." *Mamm* kept her eyes on Sadie Liz while feeding her. "Where's your *fraa*? Is she cooking breakfast?"

"No, she's still sleeping."

"Sleeping?" His mother gave him a look of disgust. "Why is she still sleeping? It's well after eight. She should be up and caring for the *boppli* so you can work." *Mamm* looked toward the barns. "Doesn't she realize you have to keep this farm running so you can support your family?"

"*Ya*, she knows what it takes to keep the farm running." Joshua's shoulders tightened in defense. "She's been up late every night, trying to help Sadie Liz figure out her days and nights. I let her sleep this morning so she could rest up some. She's still recovering from giving birth."

Mamm grunted while studying Sadie Liz.

"I don't mind taking care of my *dochder*. In fact, I'm enjoying our time together." He gently touched Sadie Liz's head. "If I let Carolyn sleep, then I get some quiet time with Sadie Liz before I start my day. I guess I'm even a little selfish by letting Carolyn sleep so I can have Sadie Liz to myself. Besides, Danny and Ben know what they're doing out there. I have complete faith in them."

Mamm lifted Sadie Liz up to her shoulder and began to pat her back. "Is Carolyn really sleeping in and recovering so she can return to that hotel?"

Joshua blinked and studied his mother's snide expression before responding. "We haven't talked about it since Sadie Liz was born, but I am assuming she won't go back to work. Why would she want to?"

"I don't know, but she didn't seem to be in any rush to quit working before the baby was born. And she told me she probably would go back. I have a hard time believing it too. Is she going to expect you to take care of Sadie Liz on the days she works?"

Joshua's lips formed a thin line, but then his face relaxed. He wasn't going to allow his mother's disparaging comments to ruin his good mood. "I don't think she expects that, *Mamm*."

"I have a feeling she will go back to work. If she does, then you'll definitely need my help. I'll come over and care for Sadie Liz while she's at the hotel."

"You really think she's going to leave the *boppli* for that job?"

His mother shrugged. "*Ya*, I do. She seems to want to keep that job, though I have no idea why."

"I hope you're wrong." He pointed toward the front door. "It's getting hot out here even if it is only May. Would you like to come inside?"

"*Ya*, that sounds *gut*."

Joshua opened the door, and his mother headed in through the mudroom to the kitchen, then sat at the table.

"Would you like some coffee?" he offered, heading to the counter.

"*Ya, danki*."

He poured two cups of coffee and brought them to the table. He sat beside her and sipped his drink while he watched his mother continue to feed Sadie Liz.

"I could stare at her for hours," Joshua said. "Of course, then no work would get done, and we'd starve."

His mother chuckled. "It is an amazing thing to hold your own *kind*." She smiled up at him. "It's even more *wunderbaar* to hold your *grosskinner*. I'm so *froh* to have more *grosskinner* in my life. You and Carolyn have blessed your *dat* and me. We had worried we wouldn't have any more *grosskinner* after Gideon died. You didn't seem interested in marriage. But the Lord has blessed us many times over, and maybe you and Carolyn will bless us again."

"I hope so, but I couldn't be happier now." Joshua sipped his coffee.

The floor creaked at the far end of the kitchen, and Joshua looked across the room to where Carolyn stood in the doorway. She was clad in a blue dress and black apron with her hair hidden by her prayer covering. Her eyes were wide as she looked at him and then his mother. The dark circles he'd seen under her eyes last night had faded, evidence that she'd slept better last night than she had the night before.

"*Gude mariye, mei liewe*," he said. "You look well rested."

"*Gude mariye.*" Carolyn looked again from him to his mother. "*Gude mariye,* Barbie."

"Nice to see you, Carolyn." His mother kept her eyes on Sadie Liz. "I was wondering if you were going to sleep all day."

Carolyn's pretty face clouded with a frown.

"Would you like me to make you breakfast?" Joshua hopped up from the table and walked over to her, hoping to distract her from his mother's comment. "I can fry some eggs and hash browns for you. How many eggs would you like? Two?"

"*Danki*, but I can make it." Her gaze seemed to search his. "I didn't expect you to let me sleep this morning. I told you last night that I could get up with you and make your breakfast. I'm feeling a lot stronger. I don't expect you to take care of me."

"It's fine." He touched her cheek. "I like taking care of you, and I don't mind letting you sleep. You looked exhausted last night after you finished the books. I'm sorry you stayed up so late working on that for me."

"I don't mind. It's my job to do the books for you." She looked toward his mother. "I didn't know you were planning to come over today, Barbie."

"I thought you could use some help." *Mamm* glanced back toward Carolyn. "But I didn't know Joshua would be caring for the baby while you slept."

Carolyn's frown deepened.

"It's fine," he whispered.

Carolyn's expression softened slightly. "Is there any coffee?"

"*Ya*, I'll pour you a cup." They walked to the counter, and he handed her a cup of coffee.

"*Danki.*" She took a long drink. "It's nice and strong, just the way I like it."

"That's why I made it that way." He smiled. "I better get outside."

"Okay." She smiled up at him, and he felt the tension in his shoulders release. "I'll think of something *gut* to make you for lunch."

"*Danki.*" He kissed her forehead before heading out the back door. As he walked toward the barn, he prayed his mother wouldn't say anything else to upset Carolyn. He also hoped she was wrong when she said Carolyn would go back to work. He was thankful to see Carolyn finally looking rested. He'd been worried at how exhausted she'd been, both before and since Sadie Liz had been born. He wanted his wife happy and healthy, along with the rest of his precious family.

· · ·

Carolyn pulled the frying pan out of the cabinet and cracked two eggs into a bowl. She hadn't expected to find her mother-in-law sitting in the kitchen this morning. While it was nice of Barbie to come over to help, Carolyn grew weary of her derisive comments. She silently prayed for strength and patience while she beat the eggs and then poured them into the pan.

"That's nice that Josh lets you sleep," Barbie commented behind her. "I think Eli did that for me a few times after each *bu* was born."

"*Ya*, it is nice," Carolyn said while the yolks fizzled and popped in the hot pan. "He's very thoughtful, and I appreciate it."

"Have you quit your job at the hotel yet?"

Carolyn moved the eggs around in the pan with a spatula. "I haven't spoken to my supervisor since Sadie Liz was born. I'm thinking about going to visit the hotel and taking her with me. I can talk to Gregg in person then."

"Why would you want to take the *boppli* to that hotel?"

Carolyn flipped the eggs in the pan while ignoring the disgust in Barbie's voice. "My friends will enjoy seeing Sadie Liz, and I want to visit them." She slipped the eggs onto a plate and sat across from Barbie at the table. After a silent prayer, she began to eat the eggs while Barbie burped Sadie Liz.

"You can just call your boss and resign from your job." Barbie rubbed Sadie Liz's back. "You don't need to take the *boppli* all the way to that hotel and tell him in person. He knows you had a baby. Didn't you say he stopped by to visit you last week?"

Carolyn nodded while she ate. "*Ya*, he did visit me, and he also sent flowers. But I want to go visit him and see how everyone is."

Barbie studied her for a moment. "Do you miss the job?"

Carolyn shrugged. Barbie would never understand how she felt about working at the hotel. She didn't miss the job, but she missed feeling as if she were working to secure Ben's future. Trying to explain it would be like speaking to Barbie in a foreign language. Her mother-in-law could never possibly understand what it felt like to be responsible for a child who didn't have a biological father to help support him.

"If you go back to work, I will have to come over to help Joshua with the *boppli*." Barbie kept rubbing Sadie Liz's back until she gave a little belch and hiccupped. "But you can't possibly want to be away from your *boppli* so you can clean hotel rooms."

Carolyn trained her eyes on her plate to avoid her mother-in-law's probing stare.

"My son makes a *gut* living here. Why would you want to work at a part-time job that you don't need? Everything you could possibly want is right here."

Carolyn sipped the coffee and tried to think of something to say that would change the subject.

"Do you think my son isn't a *gut* provider?" Barbie asked.

Carolyn's gaze snapped to Barbie's. How could her mother-in-law say something so negative and accusatory? "I never said Josh wasn't a *gut* provider."

"Then why do you need to work?" Barbie asked while

feeding Sadie Liz the remainder of the bottle. "If you have everything you need, then you should be home with your *kinner* where you belong."

Carolyn gripped her cup to prevent herself from saying something disrespectful to the older woman. "I haven't decided if I'm going back to work or not."

"It doesn't seem like it's a difficult decision to me." Barbie smiled down at Sadie Liz. "Look at you. You look just like your *dat*."

"*Ya*, she does." Carolyn's expression relaxed. At least there was one topic they agreed on.

CHAPTER 9

Carolyn was sweeping the kitchen early one morning a week later when her niece walked in from the mudroom.

"Hi, *Aenti* Carolyn," Rosemary said. "I wanted to come by to help you. I called *Onkel* Josh earlier, and he thought you might want to get away for a while today. That's why I have Aiden Monroe waiting outside in his van. Do you want to go shopping? We can take Sadie Liz with us."

"That sounds *wunderbaar*." Carolyn stowed the broom in the pantry. "I have a shopping list started. I was going to see if I could get a driver for tomorrow."

"We can go together." Rosemary turned her attention to the baby. "How are you, Sadie Liz? We're going shopping. Do you want to come with us?" Rosemary lifted her from the baby seat and looked at Carolyn. "Do you have a bag packed for her?"

"Let me put one together." Carolyn hurried to the bedroom and packed a diaper bag. When she returned to the kitchen, Rosemary was packing bottles. Carolyn added a few things to the shopping list, folded it, and placed it in her pocket with her wallet.

"Are we ready to take Sadie Liz out into the world?" Rosemary asked.

"I think so." Carolyn and Rosemary headed outside to the waiting van where Carolyn had already seen Joshua through the kitchen window helping the driver install the baby's car seat.

Carolyn smiled and greeted Aiden Monroe.

Joshua stepped back from the van. "Rosemary called earlier and asked if she could take you shopping. I told her I would pay for the driver so you could go out together."

"That's a great idea. How did you know I needed to get out of the house?"

He shrugged. "I guess I sensed your growing cabin fever."

"*Danki.*" It was just like him to know what she needed before she had figured it out herself.

"So, where are we headed?" Aiden asked. "I'm free all morning and then some, so you name the place."

"I have a list for the market," Carolyn said. "We're low on quite a few things."

"*Ya,* I had noticed that." Joshua touched Carolyn's arm. "You go on and take your time. After all, it's such a beautiful day."

Carolyn considered the idea she'd had since Barbie had visited. "I was thinking about stopping by the hotel first to see everyone and show them how big Sadie Liz is getting."

Joshua's smile faded. "You want to visit the hotel?"

"*Ya.*" She hesitated. "I just want to visit my friends. It will be a quick trip."

"I don't know if it's a *gut* idea for you to go there today," Joshua said. "You're going to be worn out just from grocery shopping, and Sadie Liz may get cranky. What if you don't make it back in time for lunch? Are you certain you want to put you both through all that in one day?"

"It will be fine. Rosemary is here to help me." Carolyn turned to Rosemary, who was standing by the fence and talking to Danny while rocking Sadie Liz in her arms. "Rosemary?" she asked, and her niece turned to her. "Do you mind if we stop by the hotel to see my coworkers?"

Rosemary smiled. "That sounds like fun."

"Josh is worried that it will be too much for Sadie Liz along with shopping at the market," Carolyn said.

Rosemary shook her head. "Oh, no. We'll be fine, *Onkel* Josh. I've taken babies out before, and they just fall asleep after a while."

He nodded slowly. "All right, but don't overdo it."

"I promise I won't," Carolyn said. "And we'll be back in time for lunch."

Carolyn and Rosemary climbed into the van, and Carolyn secured Sadie Liz in the baby seat.

Aiden steered the van down the rock driveway toward the main road.

Rosemary leaned forward toward the driver seat. "Aiden, could we please head to the Lancaster Grand Hotel first?"

"Absolutely," Aiden said as he merged onto the highway.

"How are things at the farm?" Carolyn asked Rosemary.

"Oh, they're *gut*." Rosemary turned toward her in the seat while she spoke. "*Mei dat* bought a few more cows, and David and Robert have been busy helping him."

"And how are the youth gatherings going?"

Rosemary's cheeks blushed bright pink. "They're going really well. Danny has been coming to them."

"Oh?" Carolyn smiled. "Tell me more."

Rosemary spent the remainder of the drive telling Carolyn about her friends and who was dating whom. By the time they reached the Lancaster Grand Hotel, Carolyn knew about all the couples in Rosemary's youth group.

. . .

Joshua was working with a horse in the pasture when he spotted the van parking by the house. He jogged over, paid Aiden, and then helped Rosemary take the bags into the house while Carolyn carried Sadie Liz in her car seat.

"How was your visit at the hotel?" Joshua asked as he lined the bags up on the counter.

"It was *gut*." Carolyn placed the seat on the table. "We saw all of my coworkers and then went to the grocery store. Sadie Liz fell asleep in the van on the way to the store and slept through the shopping trip. I don't think I'm ever going to get her to sleep tonight. She was passed out, weren't you?" She leaned over the seat and touched the baby's cheek.

Rosemary pulled supplies out of the bags and began

putting them in the cabinets. "I think your coworkers really enjoyed seeing the *boppli*. Even your supervisor was smiling while he talked to her. Everyone was so nice."

"*Ya*, they were *froh* that we stopped by." Carolyn smiled at Rosemary. "*Danki* for coming with me."

Joshua wanted to ask her if she'd finally resigned from her job, but he didn't want to risk upsetting Carolyn, especially in front of Rosemary. The subject of her going back to work was a sore spot for Carolyn, but he longed to hear her say she was going to quit.

Carolyn picked up Sadie Liz. "I'm going to go change her. Do you mind putting everything away, Ro?"

"I don't mind at all." Rosemary retrieved a pound of butter from the bag and slipped it into the refrigerator. "*Danki*."

"I'll come with you," Josh said. He followed her to the bedroom where she placed Sadie Liz on the changing table Sarah Ann had given her. "I'm glad you had a nice visit."

"We did have a nice time, but you were right, it was tiring for her." Carolyn slipped off Sadie Liz's dress. "It was *gut* for her to be out in the fresh air, though. And I think I did have a little bit of cabin fever. I enjoyed interacting with other people."

"Did you talk to your supervisor?" he asked, hoping to gently prod her to talk about her job. His heart would feel settled if he knew he had her at the farm full-time permanently. He didn't want to share her with the rest of the world when they had a family to raise now.

"I spoke to him briefly." She kept her gaze on the baby

while changing her diaper. "He said it was *gut* to see me and the *boppli*."

"That's all he said?" Joshua had a difficult time believing the subject of her return to work hadn't come up between them.

"He asked me to let him know if and when I'm coming back to work." He waited while she wiped Sadie Liz and applied diaper ointment, and then she went on. "He said he has someone filling in for me, and he's going to hire her on permanently if I don't return."

"And what did you say?" Joshua sank into a chair beside the bed.

"I told him I'll let him know." She pulled on a fresh diaper. "He said I should call him as soon as I decide."

She kept her eyes on their baby as she fastened the diaper and started to dress her again. *Why wouldn't she look at him? Was she avoiding his gaze? Was* Mamm *right when she said Carolyn would return to the hotel?*

"Why would you want to go back, Carolyn?" Joshua asked, praying she'd look at him. "Why aren't you *froh* here with me and the *kinner*?" He reached over and touched her arm.

"I am *froh*." Carolyn finally looked up at him. "I'm just not sure about quitting yet."

"Why aren't you certain?" Joshua searched her eyes.

"*Aenti* Carolyn?" Rosemary called from the kitchen. "Would you like me to start making lunch?"

"I need to go help Rosemary. We'll talk later, okay?" Carolyn's smile seemed forced. "I'll make you something nice for lunch."

Joshua nodded as Carolyn walked out of the room

with Sadie Liz on her shoulder. He gritted his teeth and raked his hands through his hair. Why wouldn't she tell him what she was thinking? Had he done something wrong? His father had told him to be patient with Carolyn, but his patience was wearing thin. And his mother's prediction circled through his mind daily.

He would try to talk to Carolyn again later, when they were alone. Somehow he'd make her see that she belonged at the farm with their family.

CHAPTER 10

Carolyn settled Sadie Liz in her cradle for her midmorning nap. Since the baby was sleeping soundly, she felt comfortable walking outside for a few minutes. She headed to the barn to check the phone messages, but first she stopped by her garden and noticed that the tomato seeds were finally starting to sprout. She loved watching the garden grow and flourish as the season wore on. Even as a little girl she enjoyed working in her garden with her mother and grandmother back on her brother's dairy farm.

With her hand tented over her eyes, Carolyn looked toward the pasture where she spotted Joshua, Benjamin, and Daniel repairing the far fence. She waved, and Joshua waved in response. Then she headed into the barn and checked the messages on voice mail. The first two were customers calling to inquire about horses. She listened to them and then hit the Save button for Joshua. The last message was for her.

"Hi, Carolyn. This is Linda. Last week when you stopped by the hotel, I mentioned I wanted to come by. I was wondering if tonight would be all right. I thought

I could bring something for supper. I understand if it's not a *gut* day. Just let me know. Talk to you soon. Bye!"

Carolyn rubbed her hands together. She'd been thinking about making a ham loaf for supper, and tonight would be the perfect night. She dialed Linda's number and waited for the voice mail to pick up. "Hi, Linda. This is Carolyn. I would love for you to come for supper tonight. Please come anytime. I'm looking forward to seeing you. I'm going to make a ham loaf, so you can bring whatever you'd like to go with it. See you later."

Carolyn hurried back into the house and checked on Sadie Liz, who was still sleeping soundly. She then made her way to the laundry room to run another load of clothes through the wringer washer. She hummed to herself while she worked. She enjoyed being home and taking care of her household chores. Maybe Joshua was right—this was where she belonged. After the clothes were washed, she checked on Sadie Liz and found her stirring.

"Are you awake, little one?" Carolyn lifted the baby into her arms and carried her out to the back porch. "Do you want to watch me hang the clothes on the line? Pretty soon you'll be out here handing me the clothes-pins. I used to love helping my *mamm* with the laundry when I was little."

Sadie Liz cooed and gurgled, and Carolyn laughed.

"You're in an awfully *gut* mood today, Sadie Liz. I'm certain that's because you're sleeping more at night. I'm glad you're getting your rest. I'll set you in your seat, and you can watch me work. How does that sound?"

Carolyn strapped the baby in the bouncy seat that was still on the porch from earlier that morning and continued humming while she hung the laundry on the line that extended to the barn. She moved the laundry down with a pulley that Joshua had installed for her.

First she hung Joshua's trousers and Benjamin's trousers, and next she hung their shirts. After her dresses and aprons were hung on the line, she added Sadie's diapers and onesies. Soon the line was full, and Carolyn admired how it looked with all of their clothes flapping in the warm breeze. It was a beautiful blend of colors—just like their family.

"I see you have help today." Joshua approached the porch. He lifted his hat and swiped his hand across his brow. "Are you teaching Sadie Liz about laundry?"

"I am." Carolyn smiled down at her husband. "I was just telling her how I used to hand my *mamm* clothespins. Soon she'll be handing them to me."

"I know she will." Joshua climbed the steps and leaned over the bouncy seat where Sadie Liz continued to coo. "Did she have a good morning nap?"

"*Ya*, she did. I thought she could use some more fresh air." Carolyn ran her finger over Joshua's arm. "We're going to have company for supper."

"Oh *ya*?" Joshua raised his eyebrows. "Who is going to join us?"

"Linda Zook wants to come by tonight. I thought I'd make ham loaf. Does that sound *gut*?"

"*Ya*." He picked up Sadie Liz and cradled her in his arms. "You know I love ham loaf." He turned his gaze to the baby. "Wait until you have ham loaf, Sadie Liz.

You will love it. Trust me. Your *mamm* makes the best ham loaf in all of Lancaster County."

"Don't listen to him, Sadie Liz. My *mamm* is a much better cook than I am." Carolyn looked toward the back door. "Oh, I have so much to do before Linda gets here. I need to clean the *haus* and get all of the ingredients for supper together."

"The *haus* looks fine. Didn't you just clean yesterday? You've been cleaning nearly every day."

"*Ya*, I guess I have. I've been on a cleaning frenzy since Sadie Liz started sleeping more at night. I have more energy." She smoothed her hands over her apron. "I'm so glad Linda called. I had wanted to make an especially nice meal for us. Oh, this will be fun. It's been awhile since we've had someone over for supper."

Joshua kissed the baby's head. "It's *gut* to see you smiling again. I was beginning to worry about you, but now you're back to your former self." He kissed Carolyn's cheek. "You're my *froh fraa* again. *Ich liebe dich.*" He whispered the words in her ear as if it were a secret kept between the two of them.

Carolyn felt as though her heart turned over in her chest. "I love you too."

"Josh!" Daniel called from the stable. "Can you come here and help us with something?"

"I better go." Joshua handed the baby to Carolyn. "I'll see you in a bit."

"Okay." Carolyn held Sadie Liz to her chest and sighed as Joshua loped down the steps and back toward the stable. She enjoyed every moment of her time at home with her family, and she dreaded the idea of going back to work at the hotel. She would miss mornings like this, out on the porch hanging laundry and talking to her baby.

Sadie Liz whimpered and began to cry.

Carolyn looked down at her. "Do you want a diaper change? Let's go get you fixed up and then we'll start on the cleaning."

. . .

Later, Joshua stepped into the stable and found evidence that Benjamin and Daniel were mucking the stalls. "How's it going?"

"It would go a lot faster if you lent us a hand," Daniel responded from somewhere near the back of the stable.

Joshua shook his head and smiled. Daniel and Benjamin were never afraid to speak their minds, and he appreciated their honesty. "I have *gut* news."

"What's that?" Daniel stepped out into his line of sight.

"It's noon." Joshua pointed in the direction of the farmhouse. "That means Carolyn has an *appeditlich* lunch waiting for us in the *haus*."

"Oh *gut*." Daniel started toward the front of the stable. "I'm ready for a break. It's hot in here today. It feels more like August than June."

"Make sure you wash up at the pump today," Joshua said as Daniel moved past him. "You're a mess."

"You're not so clean yourself." Daniel smirked as he headed for the house.

Joshua lingered behind and waited for Benjamin,

who emerged from a stall near the far end of the stable. "Are you hungry?"

"I'm always hungry." Benjamin met him at the door. "Is everything all right?"

"*Ya*, I just meant are you too hungry to wait up a few minutes. I want to talk to you."

Benjamin frowned. "Did I do something wrong?"

"No, no." Joshua shook his head as they walked toward the house. "I want to ask you something. Have you noticed something different about your *mamm* lately?"

Benjamin stopped walking and looked up at Joshua. "No, I haven't. What's going on?"

"She seems so *froh* these days." Joshua pointed toward the laundry swaying in the wind. "Earlier today I watched her hang out the clothes, and she was humming and talking to Sadie Liz. She was actually glowing because she seemed so content."

Benjamin nodded. "*Ya*, I have seen that. She was singing to Sadie Liz last night when she gave her a bath. I haven't seen her so relaxed in a long time."

Joshua smiled. "I was wondering if you had noticed it too."

Benjamin's stomach growled. "I'm really hungry. Can we talk about this more later?" He started toward the house.

"Wait." Joshua caught up with him. "I want to ask you something else before we go into the *haus*. Has she said anything to you about going back to work at the hotel?"

Benjamin shrugged. "No, she hasn't. Why?"

"Well, I wanted to talk about it after she took Sadie Liz to visit her coworkers, but she either won't give me a straight answer about whether or not she's going back or she changes the subject when I bring it up. I tried pushing her to talk to me, and she gets defensive. I don't want to argue with her and ruin her good mood. I wanted to get your opinion about it. I'm wondering if maybe she won't go back to the hotel now since she seems so content to be here at the farm with us. Do you think she finally feels like she can quit?"

"I really don't know." Benjamin climbed the steps to the porch. "She hasn't said anything to me about it."

"Will you let me know if she says anything to you?" Joshua asked.

"*Ya*, I will."

After washing up at the pump, Joshua followed Benjamin into the mudroom where they shucked their boots. The aroma of freshly baked cookies and bread assaulted Joshua's senses as he stepped into the kitchen. He found Carolyn standing by the table, which was clogged with platters of food.

She made a sweeping gesture. "I hope you're all hungry. I had some fun making lunch."

Joshua couldn't believe his eyes. He hadn't seen so much food since the last barn raising he'd attended.

"*Danki, Mamm.*" Benjamin washed his hands at the sink and then sat at his usual spot at the table.

"Everything looks fantastic." Joshua washed his hands, too, and sat next to Benjamin. After a prayer, he filled his plate with lunch meat, bread, pickles, pretzels, and potato salad. He glanced over at Sadie Liz in her seat and smiled. "Has she had her lunch?"

"*Ya*, she finished a bottle just before I set everything

out. She'll be ready for her afternoon nap soon, but I thought she might enjoy having lunch with you first." Carolyn sat across from him and placed a spoonful of potato salad on her plate.

While they ate, Benjamin and Daniel fell into a conversation about one of the horses. They continued talking, seemingly oblivious to Carolyn's and Joshua's presence.

"There are fresh chocolate chip and peanut butter *kichlin* and also carrot bread for dessert, so be sure to save some room. I just had time to put them in the oven before Sadie needed that bottle," Carolyn said while putting two pieces of turkey on a piece of fresh bread.

"You made *kichlin* and carrot bread too?" Joshua studied his wife. "You've been busy."

"*Ya*, I have." Carolyn shrugged. "I swept and picked up in the *schtupp*. The *haus* is all ready for when Linda arrives." Her cheeks flushed. "You're staring at me."

"I was just admiring you. You're glowing." He picked up a pretzel from his plate. "You seem to be really settled in our new life."

"What do you mean?" She added mustard and mayonnaise to her sandwich. "I've been settled in at the farm since we were married."

"I don't mean that. I mean you seem happy to be here all the time and not working part-time at the hotel."

Her smile faded slightly. Why did he have to bring up the subject? She had looked so happy and now he had ruined it.

"I am enjoying being home." She cut the sandwich in

half. "I was thinking of making a pie for dessert tonight. Do you have a preference?"

"How about crumbly peach pie?" he asked, hoping to lighten her mood again. "You haven't made one of those in a long time."

Her smile was back. "That's a *gut* idea. I'll make that for Linda."

"I thought you would make it for me." He winked at her, and she laughed. Her sweet laughter was a melody to his ears. He hoped to hear her laugh more often.

CHAPTER 11

Carolyn put the ham loaf in the oven and began setting the table for supper. Sadie Liz sat nearby in her seat and cooed while Carolyn worked. She lined up the plates and pulled out the utensils.

"Dinner is going to smell *wunderbaar* tonight," she told the baby. "You won't believe how *gut* until you smell it."

Carolyn heard a knock on the back door and went to open it.

"Hi, Carolyn!"

"Linda!" Carolyn hugged her friend. "I'm so glad you came. I just put the ham loaf in the oven."

"That sounds fantastic." Linda pointed toward the bag she had in her other hand. "I brought a seven-layer salad."

"Thank you. I am sure it will be delicious."

Linda followed Carolyn into the kitchen, where she took her casserole dish out of the bag.

After cooing over the baby for a few moments, Linda looked at Carolyn. "How are you? You seem different."

"What do you mean?" Carolyn asked.

"You look younger, if that's possible." Linda paused,

tapping her finger to her lip. "Well, that's not it exactly. You're radiant. You just seem more cheerful and more youthful. It's as if something's happened to you. You've been transformed."

Carolyn chuckled. "You could say I've been transformed. I did just have a *boppli*." She motioned toward Sadie Liz, still contented in her baby seat. "It's just part of having a *kind*."

"No, it's more than that. Something has changed for you. What is it?"

Carolyn shook her head as she took the salad to the refrigerator. "I'm not sure what it could be other than I had a really great day. I got a *gut* night's sleep because Sadie Liz is sleeping much more during the night lately. I did the laundry, cleaned, and baked. I made a special lunch for Josh, Ben, and Danny, and I got to plan this meal for you. I guess I spent the day doing all of my favorite things."

Linda snapped her fingers. "That's it. You're doing what you truly love. I think you've been craving this family life for a long time. You told me you thought you'd never find someone to love you completely because of Benjamin. You not only found and married Josh, but now that you have Sadie Liz, you feel as if your life is complete, right?"

"Maybe it is that." Carolyn leaned back against the counter and folded her hands over her apron. "I do feel complete now. I have my family, my husband, and my two *kinner*. We have this wonderful home. I didn't think I deserved a life like this after I became a mother when I was sixteen. Now I see that I have everything

I ever wanted. I'm so thankful for all that I have now. Today I felt like I couldn't stop smiling."

She gazed at Sadie Liz, who cooed from her bouncy seat.

"*Ya*, I know you went through a hard time before you met Josh, but God had the perfect timing for you both. He answers our prayers." Linda tapped her finger on the counter. "It's like those Scripture verses in First Thessalonians say. 'Rejoice always, pray continually, give thanks in all circumstances; for this is God's will for you in Christ Jesus.' We always have to keep praying and thanking God. Even when we think things won't work out for us, God is in control. He will never abandon us. In the end, He's with us, protecting us and loving us."

"That's very true."

"Now, what can I do to help you get ready for supper?" Linda asked.

Carolyn scanned the table. "We need glasses."

Linda turned to the cabinet and pulled out four glasses. "Gregg asked about you yesterday. He wanted to know if I'd heard from you."

Carolyn's shoulders tensed. "What did you tell him?"

"I told him we hadn't talked about it, but I promised to let you know he asked."

"He hasn't offered my job to the other woman yet, has he?"

"No, but I heard her asking him about it. She said she really needs to find a stable part-time job. She's very nice. She's *English*, and she lives over in Bird-in-Hand." Linda retrieved a pitcher of water from the refrigerator.

"You're not still considering coming back to the hotel, are you?"

Carolyn hesitated but decided to be forthcoming with her friend. "I don't want to go back, but I know I need to."

"Why would you have to come back?" Linda filled the glasses. "You just finished telling me how happy you are here. Why would you want to leave this?"

"I need to work for Ben." Relief flooded Carolyn as she said the words out loud. "I have to make sure he has everything he needs."

"What do you mean?" Linda shook her head.

"Ben isn't Josh's biological son."

"I know that."

"That means Josh may not feel like he has to help Ben when he's ready to buy his own farm or build his first *haus*. If I keep working part-time at the hotel, I can put money away for Ben to secure his future. I have an obligation to my son, and I have a savings account where I put a little bit of money away for him every time I get paid."

Carolyn pulled out a stack of paper napkins and started folding them. "I want him to have the same opportunities Sadie Liz will have when she's older. I'm certain Joshua will make sure Sadie Liz has everything she needs when she's ready to move out and have her own *haus*. I don't want Ben to resent Sadie Liz or any of his other future siblings if they get more than he did. It wouldn't be right for him to feel as though he's not as important as they are."

"Carolyn." Linda placed her hand on Carolyn's arm.

"Josh loves you, and he loves Ben. I'm certain he wouldn't give more to Sadie Liz than he'd give to Ben. Why aren't you certain?"

"I don't think he would do it deliberately." Carolyn started setting the folded napkins under the utensils. "I think it might be subconscious. He may not even realize it if he favors his biological *kinner* over Ben. I can't run the risk of Ben resenting his other siblings or not having as much as they have. It's not Ben's fault that he came into the world the way he did."

"You need to stop punishing yourself for having Ben when you were sixteen. You're a great *mamm*, and Josh is a great *dat*," Linda said while placing the water pitcher back in the refrigerator. "I've noticed how Josh and Ben interact at church service, and it's obvious they have a great mutual respect for one another. I don't think Ben is missing out on not having his biological *dat*."

Carolyn nodded, but she couldn't stop the doubt from filling her mind.

"Carolyn, please look at me."

She turned to her friend.

"You told me Josh adopted Ben, and he calls Josh *Dat*, right?" Linda asked. Carolyn nodded. "What else does he need to do to prove to you that he considers Ben his son?"

The question was simple, but Carolyn answered, "I honestly don't know."

"Carolyn, I don't think you need to work at the hotel to try to prove anything else. I think you're already doing everything the best you can, without that extra income." She paused. "And I don't think the problem is Josh. I get the feeling you're still blaming yourself for becoming a *mamm* at such a young age. You've been forgiven, and you can trust God to provide for you and also for Ben's needs. Stop punishing yourself for your mistake. God has forgiven you, so now you need to forgive yourself, once and for all."

Carolyn sighed. "*Danki* for trying to help me sort out my feelings, Linda. I appreciate it."

Linda's words circled her mind. She needed to let them settle in her soul. Was Linda right? Did she still need to forgive herself, once and for all? Is that why she was so concerned about Ben and whether Josh would truly treat him as a son?

She had a lot to contemplate, and she was thankful for her friend's honest conversation.

. . .

Linda's words were still echoing through her mind while she rocked Sadie Liz later that evening. She held her baby close to her chest while she nursed. Was she overcompensating by trying to go back to work at the hotel? She still felt responsible for Benjamin, that she had to be the one to ensure his future, and she couldn't earn money for him staying at home. Some women like her mother and Sarah Ann earned some money sewing or quilting, but she didn't think her skills were as good or marketable as theirs. And neither of them had small children to care for now, so they had more flexibility.

No, working at the hotel still made sense, even though

she despised the thought of going back and she felt more confused about making a decision than ever.

"Dinner was *wunderbaar* tonight." Joshua sat on the edge of the bed, which creaked under his weight. "I think Linda had a nice time."

"*Ya*, she did." Carolyn looked up at him. "I think she liked her crumbly peach pie."

"I still say it was my pie." Joshua smiled at her, and then his eyes seemed to question hers. "You look like you have something on your mind. Do you want to talk about it?"

"No, I'm fine. I'm just tired." She cupped her free hand over her mouth to cover a yawn. "It's been a long day."

"You stayed busy all day long." His gaze moved to Sadie Liz. "She seems *froh* there. Are you going to try to keep her up for a little bit?"

"*Ya*, I am. I'm hoping to get even more sleep tonight than I did last night."

"As hard as you worked today, I'm certain you need it." He watched Sadie Liz for a moment, and she wished she could read his thoughts. "But you've seemed happy. Even Ben has noticed how happy you've seemed lately."

"He has?" she asked, and he nodded. "Ben hasn't said anything to me."

"He's a teenage *bu*. What do you expect him to say?"

"You're right." She looked down at Sadie Liz. "You can go to bed. You don't need to sit up with us."

"I don't mind. I can wait for you."

They sat in silence while Sadie Liz finished nursing and then burped. Joshua leaned over and touched

Carolyn's knee while keeping his eyes on the baby. Carolyn enjoyed having his company while she cared for Sadie Liz. She felt safe with Joshua near her side. Joy filled her as she enjoyed the quiet, intimate moment with her newborn and her husband.

Once Sadie Liz began snoring quietly, Carolyn gently placed her in the cradle and tucked her in. Then she climbed into bed beside Joshua, and he snuffed out the lantern.

"*Gut nacht*," he whispered before kissing her cheek and resting his hand on her arm.

"*Gut nacht*," she repeated. As she rolled onto her side, she opened her heart to God.

Lord, please guide me in my decision about returning to work at the hotel. I'm so confused by all of my feelings. While I still believe I need to build up a nest egg for Ben, I'm beginning to wonder if Linda is right. Do I need to trust that Josh will provide for all of our kinner, including Ben? And am I not seeing that I deserve complete forgiveness for my mistakes? Please guide my heart to the right decision. In Jesus' holy name. Amen.

CHAPTER 12

Carolyn held Sadie Liz while she stood in Barbie's kitchen the following Sunday afternoon after service. Sadie Liz cooed and grunted while Carolyn gently patted her back. Lillian Glick, Joshua's niece, moved through the knot of women serving the noon meal and sidled up to her.

"She is getting so big, *Aenti* Carolyn." Lillian held up her hands. "I just washed my hands. May I hold her?"

"Of course." Carolyn handed her the baby. "I just finished nursing her, so she's *froh* and full."

Lillian smiled down at Sadie Liz. "Isn't it amazing how quickly babies grow? It seems like only yesterday that we were waiting for her to come into the world."

"*Ya*, I know." Carolyn sighed. "I can't believe she's a month old already. It feels like she was born only a few days ago."

"Carolyn." Her mother came up behind her. "How is my Sadie Liz?"

"She's doing great," Carolyn said. "She's enjoying her cousin right now."

Mamm touched Sadie Liz's hand. "Look at you. You're so big. Is she sleeping better at night?"

"Oh, *ya*. She slept a four-hour stretch last night. It was

wunderbaar." Carolyn nodded at her mother and then spotted a tray of peanut butter spread in her hands. "Do you need help serving the meal? Lily can hold Sadie Liz, and I'll help you."

Her mother pointed to a coffeepot on the counter. "You can fill coffee cups if you want."

"Okay." Carolyn turned to Lillian. "Do you mind holding her awhile longer?"

"Oh, no, not at all. I'd love to," Lillian said. "I'll take *gut* care of her."

Carolyn fetched the coffeepot and walked outside with her mother.

"The service was nice today," *Mamm* said as they walked toward the large barn where the benches were set up for the noon meal.

"It *was* nice," Carolyn agreed. "I missed part of it while I was walking with Sadie, but I enjoyed the parts I was able to hear."

"You seem completely relaxed today." Her mother studied her. "You didn't even hesitate when you asked Lillian to hold Sadie Liz."

Carolyn shrugged. "I know Lily is great with *kinner.* I've seen her with other babies, and she does a *wunderbaar* job. I know I don't have to worry when she watches Sadie Liz."

"No, that's not it." *Mamm* stopped walking and faced her. "You're different, Carolyn. You've changed since you've had Sadie Liz."

"I keep hearing that." Carolyn held the coffeepot by her side. "Even Ben and Josh have said I'm different, and I don't understand. I still feel like the same person, but everyone has been telling me I'm not. How am I different?"

"You were so worried before Sadie Liz was born, but you don't seem to be as worried anymore. You're almost always relaxed and positive about things. Every time I look at you, you smile. I'm so relieved to see you like this. I was concerned about you."

"You were?" Carolyn asked. "I'm sorry I worried you."

"Oh, no. You don't need to apologize. It's my job as your *mamm* to be concerned about you and your *bruder*. You were just so exhausted, and you didn't seem ready for Sadie Liz."

"I have my strength back, and that has made a big difference in how I feel."

Mamm tapped her chin with her free hand as she balanced the tray with the other. "But something was bothering you. You told me you were anxious about how Ben would fit into the family after Sadie Liz was born, but now you don't seem to be apprehensive about that anymore."

Carolyn shook her head. "No, I'm not. Ben is adjusting fine, and he loves his baby sister." *But I don't want to go back to work at the hotel. I haven't figured that out yet.*

Mamm touched Carolyn's arm. "I'm glad you're feeling better. And I'm proud of you. You're a *wunderbaar mamm*."

"*Danki*." Carolyn's eyes misted over. "We'd better take in this food before the men start asking for the peanut butter spread. They also won't be happy if I fill their cups with cold coffee."

Carolyn and her mother entered the barn where the men were sitting at the benches to eat lunch before the women and children. While her mother delivered the bowls of peanut butter spread, Carolyn filled cups at several tables before she arrived where Joshua sat with her father and Benjamin.

"*Danki*, Carolyn," *Dat* said with a smile as she filled their cups as well.

"Where's Sadie Liz?" Joshua asked.

"Lily is holding her," Carolyn said. "I thought I'd help serve today."

"*Danki*." Joshua winked at her.

Once the coffeepot was empty, Carolyn started back toward the house.

"Carolyn." Barbie walked beside her. "*Danki* for helping with the coffee."

"*Gern gschehne.*" Carolyn smiled at her mother-in-law. "I enjoy helping the other ladies serve the meal. It gives me a chance to say hello to everyone."

"I saw Lily rocking Sadie Liz on the porch. They both looked content." Barbie pointed to where the pair sat. "Josh told me you've got Sadie Liz in a *gut* routine, and she's sleeping longer at night. You're doing a great job with her."

Carolyn stopped walking and swallowed a gasp as she looked at Barbie. "*Danki.*"

Barbie gave her a stiff nod and continued toward the house.

Carolyn gripped the coffeepot in her hand and wondered if that was a sign from God for what she should do. If even her censorious mother-in-law thought she was a good mother, was she meant to stay at home with the children full-time, no matter her fears about Ben's future?

. . .

Joshua and his father leaned on the pasture fence and watched as a line of buggies drove toward the main road. The noon meal was over, and families were headed back toward their homes.

"It was a *gut* day," *Dat* said while wiping his hand across his brow. "It sure is warm today. I enjoy hosting church, but it is a lot of work. *Danki* for helping us get the barn ready yesterday. I appreciate your help."

"You're welcome. *Ya*, it is a lot of work." Joshua took a long drink of water from a paper cup. "Do you need help with anything else before I go? I can help you take care of the animals."

"No, it's fine." His father waved off the question. "I'll check on them later. I'm going to go sit on the porch and enjoy this *schee* summer day."

"That sounds like a *gut* plan." Joshua and his father walked together toward the porch, where Josh thought he would find his family so they could head home.

"Josh," *Dat* said. "I've been meaning to ask you something. Right before Sadie Liz was born, you were concerned about Carolyn. You said she was worried about how Ben would fit into the family after the *boppli* was born. Is she still worried about that?"

Joshua shook his head and smiled. "No, she's been

more relaxed than I've ever seen her. She walks around humming, and she seems to have boundless energy. She hasn't asked me anything like that again."

"*Gut*." *Dat* nodded. "I'm glad to hear that. I know you're relieved that things are back to normal. Well, as normal as anything can be when you have a newborn."

Joshua chuckled. "It's amazing, *Dat*. God is so *gut*. I've never been more grateful."

"That's *gut*. I told you just to be patient with Carolyn."

"*Ya*." Joshua tugged on the brim of his hat as his thoughts returned to a conversation he had with his mother shortly after Sadie Liz was born. "I'm a little concerned, though. Carolyn still hasn't told me that she's quitting her job at the hotel. I'm not certain she's going to quit."

"What do you mean?"

"She hasn't told her boss that she isn't going back."

"Why would she go back to work?" *Dat* crossed his arms over his chest. "You've told me the farm is secure, so why would she have to work?"

"That's what I can't figure out. *Mamm* told me she thought Carolyn would return to the hotel. I'm hoping *Mamm* was wrong. I'm hoping Carolyn will realize she doesn't need that job. Today during the service I prayed and asked God to help guide her heart to the farm. I'm hoping she will finally see that the *kinner* and I need her home full-time."

"I'm certain she will." *Dat* patted Joshua's arm. "You're a *gut* man, Josh. She'll figure it out."

"*Danki*." Joshua spotted Carolyn sitting on the porch

with Lillian and his mother. She looked toward him and waved, and his heart seemed to flutter. He hoped Carolyn was as content as he was.

. . .

The following morning Carolyn rocked Sadie Liz in her bedroom and hummed softly. She enjoyed hearing the quiet rhythm of her baby's snores, and she didn't want to put her down in her cradle. Not just yet.

Closing her eyes, she allowed her thoughts to focus completely on the sounds coming from her daughter. Her thoughts moved to the prayer she'd sent up to God a little over a week ago. She still hadn't felt the answer to her most heartfelt question. She didn't want to leave her baby and go back to work, but she still felt the need to go. What did God want her to do? Where did she belong?

She longed to spend the entire day just watching Sadie Liz sleep, but there was work to be done. She needed to clean up the kitchen, sweep the porch, and check on her garden.

Carolyn gingerly lowered Sadie Liz into her cradle and then walked to the kitchen. She would have about two hours before Sadie Liz was awake again. After the breakfast dishes were washed and put away, she headed out to the porch with her broom in her hand. She was sweeping when her gaze moved to the stables. She wondered what Joshua and Benjamin were doing. She was surprised they weren't already out in the pasture working with horses.

Carolyn leaned the broom against the railing and walked back into the house. After lifting Sadie Liz from the cradle, she held the sleeping baby close to her chest, slipped back outside, and headed down the path toward the stables. She stood in the doorway and peeked into the stable.

"So, I've been thinking about something, Ben." Joshua's voice sounded from the stalls near the far end of the stable. "And I'm ready to discuss it with you."

"What's that?" Benjamin asked.

"In five years, you'll be ready to officially be my business partner, if that's what you want," Joshua said, stepping out into the main area of the stable with his back to Carolyn. "We can build a house for you beyond the pasture. You just let me know how many acres you want, and your *mamm* and I will sign them over to you. We can even change the name of the business to Glick and Son if you'd like. Of course, if your *mamm* and I have another *bu*, then we'll have to call it Glick and Sons."

"You want me to be your partner?" Benjamin's expression brightened with excitement and surprise. "That would be *wunderbaar, Dat*! I don't know how to thank you. I'd be honored to be your partner. I love working with you, and I love the horses so much. I never felt like I fit in at my *onkel's* dairy farm, but I feel like I belong here. I want to work here with you for the rest of my life. This is a dream come true for me."

"*Gut, gut*," Joshua said with a nod. "I'm glad to hear you say that, Benjamin. That's what I'd hoped you'd say. We'll tell your *mamm* together. I wanted to be sure the farm was prospering long term and that partnering with me was what you wanted before I said anything to her about this plan."

Carolyn gasped and cupped her hand to her mouth. God had answered her prayer! She knew at that moment where she should be, and it was with her family, not at the hotel three mornings each week.

And it seemed as if the answer had been right in front of her all along. Just as Linda and her mother had said, when Joshua adopted Benjamin, he truly made the boy his son. It was more than just a legal formality; it was a true declaration of his love.

By asking Benjamin to be his business partner, Joshua was declaring Benjamin a part of the family she had built with Joshua, and that meant he would support the boy in every way he would support their biological children. Benjamin was just as important to Joshua as their new baby girl was to him.

"Thank You, God, for showing me that I need to stay home," she whispered as tears spilled from her eyes. "I can hear Your voice, God, and I understand now. I'm sorry I didn't trust You." She hugged the sleeping baby closer to her body.

Joshua turned toward the door, and his eyes rounded. "Carolyn? I didn't know you were standing there. Is everything all right?" He rushed over to her and stroked her arm. "Is something wrong with Sadie Liz?"

"No. Everything is fine." She wiped an errant tear from her cheek. "Actually, everything couldn't be any better."

"I don't understand." He shook his head while studying her.

"Let's walk outside so we can talk in private." She led him out of the stable and back toward the house where they climbed the porch steps and sat beside each other on the swing. "I've made a decision. I'm ready to call Gregg and tell him that I quit. I belong here at the farm with you and the *kinner*."

"Oh, Carolyn." His smile was wide. "I'm so thankful to hear you finally say that." His smiled faded slightly. "But what made you realize that you belong here? And why are you crying?"

"I've been worried that you might not feel you could support Benjamin financially like you would support your biological *kinner*." Carolyn wiped her wet cheeks with one hand as she settled Sadie Liz in her lap. "I had convinced myself that I needed to work and save money so I could be the one to help Benjamin when it came to help him get his own home. I felt responsible for his future. I think my insecurities go all the way back to when Benjamin's father rejected me. I was afraid you'd, in a way, reject Ben."

"Carolyn—" Joshua began.

"Please let me finish." She touched her finger to his lips to stop him from talking. "I had convinced myself I had to work no matter what, even though you've been trying to tell me all along that you love Ben and will always love him. I prayed and asked God to show me clear direction for whether I should work or stay home with the family. He provided that for me just a few moments ago."

She nodded toward the stalls. "I heard what you said to Ben about making him your partner and giving him land to build a home. That was the sign I needed to realize how much you love Ben and how you will also support him because you do consider him your son." She kept a hand on Sadie Liz's tummy while she spoke.

"That's exactly right." Joshua's eyes were warm and tender. "I told you that when I adopted Ben, he became my son. I meant it, and I will always mean it."

"I know." Carolyn reached up and touched his cheek. "I see that now. I'm sorry for doubting you. You've been trying to show me how much you love Ben and me all along. I'm sorry I was too stubborn and scared to see it. Linda told me God has already forgiven me for how Ben came into the world and that I need to finally forgive myself. She was right. I had to let myself believe that I've moved past my mistakes and that I'm worthy of love."

Josh took her hand in his and kissed it. "Of course you're forgiven and worthy of love. I promise you that I will always take care of you, Ben, and the rest of our *kinner*, no matter how many we have. *Ich liebe dich*."

"*Danki*, Josh." Carolyn smiled as fresh tears splattered her cheeks. "I love you too."

Joshua draped his arm around Carolyn, and she rested her head on his shoulder as she pushed the swing into motion with her foot. At that moment, she knew without a doubt that she and Joshua would always keep their children safe and provide for their future, together.

DISCUSSION QUESTIONS

1. Carolyn feels it's her obligation to plan for Benjamin's financial future without Joshua's help. She worries that Joshua won't love and support Benjamin as much as he will love and support his biological children. Do you think her feelings are justified? Take a walk in her shoes. How would you have handled this situation if you were Carolyn? Share this with the group.

2. Linda finds encouragement in 1 Thessalonians 5:16–18. (Write out the passage.) What do these verses mean to you?

3. Barbie has criticized Carolyn since before she married Joshua. By the end of the story, however, Barbie finally admits that Carolyn is a good mother. Have you ever been criticized by a close family member? If so, how did you handle the criticism? Share this with the group.

4. Joshua doesn't understand why Carolyn feels she has to continue working at the hotel to help the family financially since the horse farm provides everything that they need. He is determined to convince Carolyn that he wants her on the farm with him. Joshua feels lost as to how he can help

Carolyn realize that she doesn't need to work. What, if anything, do you think Joshua should have done differently?

5. Carolyn is irritated by Barbie's constant remarks about Benjamin not being Joshua's biological son. Due to a mistake she made when she was sixteen, Carolyn feels she's been judged much of her life by her community that is supposed to be Christlike. Do we do this in our own church communities—judge and gossip about our fellow Christians without considering the consequences?

6. Which character can you identify with the most? Which character seemed to carry the most emotional stake in the story? Was it Joshua, Carolyn, Benjamin, or someone else?

7. Before Joshua met Carolyn, he was certain he would never get married and have a family. He feels that God gave him a second chance when he fell in love with Carolyn, and he is delighted that they are going to be blessed with a family. Have you ever experienced a second chance?

8. What did you know about the Amish before reading this book? What did you learn?

ACKNOWLEDGMENTS

As always, I'm thankful for my loving family. Special thanks to my special Amish friends who patiently answer my endless stream of questions. You're a blessing in my life. I'm grateful to Stacey Barbalace for her help with the recipe and research.

To my agent, Sue Brower—you are my own personal superhero! I can't thank you enough for your guidance, advice, and friendship. I'm thankful that our paths have crossed and our partnership will continue long into the future. You are a tremendous blessing in my life.

Thank you to my amazing editor, Becky Philpott, for your friendship and guidance. I'm so grateful to Jean Bloom for her help polishing this novella. I also would like to thank Laura Dickerson for tirelessly working to promote my books. I'm grateful to each and every person at HarperCollins Christian Publishing who helped make this book a reality.

To God—thank You most of all for giving me the inspiration and the words to glorify You. I'm grateful and humbled You've chosen this path for me.

A LOVE FOR IRMA ROSE

BETH WISEMAN

To Larry Knopick

Pennsylvania Dutch Glossary

ab im kopp—off in the head; crazy
ach—oh
daed—dad
danki—thank you
Englisch—non-Amish person
fraa—wife
gut—good
haus—house
kapp—prayer covering or cap
kinner—children
maedel—girl
mamm—mom
mammi—grandmother
mei—my
mudder—mother
nee—no
Ordnung—the written and unwritten rules of the Amish; the understood behavior by which the Amish are expected to live, passed down from generation to generation. Most Amish know the rules by heart.

rumschpringe—running-around period when a teen-
    ager turns sixteen years old
sohn—son
wunderbaar—wonderful
Wie bischt—How are you?; Howdy
ya—yes

PROLOGUE

Jonas glanced around the small cemetery, sprigs of brown poking through the melting clumps of snow. Sunshine beamed across the meadow in delicate rays, as if God were slowly cleaning up after one season, in preparation for the next. Soon it would be spring, Irma Rose's favorite time of year, when new foliage mirrored hope for plentiful harvests, when colorful blooms represented life, filled with colorful variations of our wonderment as humans.

"I love you, Irma Rose. I've loved you since the first day I saw you, sittin' under that old oak tree at your folks' house, readin' a book. You musta been only thirteen at the time, but I knew I'd marry you someday."

—FROM *PLAIN PROMISE*, BOOK THREE IN THE
DAUGHTERS OF THE PROMISE SERIES

CHAPTER 1

Jonas clutched the reins with sweaty hands, his fingers twitching as he waited for Amos Hostetler to blow the whistle, signaling the start of the race. He glanced to his right and scanned the crowd, at least fifteen onlookers—including Irma Rose Kauffman. This buggy race down Blackhorse Road was more than a friendly competition. More than just a group of Amish kids enjoying their *rumschpringe* on a Saturday afternoon.

He peered to his left at Isaac Lapp's flaring nostrils, knowing that his rival for Irma Rose's affections wanted to win as badly as he did. Jonas knew that pride was a sin, as Isaac surely did, but when it came to Irma Rose, Jonas figured Isaac's thoughts were as jumbled as his own. Jonas had been waiting to court Irma Rose for three years, since right after his father died. He recalled the way she lit his soul at a time when his grief threatened to overtake him. And now that she was sixteen, her parents were allowing her a few freedoms. Buggy races were looked down on by the elders in the community, but the young members of the district still gathered at the far end of the road most Saturdays to see who had the fastest horse and buggy.

"That ol' horse of yours ain't gonna be able to keep up with Lightning." Isaac smirked from his topless buggy, the type used for courting. Jonas hoped he never had to see Irma Rose riding alongside Isaac.

"*Ya*, well . . . we'll see about that." Jonas kept a steady hand on the reins while he and Isaac waited for the spectators to start loading into their buggies. They would wait about ten minutes, until everyone reached the finish line down by the old barn at the far end of the King property. Then Amos would blow the whistle to start the race.

Jonas sat taller, raised his chin, and tried to ignore that his own horse chose this moment to relieve himself. Bud was a fine animal. And fast. But Bud pooped more than any other horse around, and always at the wrong time, as if he was showing off. Or just trying to irritate Jonas.

Luckily the whistle blew before Isaac had time to make a joke, and Jonas slapped the reins. "*Ya!*" Within seconds, he was several yards ahead of Isaac, squinting as the late-afternoon sun almost blinded him. But he kept pushing Bud, anxious to see Irma Rose standing at the finish line, hopefully cheering him on.

Competition was against the *Ordnung* and everyone knew it, but there was a certain thrill about being victorious, even though deep down, Jonas knew God wouldn't approve. As he crossed the finish line two buggy lengths ahead of Isaac, God wasn't the one on his mind. As he pulled back on the reins, he looked to his right, searching the crowd standing in the grass on the side of the road.

Bud was completely stopped—and relieving himself again—when Jonas finally located Irma Rose. Even though the women in his district all dressed similarly, Irma Rose was easy to spot. She was tinier than most of the women, with dainty features. Loose tendrils of golden hair framed her face from beneath her *kapp*, and if a man was lucky enough to attract her gaze, he could feel her green eyes searching his soul. Even though she was petite and flowerlike, she had the perfect balance of femininity and strength. But she wasn't even looking toward the road. Instead of watching Jonas whup Isaac in the race, she was standing way off to the side of the crowd, smiling and seeming to enjoy the company of someone who threatened Jonas's potential courtship with Irma Rose way more than Isaac or anyone else. Jake Ebersol.

. . .

Irma Rose hung on Jake's every word. He was so wise and knew more about Scripture and the teachings of the *Ordnung* than anyone she knew. He was only nineteen, but he had the mind of someone much older. When Jake Ebersol spoke, people listened. And it didn't hurt that he was quite handsome. His big brown eyes peeked from beneath sandy-blond bangs cropped high on his forehead, and his face was bronzed from his work outdoors. Jake was tall and muscular, his suspenders tightly fitted atop his blue shirt. He was everything an Amish girl could want.

"I'd love to go with you to the singing next Sunday."

Irma Rose blinked her eyes a few times, unable to control her reaction to his invitation as a smile spread across her face. She'd been waiting for Jake to ask her to a singing since she'd turned sixteen last month. She loved when someone hosted a singing for the young people in her district, a time for fellowship, prayer, and singing. And best of all, it was a time to socialize without adults hovering nearby.

"Gut, gut." He pushed back the brim of his straw hat, smiling, then he brushed a clump of dried dirt from his britches. Several of the men who were standing too close to the race had been splattered with mud.

Irma Rose snuck a peek at Isaac, who was standing a few yards away. He'd been staring at her most of the day. She'd known for a long time that he was interested in courting her, and he was nice enough . . . but in her mind, there was only Jake. She offered Isaac a quick wave before she turned her attention back to Jake. A smile lit his face again, and she was basking in the moment when Jonas Miller walked up.

"I won. Ol' Bud came through for me." He smiled as he looped his thumbs beneath his suspenders, which were not doing a very good job holding up his britches.

Irma Rose hoped Jake would make pleasantries with Jonas so she didn't have to. Jonas was wild and reckless, and Irma Rose could often smell the lingering scent of cigars when she was around him. He was the same age as Jake, and while Jonas was handsome in his own way, he was certainly not Irma Rose's type.

"It was a *gut* race," Jake said, smiling. "Congratulations on the win."

Irma Rose was thinking about sitting next to Jake in his buggy on Sunday and wondering if he'd kiss her at the end of the night. She became aware that Jonas was speaking to her.

"Did you ask me something?" She blinked her eyes a few times, then brought her hand to her forehead to block the sun.

His firm mouth curled as if always on the edge of laughter, and Irma Rose found it unsettling. As his dark eyes raked boldly over her, she felt her cheeks reddening, the way they always did around him. He caused a tingling in the pit of her stomach that made her uncomfortable. Jonas was tall, but unlike Jake, he was thin, like he hadn't yet grown into his height. Jonas had the biggest feet she'd ever seen, and she'd heard that Mr. Tucker at The Shoe Barn had to order his black leather loafers from another state. Jonas took a step closer to her, and she noticed the stubble on his jawline. It seemed that no matter what time of day or night, he was never quite clean-shaven. Maybe because his hair was as black as a starless sky.

"I asked what you thought about the race." Jonas's smile grew and so did the funny feeling in Irma Rose's stomach.

She lifted her chin. "I don't think such competition is necessary." She shrugged and smiled back at him. "It's just silly." She turned to Jake, wishing he'd reach for her hand—something to let Jonas know that Jake would be courting her. Or at the least, taking her to the singing next Sunday.

"I'll be back," Jake said as he pointed to his right. "*Mei* sister is yelling for me." He extended his hand to Jonas. "Congratulations again. Bud is a fine animal."

Irma Rose glanced around, looking for a way to escape being caught in a conversation alone with Jonas, but everyone seemed involved in their own conversations. She twisted the tie on her prayer covering, hoping Jake would return soon. And that Jonas would mosey along.

"I was wondering . . ." Jonas grinned as a river of sweat flowed down both sides of his face. ". . . if you'd like to go with me to the singing on Sunday?"

Irma Rose pulled a hand-stitched handkerchief from the pocket of her apron and dabbed at the perspiration beading on her forehead. She cleared her throat, her heart hammering against her chest. She hated that he had this effect on her. "*Nee*, I can't," she finally said, fighting the knot rising in her throat. "I'm going to the singing with Jake."

Jonas took another step closer, his tall build casting a protective shadow over her, shielding her from the setting sun behind him. July had never felt so hot. "I think you should go with me instead."

Irma Rose stepped back as she tried to get control of her uneven breathing. "I just told you . . . I'm already going with someone else." She turned away to find Jake.

She could feel Jonas's eyes on her as she rushed away. Blotting her forehead with her hankie again, she picked up the pace.

. . .

Jonas took a step to go after her, but stopped himself. He rubbed the stubble on his chin and took a deep breath, knowing he had to make Irma Rose see that they were meant for each other. Jake Ebersol was a likable fellow, a pillar in the community, and everyone thought he'd follow in a long line of footsteps and become a deacon or bishop someday, like his father and grandfathers. But Jake wasn't the right guy for Irma Rose. Jonas had watched her for three years. She had a fire for adventure. He'd watched her jump from the highest peak into Pequea Creek, and she could run faster than any girl he knew. She could swing a baseball bat and knock a volleyball over the net with ease, and her laughter stole his breath.

Irma Rose was beautiful. Great with the *kinner* in the community. And she was going to be the mother of his children.

She just didn't know it yet.

CHAPTER 2

Irma Rose sat with her girlfriends—Hannah and Mary—at the soda shop, as they did every Tuesday after they went to the market. They all shared a strawberry malt at the counter while watching the television—knowing their parents wouldn't approve.

Hannah's father would be particularly upset, whether it was their *rumschpringe* or not. He'd ground her for sure if he knew. Irma Rose was an only child, and her parents wouldn't be happy, but they weren't as strict as Hannah's. Most likely, Irma Rose would just get a good talking-to. Unless, of course, they caught her watching something inappropriate—like Elvis Presley or Jerry Lee Lewis. Then there would be trouble. As for Mary, she always said her parents had more children than they could keep up with—fourteen—so she figured her chances of getting caught were slim.

Today, the sound on the television was turned down so low they could barely hear it, and the daytime soap opera *As the World Turns* was on, which didn't interest the girls much.

"I hope it doesn't rain on the way home." Mary leaned

forward and slurped from one of the three straws. "We should have brought one of the covered buggies."

Irma Rose glanced out the plate glass window facing Lincoln Highway and toward the dark clouds in the west. They'd ridden into the town of Paradise together in Hannah's topless buggy. She looked down at the floor beside them where their few grocery bags were. "*Ach*, I've got flour in my bag. That won't do well in the rain."

"We'd better go." Hannah reached into her pocket for some coins. It was her turn to pay for the malt. She was waiting for change when the bell above the door rang, drawing their attention to a tall Amish man walking in.

Mary gasped, then covered her mouth with one hand. "It's Jonas Miller," she whispered.

Irma Rose sat up straighter and quickly looked away. Mary fancied Jonas—although Irma Rose couldn't understand why. Mary said he was rough around the edges, but that all he needed was a *gut fraa* to tend to him. Irma Rose was pretty sure he needed more than that. She cut her eyes in his direction. For starters, he needed a haircut and, as usual, a shave. And someone in his house needed to mend the missing button on his blue shirt. Irma Rose could already smell the stale stench of cigar, yet a brief shiver rippled through her.

"*Wie bischt*, ladies?" He stopped right in front of Irma Rose. "Have you reconsidered going with me to the singing next Sunday?"

Irma Rose glanced at Mary, whose expression immediately fell, and she wanted to smack Jonas for hurting her friend like that. Didn't he suspect how Mary felt about him? "I already told you . . ." She took a deep breath as the pit of her stomach churned. "I'm going with Jake."

Jonas's edgy grin crept up one side of his face. "I was just making sure you hadn't changed your mind."

"*Nee*. I have not." She forced a thin-lipped smile. "Maybe Mary would like to go with you though."

Mary hung her head as her face reddened, but she quickly lit up when Jonas said, "Sure. Mary, do you want to go with me on Sunday?"

Irma Rose felt her pulse beating in her throat as she watched Mary nod. Mary was a quiet girl, pretty with wavy brown hair and rosy cheeks. She had big blue eyes and long lashes that she was batting at Jonas.

"We have to go." Irma Rose stood up from the stool, leaned down, and began gathering her share of the bags. "*Danki*, Mr. Weaver," she said to the soda shop owner, who waved and nodded.

"Here comes the rain." Hannah pointed at the window that ran the length of the soda shop. "Your flour isn't going to make the trip home in my topless buggy." She turned to Jonas. "Since you brought a covered buggy, can you cart Irma Rose to her *haus* so her flour doesn't ruin?" She nodded toward the window, and Irma Rose looked in that direction. Jonas's buggy was parked in front of the store, Bud tethered to the hitching post. Jonas's buggy was easy to spot. It was the only one with bullet holes in it. There were all kinds of stories floating around about what happened, but Jonas would never confirm or deny any of them.

Irma Rose clutched her bags to her chest. "*Nee*. It will be fine."

Mary spoke up too. "Hannah's right. You should let Jonas carry you home."

Looking down at the five-pound bag of flour, Irma Rose considered her options. Riding two miles in the buggy alone with Jonas, or showing up at home with wet flour and having to endure a lecture about reading the weather forecast in the newspaper before heading to town. "Fine," she said stiffly as she lifted her eyes to his.

Jonas tipped the brim of his straw hat toward Mary. "And I'll see you on Sunday."

Irma Rose pursed her lips and said good-bye to Hannah and Mary. Jonas picked up the bag of flour, then Irma Rose followed him to his buggy carrying a brown paper bag of groceries. They placed the items in the backseat, then Jonas offered his hand to help her into the buggy. Ignoring the gesture, she heaved herself onto the bench seat and folded her hands in her lap.

Jonas had barely closed the door on his side when the rain started in earnest. He clicked his tongue and set the horse in motion, and Irma Rose prayed silently that it would only be rain and not a storm. Not only was she frightened of lightning and thunder but sometimes the horses got spooked, and they were going to have to cross Lincoln Highway to get home.

She was particularly worried about Hannah and Mary, and she could see her friends getting soaked in the topless buggy. "Can you follow Hannah and Mary to Mary's *haus* before you take me home?"

Jonas began crossing Lincoln Highway behind Hannah. "*Ya*. Planned on it." He turned to her and grinned. "Someone forgot to check the weather."

She ignored him for a few moments, then turned to face him. "What were you doing in the soda shop, anyway?"

He didn't answer at first, concentrating on getting across the highway safely. Once Bud was trotting behind Hannah's buggy and away from the traffic, he turned to her. "I was looking for you."

"I don't know why," she said dryly as she rolled her eyes, aware of how close they were in the small buggy.

Jonas smiled but didn't say anything. Either he was the happiest man on the planet, or he just liked to make her uncomfortable.

They were quiet as both buggies made their way down Black Horse Road in the pouring rain. Irma Rose needed a distraction, something to keep her from focusing on the flashes of lightning up ahead.

"That was nice of you to ask Mary to the singing." Irma Rose kept her eyes straight ahead, knowing she was fishing for information. Would Jonas say that he'd had to settle for his second choice? *And why does that matter?*

"Mary is a sweet *maedel*." He wasn't smiling anymore, and his jaw tensed as he strained to see through the windshield. The wipers were working hard, but it was still difficult to see.

Irma Rose jumped and covered her eyes when she saw a rod of lightning not too far ahead. *One, one thousand . . . two, one thousand*, then BOOM! She pressed her hands against her ears and fought the tears forming in the corners of her eyes.

"That was close," Jonas said in a whisper, then she felt a hand on her arm. "Are you okay?"

She pulled her hands from her ears, nodded, and bit her trembling lip.

"Don't worry, Irma Rose. I'll get you home safely."

His voice was so strong and determined that she believed him. She was relieved when she saw Hannah and Mary turn into Mary's driveway. She knew Hannah would wait to leave until the storm was over.

Another bright burst of light shone ahead of them, and she wondered if maybe they should ride out the storm at Mary's house, too, but by the time she thought to suggest it, Jonas had Bud in a good trot and was passing Mary's house. Irma Rose's heart was pounding in her chest, and with one loud, thunderous boom after another, she fought the urge to cry.

Then Jonas shouted, "Bud!" He pulled back on the reins so hard the horse's front feet came off the ground; the horse waved his hooves in the air until Jonas stopped pulling on the reins and they were at a complete stop.

"That was close!" Jonas let out a long breath and stared at the tree lying across the road in front of them.

"Should we go back the other way?" Irma Rose had both hands on the dash as she peered through the rain. Then she turned around and, in the distance, could see water starting to flow across the road in front of Mary's house, an area that flooded easily.

Jonas slammed a hand against the dash of the buggy, causing Irma Rose to jump.

"I should have left you at Mary's," he said, shaking his head.

"You couldn't have known that a tree would fall in front of us." She paused, turning to look at him. His forehead was creased, but she covered her ears when another bolt of lightning flashed up ahead with a quick, thunderous follow-up. Jonas put an arm around her and pulled her close, and Irma Rose buried her face in his chest.

"Everything's okay, I promise. The lightning is still a ways off, and it's moving to the east. We'll just have to wait here a little while." He rubbed her arm, and she could feel his heart beating against her ear. She knew hers was pounding twice as hard, but the nearness of him gave her comfort. And something else. Something she wouldn't examine until later.

She lifted her face to his, gazed into his eyes, and tried to figure out what it was about Jonas that left her feeling light-headed. He slid a finger along her cheek, pushing back a strand of hair, and for a few seconds, she was sure he was going to kiss her. She quickly wrenched herself away, straightened her *kapp*, and took a deep, cleansing breath.

"I think the rain is easing up." She stared straight ahead but eventually turned to face him. He was grinning again—that irritating, all-knowing quirky smile. "What's so funny? Why are you looking at me like that?"

"I almost kissed you." He paused, his smile fading as he gazed into her eyes. "And one day, I'm going to marry you."

Irma Rose's jaw dropped as she turned to face him. "You are *ab im kopp*! And arrogant. You think everyone wants to be with you! You've always been like that, Jonas Miller." She chuckled. "I'm not one of those people."

"Whatever you say, Irma Rose." He smiled again,

winked at her, then turned and looked over his shoulder. "The water's going down." He eased Bud around until the buggy faced the opposite direction. The rain had all but stopped, and when they got closer to the small stream of water moving across the road, it was easy to see that it wasn't more than an inch deep, and Bud easily got them safely through it.

She couldn't look at him, so she kept her eyes on the road in front of them as they passed Mary's house. Jonas took an alternate route to Irma Rose's house. When he finally pulled into her driveway, she knew she had to thank him for the ride, but she wasn't about to look at him. "*Danki.*" She pulled on the door to open it, but he caught her arm, causing her to stop breathing for a moment.

"Go with me to the singing on Sunday. Please."

She eased her arm out of his grip and released her breath. "I'm going with Jake." She opened the door, stepped out, then turned to face him. "And you're going with Mary."

. . .

Jonas watched her walk up the porch steps, open the door, and go inside her house. She didn't turn around. After a few seconds, he eased Bud into a light trot and headed for home.

He'd known Irma Rose was the one for him when he first met her three years ago, and he suspected that she'd felt that spark too. Even though she'd been too young for courting at the time, it was easy for him to envision the woman she would become someday. Jonas's father had just died, and despite his strong faith, he was struggling to find joy, even just a reason to smile. Irma Rose had been sitting in the grass, reading a book. When she looked up and saw him, she closed her book, her cheeks filling with color. She was soft-spoken but confident as she told him about the book she was reading, and he'd listened to the gentleness of her voice, even though he had read this same book nearly a dozen times, as recommended by his father. And when she'd tenderly lifted a baby grasshopper into the palm of her hand, coddling it as if it were a newborn baby, something inside of Jonas changed forever. He would wait for her.

But he was going to need to do something extra special to convince her to give him a chance. Jake was stiff competition. All this time, he'd been worried about Isaac. And somehow Jake had snuck up and stolen her affection.

When he got home, he settled Bud in his stall, then set to work on all the chores he'd missed while he was out. As he dumped a bucket of feed into the pigpen, he thought about what he would have done if anything had happened to Irma Rose. *Thank You, Lord . . . for getting us home safely.*

After he'd tended to the pigs, he took to milking the cows. That's how it was when you had all sisters and no father. His *mamm* and four sisters took real *gut* care of him, so he tried to make sure they had everything they needed and that the farm was kept up the way his father would have wanted. He didn't really have time to be chasing after a *maedel*. But Irma Rose wasn't just any girl.

He'd almost finished his late-afternoon chores when Missy came running out of the house. His four-year-old sister was a bundle of energy. She most likely was coming out to tell him what was for supper, that it was ready, or maybe just to fill him in on her day. He tried to be a father to her as much as a brother. His other sisters were a little older, and he was thankful for that, for his mother's sake. At least they were able to help *Mamm* with laundry, cooking, and tending to the many tasks it took to keep things running smoothly.

Mae was ten; Annie, eleven; and Elizabeth, thirteen. Jonas's father used to jokingly tell Jonas, "It took us six years to have Elizabeth. I reckon the good Lord thought you were plenty a handful on your own back then." Jonas smiled as he recalled memories of his father.

"*Mamm's* sick!" Missy screamed, and because of the tears in her eyes, Jonas was already moving toward her. He scooped her into his arms as he hurried to the house.

"Now, now. What's wrong?" Jonas's heart was pounding as he picked up his pace.

"Elizabeth said to come get you. *Mamm* is throwing up red. What's wrong with her, Jo Jo?"

He set Missy on the porch steps and ran into the house. He didn't know what he'd do if the Lord saw fit to take his mother too.

CHAPTER 3

Irma Rose huffed as her mother packed a variety of baked goods to take to the Millers' house. She leaned against the kitchen counter and folded her arms across her chest, sighing heavily.

Mamm added a loaf of bread to the bag. She paused and looked over her shoulder at Irma Rose. "Why are you giving me fits about taking this to the Millers? I told you that Sarah Jane is going to be in the hospital for a while, and I'm sure the girls and Jonas have their hands full in her absence. That little *maedel*, Missy, isn't even five yet, and without a father, I know they will need some help. Their oldest girl is only thirteen."

Irma Rose thought the name Sarah Jane was the prettiest name she'd ever heard. *I'm going to name my daughter that someday.* She couldn't wait to be a mother, and for a few moments, she allowed herself to imagine a life with Jake and lots of *kinner*. "I know," she finally said as she chewed on a nail. Maybe Jonas wouldn't be there when she made the delivery.

Mamm handed her the bag of pastries, breads, and cookies. During the summer, they tried to do all of their baking early in the day, but the kitchen was still stifling. "Tomorrow I'll send a casserole or something easy for them to have for supper. But I know Widow Zook took care of their supper for tonight."

Tomorrow? Was she going to be carting food to the Millers every day? Guilt nipped at her for having the thought. Of course she wanted to do what she could to help their family. Jonas would probably be working in the fields anyway.

Ten minutes later, she pulled into their driveway. She loved the Miller homestead. Not only was it pristine but it had just the right mix of wide open fields as well as areas that were slightly wooded, keeping the house and other structures out of view from the road. Once you laid eyes on the home and property, it took your breath away, especially this time of year. Sarah Jane and her daughters had filled the many flower beds with colorful blooms, a reminder to Irma Rose that her own beds needed sprucing. The house always looked freshly painted; she knew Jonas could be credited for that. Since his father had died three years ago, Jonas had worked hard to keep the property up. Wild and reckless, yes. But not lazy.

As she tethered her horse, she tried to figure out what it was about Jonas that bothered her so much. She always came back to the same conclusion. He made her feel uncomfortable because he assumed she had feelings for him that she didn't have. He acted like he knew her better than she knew herself. His arrogance put her on edge. She carried the bag through the plush green grass, wishing she was barefoot so she could feel the warm dewy blades tickling her toes. She knocked on the door and waited. A few moments later, Elizabeth answered the door with Missy standing beside her.

"*Wie bischt,* Irma Rose. Come in." Elizabeth swung the door wide and stepped aside so Irma Rose could enter the living room.

Since all of the Miller girls were younger than Irma Rose, she didn't know them all that well. But the age differences hadn't been the only reason Irma Rose avoided coming here if she could, and she'd been doing so for the past three years. Ever since Jonas showed up at her house while she was sitting underneath a tree reading a book. He'd struck up a conversation with her after returning a serving bowl to her mother, and not only did her hands get clammy that day but she'd stuttered while talking with him, something she'd never done. And after only a few moments, she'd broken out in a rash on her face. At thirteen, she'd been sure she was allergic to Jonas Miller. She didn't break out in hives around him anymore, but her hands still became sweaty sometimes.

"*Mei mamm* sent some baked goods to help out while your mother is in the hospital." She handed the brown paper bag to Elizabeth. "And she said she would send supper for tomorrow night." She leaned down and said hello to Missy.

"*Ach,* this is so kind. *Danki.*" Elizabeth smiled, but Irma Rose saw the black circles underneath the girl's eyes. It had to be a lot of work taking care of this huge place and three younger sisters. Irma Rose suspected Mae and Annie spent half a day at summer Bible school, like most of the *kinner* that age, so that left Elizabeth home alone with Missy while also taking care of everything else. Even after just a couple of days, the schedule looked to be taking a toll on Elizabeth. And the poor girl must be so worried about her *mamm* too.

"I was just making Missy a sandwich," Elizabeth said as she headed back toward the kitchen. "Can you come in and visit a few minutes?"

Irma Rose followed Elizabeth and Missy across the spacious family room, and just before they rounded the corner to the kitchen, Irma Rose heard someone cough, but it was too late to turn back.

"Please tell your *mudder danki*, but there is no need to send supper tomorrow." Elizabeth smiled as she nodded to the kitchen counter, filled with bowls and casserole dishes. "I'm still trying to fit everything into the refrigerator. But I'm very grateful for all of the kindness everyone in the community has shown our family."

Guilt gnawed at Irma Rose again because of the relief she felt over not having to return tomorrow. She avoided Jonas's eyes as he stood up from the kitchen table. His dark hair was flattened on top of his head, like he'd just taken off his hat, and after a few moments, her eyes drifted to his. "*Wie bischt*, Jonas." She held her head high, determined not to let him get the best of her today. She glanced at her hands, then back at him. "I'm sorry to hear of your *mudder's* illness."

"*Danki*." He smiled slightly, the familiar dark shadow across his jaw. Maybe he just needed a better razor. "Irma Rose . . ." He scratched his head for a moment. "I think it's best that I not go to the singing on Sunday. Will you be seeing Mary? Might you be able to get word to her?"

"*Ya*, I can go by her—"

"*Nee*," Elizabeth interrupted. "The *Englisch* doctor said *Mamm* is going to be okay." She glanced at Irma Rose. "She has an ulcer in her stomach, a bad one." Elizabeth turned back to Jonas. "But she might even be home before Sunday afternoon. Don't cancel your plans with Mary. I can take care of things here."

Jonas took in a deep breath and blew it out slowly. "I don't know . . ." He looked down at the floor, then back up at his sister. "But if she's not home, I'd be here to help you."

Elizabeth shook her head, frowning. "I can do this, Jonas." She glanced at Missy, who was busy sneaking a cookie from a tin on the counter, then looked back at her brother. "I'm old enough to take care of everything."

Irma Rose wondered if that was true, but she stayed quiet as they waited for Jonas to respond. He finally nodded, and Elizabeth began slathering a slice of bread with peanut spread. She waited for Elizabeth to get out the homemade cheese spread, but instead, she stacked on a bunch of pickles before slapping the other slice of bread on top.

Jonas laughed. "It looks terrible, *ya*?"

Irma Rose pulled her eyes from the sandwich, looked at Jonas for a moment, then glanced down at her hands. She turned to Missy and waited for the little girl to finish praying silently, then flinched when Missy took a big bite.

"Can I make you a sandwich, Irma Rose?" Elizabeth didn't look up as she slathered another piece of bread with more of the peanut spread. Followed by more pickles.

"*Nee. Danki*, though." Irma Rose swallowed hard. Just the thought of eating that sandwich caused her stomach to rumble a warning.

Elizabeth put the other slice of bread on top of the pickles and handed the plate to Jonas. He took a large bite, swallowed, and smiled.

"I said it *looks* awful, but it's *gut*." He took another hefty bite and winked at Irma Rose. She pulled her eyes away as her heart thumped against her chest.

"I guess I should be getting home. Please let us know if you need anything, and I hope that your *mamm* will continue to be on the mend."

Jonas almost knocked his chair over as he stood up, still chewing the last of his sandwich, which he'd practically inhaled. "I'll walk you out."

"*Nee.* No need." She gave a quick wave to Elizabeth before she hurried out of the kitchen. She'd almost made it to the front door when Jonas edged up beside her and pushed the screen open.

She didn't look back as she made her way across the yard toward her buggy, but she could hear Jonas's big feet tromping through the grass behind her.

"Irma Rose."

She stopped a few feet from her buggy and slowly turned to face him. "*Ya?*"

Jonas scratched his forehead and knitted his eyebrows. "Do you think it's wrong of me to take Mary to the singing? You suggested it, but it wonders me if maybe it ain't right."

Irma Rose didn't want to see Mary get hurt, but the situation was becoming awkward. "And—and why is . . .

that?" She tried to avoid his dark eyes peering down at her, but she felt like a piece of metal drawn to a huge magnet. If she ever let herself get too close to him, she might be stuck with him. Forever. And that thought terrified her.

As he inched closer to her, she took a step backward, recalling the moment in his buggy when he admitted he'd almost kissed her. And even more wildly inappropriate, him saying he would marry her someday.

"You're the person I want to date. Not Mary. But if you really don't want anything to do with me, then I'll do my best to get to know Mary better."

She blurted out the first thing that came to mind, and she spoke through a slight chuckle. "So much for marrying me, *ya*?"

Right away, she felt the color drain from her face, but there was no taking it back, so she faked a smile before turning to leave. He was on her heels again, and this time he latched onto her arm before she could get in her buggy.

She shook loose of his hold. "Go with Mary to the singing. Date Mary. She likes you, Jonas. And—and . . ." She searched her mind for a way to tell him that he just wasn't right for her, but there was no kind way to do so. "I'm dating Jake. He's the man I'll marry someday." She folded her arms across her chest.

The only thing she was sure of was her uneasiness when she was near Jonas, and she couldn't live her life feeling like that. She'd no sooner had the thought when she remembered how safe she'd felt with him during the storm, the gentle way he'd held her, the tenderness in his voice, the feel of his heart beating against her ear. She held her breath and waited to see if he would argue, but instead he was quiet, his expression masked.

He took a long, slow step backward, lifted his hand to his forehead to block the sun, and said, "Okay." He kept his eyes on her as he took a couple more steps, but when he turned around, his pace quickened as he went up the steps and disappeared into the house.

Irma Rose couldn't move for a few moments as she pondered exactly what it was that she wanted from Jonas Miller. She didn't want to be with him, but she wasn't sure she wanted him with anyone else either.

• • •

Jonas towel-dried his hair, tossed the towel on the floor, and sat on his bed. He raised the flame on the lantern, then opened his copy of *The Rawhide Kid*, sure his mother would blow her top if she knew he'd snuck the comic book into the house. Especially since it was about a heroic gunfighter from the nineteenth century who was unjustly wanted as an outlaw.

He opened the book and started where he'd left off, but he couldn't concentrate. Something about taking Mary to the singing on Sunday just didn't feel right. He had to assume that Irma Rose was telling the truth, that she intended to marry Jake Ebersol someday. The thought caused him to shiver. But if that were the case, then it would be best for him to get to know Mary better. Jonas had known for a while that Mary fancied him. She was a sweet girl, a pretty *maedel* who was a bit quiet for Jonas's liking.

Tossing the book to the end of the bed, he lay down. The room was stuffy and humid, and he was already sweating again. Summer was *Mamm's* favorite time of year, and she never seemed bothered by the heat that settled over Lancaster County. Jonas preferred the sharpness of a cold winter. Maybe because it allowed for more time in the house, a fire in the fireplace, and extra family time. It wasn't the same without his father, but he enjoyed the togetherness and reading to the girls more during that time of year.

He closed his eyes, trying to envision himself and Irma Rose with a family of their own. But he was having trouble concentrating on that as well. He was worried sick about his mother, and for the hundredth time, he begged the Lord not to take her. The doctors had said she'd be just fine, but that's what they'd said about his father too.

CHAPTER 4

I rma Rose walked into the Lapp basement with Jake at her side. About fifteen teenagers were gathered around a table of food in the middle of the room. Once everyone was full, they'd likely break off in small groups at first to chat, then someone would suggest a song. This was the only time they would be able to harmonize since it wasn't allowed during worship service. Irma Rose loved to sing songs that glorified God.

She scanned the room until she saw Isaac. She was glad to see him chatting with several girls on the other side of the room. As she continued to look around, she noticed something in the corner of the room was covered with a sheet. It wasn't hard to tell that it was a radio. One of the large, box types from the 1930s or '40s. No one would speak of it, but plenty of families kept a radio hidden from plain view. Mostly transistor radios these days, but some folks held on to the older models. They'd say it was for listening to President Eisenhower talk about world events, but Irma Rose's mother had said some women she knew admitted to listening to variety shows. Irma Rose's family had never owned a radio.

"I'm going to go talk with Isaac for a minute. Be right back." Jake smiled at Irma Rose before he walked off. She greeted several friends hovering around the food, then reached for a chocolate-chip cookie before she scanned the room. Her eyes landed on Mary. Her friend was alone in the corner of the room, munching on a whoopie pie.

Irma Rose sidled up to Mary. "Where's Jonas?"

"I have no idea." Mary spoke with her mouth full, and before she had even swallowed, she stuffed another chunk of the dessert in her mouth. "He never showed up, so I rode with Jacob and John."

Irma Rose glanced around the room and saw Mary's two brothers standing away from the table of food and talking with two girls whom Irma Rose thought might be a bit too young to be here. "Hmm . . ." Jonas wasn't dependable; she'd add this to her list. "Awfully rude of him."

Mary finally swallowed the last of the pie. "Maybe it's his *mudder*. She's not well. She's in the hospital."

"*Ya*, I know." Irma Rose felt bad that she'd assumed the worst about Jonas without considering the situation with his mother. "I hope everything is all right."

"Me too."

"He still should have gotten word to you." Irma Rose looked around again until she saw Jake. He winked at her, and after a few minutes, he cozied up beside her. Mary excused herself and said she was going to get another whoopie pie.

"Didn't she just eat one of those?" Jake whispered to Irma Rose as he nodded toward Mary.

"*Ya.* Mary has always liked pies and cakes. But I'm not really one to talk. I have a sweet tooth too."

Jake grimaced. "I'm not much of a sweets eater."

Irma Rose nudged him gently. "*Ach*, I bet you'd eat my shoofly pie. *Mamm* says I make better shoofly pies than *mei mammi* did."

Jake shrugged. "*Nee.* I'd rather have something salty, like a pretzel."

Irma Rose rocked from heel to toe a couple of times, searching her mind for something to talk about. She'd waited a long time for Jake to ask her out, and now that she was sixteen, she'd hoped they would become a couple. Taking a girl to a singing was almost as good as announcing to the world that you were dating. But when Jake didn't offer up any conversation either, her mind became preoccupied with Jonas. *I hope he is okay.* She hoped his mother hadn't taken a turn for the worse.

She pulled a handkerchief from the pocket of her apron and dabbed at the sweat starting to bead on her forehead. "I'll be glad when summer is over and it cools down. And I can't wait until the first snow after that. I love to make snow angels, then curl up in front of a fire and drink hot cocoa."

Jake frowned as he shook his head. "Not me. I'll take summer over winter any day."

Irma Rose had thought she'd feel different standing here with Jake. She tried to talk to him about a book she was reading, but he said he didn't do much reading. He wasn't much of a talker either.

By the end of the evening, her emotions were all over the place. For more than a year she'd waited to be old enough to date. But her first date hadn't been at all what she'd hoped for. Jake was handsome, polite, hardworking, and would make a wonderful husband and father one day. But as he pulled into Irma Rose's driveway at the end of the night, another word came to mind. *Boring.*

Now, as he walked her to her front door, she worried he might try to kiss her, and she wasn't sure how she felt about that anymore.

"*Danki* for taking me to the singing, Jake. I had a really nice time." That wasn't a lie. She'd enjoyed talking with everyone, and Ida Lapp was one of the best cooks in their community, so the food had been wonderful. She looked up at Jake and smiled. In one swift movement, he leaned down and pressed his lips to hers. As only their lips touched, Irma Rose stood frozen. Should she put a hand on his arm? Why wasn't he cupping her cheek or the back of her neck? She'd heard that's how it was done. Her discomfort bordered on painful, and when Jake finally pulled away, Irma Rose reached up and dabbed at her lips.

Jake stood taller, looped his hands beneath his suspenders, and grinned as if he'd just set Irma Rose's world on fire. As if fireworks would burst into the sky at any moment. He winked at her again, but instead of finding it endearing, she fought a frown. She halfway expected him to start beating his chest triumphantly. Waving, he left her standing on the front porch. If that was how kissing was done, she didn't know what all the excitement was about.

• • •

Irma Rose walked onto the front porch the following Friday, then bounced down the steps and into the yard. It was a beautiful summer day, and she decided to deliver some freshly baked cookies to the Millers. But she was on a bit more of a mission than she cared to admit to her mother. Yesterday, at the malt shop with Mary and Hannah, Mary said she'd never heard from Jonas and that Sarah Jane Miller was still in the hospital. "No one has laid eyes on Jonas in almost a week," Mary had said.

Irma Rose wondered if members of the community were still taking food to the family, so she'd told her mother she would make a delivery. Mostly, she wanted to find out where Jonas was hiding.

When she pulled into their driveway later that morning, she noticed his buggy sitting alongside two others the family owned. She knocked on the door, and Elizabeth answered.

Irma Rose's jaw dropped when she saw the girl. No *kapp*, and not even a scarf over her head. Her blue dress was a wrinkled mess, and she had a smudge of flour on her chin.

"*Wie bischt*, Irma Rose?" Elizabeth brushed several strands of hair from her face. "Would you like to come in?" Her voice was almost a whisper, and Irma Rose hesitated but finally stepped across the threshold. "Please excuse the mess," Elizabeth added and then sighed.

Mess? Irma Rose gulped. This was much more than a mess. It was a disaster, with toys everywhere, a half-eaten sandwich on the coffee table next to a spilled glass of orange juice, and at least two piles of clothes sitting on the couch waiting to be folded.

Elizabeth nodded to the clothes. "Mae and Annie will help me with those when they get home. They're at a friend's house. I could tell they were worried about *Mamm*, and I thought some playtime might distract them from their worries." She picked up the overturned glass and blotted up the spilled juice with a clean towel from the pile.

"I brought you some cookies." Irma Rose eyed the rest of the room. Muddy shoes in the middle of the floor, and it looked like someone had walked across the living room in them.

"Danki." Elizabeth accepted the bag from Irma Rose and rushed to the kitchen. Irma Rose followed her, stepping over two pots in the entrance to the kitchen, with a large metal spoon nearby. Maybe Missy had been playing the drums. Irma Rose couldn't even see the countertops. But instead of an overabundance of food like the last time Irma Rose visited, there were dirty dishes, an opened box of crackers, spilled coffee, and a platter of pastries that were a tad green on the edges.

Irma Rose remembered when her grandmother died. For a while, everyone took meals to her grandfather, but after a time, the visitors stopped coming. Maybe no one realized that Sarah Jane was still in the hospital. Irma Rose wished she'd brought more than just cookies. "Where is Jonas, Elizabeth?"

"Um . . . what?" Elizabeth faced the counter and began gathering dirty dishes and putting them in the sink. Irma Rose walked to her and gently latched onto Elizabeth's arm until the girl turned to face her.

"Where is Jonas?"

Elizabeth's eyes filled with tears. "I-I can't say."

Irma Rose's heart flipped in her chest. "Where is Missy?" She realized she should have asked that as soon as she saw the living room.

"Missy is upstairs napping." Elizabeth sniffled. "Are you going to tell anyone that I've let things get in such a mess?"

Irma Rose began rolling up the sleeves of her blue dress. "*Nee.* I'm going to help you get all this cleaned up."

"*Nee, nee.* I can do it." Elizabeth straightened, still sniffling. "I just got behind on my chores."

Irma Rose scratched her forehead for a moment. "Do you not *know* where Jonas is?"

"Um . . . that's not what I said." Elizabeth turned away from her and picked up two dirty glasses at the far end of the counter.

"You said you can't say. So, what does that mean? That you know where he is and won't tell me? Or you can't say because you don't know?" Irma Rose stared at Elizabeth until Elizabeth looked her in the eye. "Tell me, Elizabeth."

"I told Jonas I wouldn't tell anyone." She covered her face with her hands for a few moments before she wiped her eyes and looked back at Irma Rose. "Please don't ask me again."

Elizabeth was so upset that Irma Rose just nodded. "Can I go check on Missy?"

"It's just as messy up there."

"It's okay." She hurried up the stairs and spied on Missy, who was sleeping soundly. She walked back to the kitchen.

For the next two hours, Irma Rose helped Elizabeth clean and put the house back together, and when they were finally done, Elizabeth made them both a glass of tea and they sat down at the kitchen table.

"Much easier with two people doing it," Irma Rose said as she smiled at Elizabeth.

"*Ya. Danki* so much, Irma Rose. I've been staying up late finishing chores from the day before. I overslept this morning, and everything just piled up on me. But I'm sure I'll be able to keep up now."

Irma Rose sipped her tea. "Do you know when your *mudder* will be home?"

Elizabeth shook her head. "We thought she would be home last weekend, but the doctor said she was bleeding inside her stomach, and now she has some sort of infection too. She would be so upset with me if she knew the *haus* was like this, and that you saw it this way." Her eyes rounded as she shook her head. "I've been going to see her every day; that's another reason I got so behind around here. I never stay long because I worry about the girls being alone, especially Missy. I sometimes bring her with me to the hospital."

Irma Rose chose her words carefully, wondering exactly how sick Sarah Jane was. "Did they give you a time frame, a day she might be coming home?"

"*Nee*. But when I went to see her yesterday, she looked much better and said she was feeling better. I hope she'll be able to come home soon."

Irma Rose couldn't stand it anymore. "Elizabeth, you must tell me where Jonas is. Even if he told you not to. This is too much responsibility for you."

Elizabeth covered her face with her hands again. "I promised I wouldn't."

"Jonas would want you to tell me if he knew that you were having such a hard time. When is the last time you talked to him?"

Elizabeth uncovered her face, sniffled, and swiped at her eyes. "When he called me last Friday."

"Was he okay?"

Elizabeth nodded. "*Ya.* I think so."

"Where was he?" She waited, her heart thumping in her chest. "Where was he, Elizabeth?"

Elizabeth's eyes filled with tears again. "Jail."

CHAPTER 5

Y ou have a visitor," the young jailer said as he put a key in the lock, then opened the door. Jonas stood up from the soiled mattress in the corner of his cell where he'd been sitting.

They exited the cell, Jonas getting in step beside the man.

"Personally, I don't think it's right for an Amish girl to be in a place like this, but I reckon it's your business." The guard, dressed in all black, didn't look much older than Jonas.

Elizabeth was the only person who knew he was here, and Jonas didn't want her in a place like this either. He glanced down at his orange slacks and shirt, thankful the jailer hadn't put handcuffs on him. They'd let him keep his black loafers, but they'd taken his straw hat. "I'll tell my sister this isn't a *gut* place for her to visit," he finally said as they rounded the corner toward the front of the building.

"The normal place for visits is down the hall, but there's a plumbing problem down there, and we got repairmen working on it." They walked around another corner. "I seriously doubt that your sister is going to try to slip you a nail file in the box of whoopie pies she brought." He turned to Jonas and grinned. "Which are mighty good, by the way."

"Elizabeth is a *gut* cook."

The guard stopped and faced Jonas, narrowing his eyebrows. "Elizabeth? This woman said her name was Irma Rose." He scratched his head. "Maybe she is here to break you out after all, if she's giving a fake name." The man chuckled.

Jonas's heart thumped against his chest as he looked down at what he was wearing again before looking at the guard. "I don't want to see Irma Rose. She's a friend, but I don't want her to see me like this."

The guard laughed again. "Friend, I'm not sure what you're wearing is any worse than the getup you wore when you came in, but suit yourself." The guard spun around and took two steps, but Jonas didn't follow. This might be the only time he'd get to hear how his mother was. Irma Rose might have information. And as much as he didn't want Irma Rose here, it was probably better than Elizabeth, if for no other reason than Irma Rose was older than his sister.

"*Nee.* I need to speak with Irma Rose."

The guard shrugged as he walked back to Jonas, and they took a few more steps to a door on the right. The man let Jonas walk in first. There was a table and two chairs in the middle of the room, and that was all. Except for a box of whoopie pies and Irma Rose.

"This is normally where we interrogate people, but it'll do for now. You've got ten minutes, and we can see you through that two-way mirror over there."

Jonas didn't look away from Irma Rose as the guard spoke. Her eyes were teary and she stood up as he walked closer. He wanted to run into her arms. He wanted to cry.

"Is my mother okay?" He folded his arms across his stomach, feeling like he might throw up.

"*Ya, ya.* She's much better. She doesn't know you're in jail. Elizabeth didn't want to worry her." Irma Rose blinked her eyes a few times. "Are you okay?"

Jonas nodded, fighting the urge to run around the table and into her arms. "*Ya,* I'm okay. But why . . . ? How—how did you know I was here?" He looked down, then back up at her. "I'm sorry for you to see me like this." He motioned for her to sit down, and he did the same.

. . .

Irma Rose had planned what she was going to say during the ride to the jail. Her hired driver had wanted to chat and seemed particularly curious why an Amish girl would ask to be taken to the county jail. Irma Rose had answered politely, but she'd also stayed busy trying to script her conversation. And now, with Jonas sitting in front of her, she couldn't recall any of her thoughts, so she asked the question heaviest on her heart.

"What did you do?" She brought a hand to her chest, drew in a breath, and held it.

Jonas hung his head for a few moments before he looked back at her. "Are Elizabeth and the girls all right?"

Irma Rose nodded.

Jonas slouched into his chair and leaned back, sighing. "I'd rather not say."

Irma Rose let out the breath she was holding and dropped her hands to her lap. She sat taller and spoke to him in the firmest voice she could muster. "Jonas Miller, you listen to me . . ." She started to tell him about the disarray at his house and how much trouble Elizabeth was having, but then she thought about Sarah Jane in the hospital, and the expression on Jonas's face was one of genuine pain. There was no half smile, and his dark eyes were moist. The whiskers on his face were more than just a dark shadow, almost a beard.

"I asked for a razor, but no one brought one," he said, as if reading her mind.

Irma Rose leaned forward in her chair, frowning. "What did you *do*?" She'd only known one Amish person who'd gone to jail, and it had been a case of mistaken identity. "Do they think you are someone else?" Hope filled her at the thought, until Jonas shook his head. "Then what?" She raised her shoulders, left them there, then let them fall when Jonas looked away.

Jonas scratched his scruffy chin, squinting. "If I tell you, you gotta promise not to get mad."

"I won't get angry," she said quickly, hoping it was a promise she'd be able to keep.

"Well . . ." He cringed. "There's this guy named Lucas. He's *Englisch*." Jonas paused and locked eyes with Irma Rose, as if waiting for a reaction. Irma Rose knew *Englisch* people, so this didn't seem odd. "He's a fine Christian. A *gut* man. He's about my age, maybe a year older, maybe twenty or so."

Irma Rose let out an exaggerated sigh. "And . . ."

"And he's got this car, a Chevy 210 Delrey." He paused, the familiar half grin returning. "And it's real fast, Irma Rose. He special ordered it; it's a powerful machine. I've watched him race it before at a little place on the outskirts of Paradise." His smile grew. "And he was going to race it against Andy Smith. I don't expect you to know him. Smith is a common name, but anyway . . . Andy has a Pontiac Bonneville, and it's fast, too, and . . ."

"Jonas!" Irma Rose slammed a palm on the table. "Did you hear that man say we only have ten minutes?"

Jonas lost his animated expression right away. "Lucas was racing Andy, and Andy asked me if I wanted to ride along. And I did. The police came. I didn't know there was beer in the back of Lucas's car. I got arrested because I'm underage and drag racing. And here I am." He shrugged before a big smile filled his face. "Remember, you said you wouldn't be mad."

Irma Rose slowly lifted herself out of the chair and raised her chin, choosing her words carefully. "I'm not mad, Jonas. I am disappointed in you. Your mother is in the hospital. You've left poor Elizabeth by herself tending to the house and your younger sisters. All because of your silliness with things that go fast. You are irresponsible. Couldn't you have just paid a fine?"

"The fine is over a hundred dollars. I can't get that kind of money, and I didn't want to worry *Mamm* while she's in the hospital. They told me I could go to jail for two weeks instead. So that's what I decided to do. I know *Mamm* will find out when she gets home and

I'm not there, but I didn't want this news to hinder her recovery. I figured she'd be home by now. And I talked to Elizabeth about it. She said she'd have no problem handling everything." He paused, searching her eyes for approval, but Irma Rose just looked away, knowing she had to tell him the truth. "The other guys chose to pay the fine," he added.

"Elizabeth is having a very hard time. The children are all fine, but it's a lot of work. She's very tired. And the house . . ." She chewed on her bottom lip, not sure how much more to say. It wouldn't change the situation. "I will help Elizabeth until you are freed. Annie and Mae are still going to Bible school at the Stoltzfuses' *haus* in the mornings."

"I will make this up to you, Irma Rose. I don't know how, but I will. Tell Elizabeth I'm so sorry."

She rolled her eyes as Jonas stood up. "I have to go." She turned toward the glass window, wondering if people were listening to their conversation or just watching them. She turned back to Jonas. "We are not going to tell anyone about this." She hurried to the door, leaving the box of whoopie pies on the table.

"Irma Rose?"

She waited while Jonas walked toward her. He stopped in front of her, and she dabbed her forehead with a sweaty hand, despite the coolness in the room. "What?"

"Everything that happens is God's will, part of His plan."

Irma Rose grunted. "Jonas, I can't think of one reason why the Lord would have you leave your family in a time of need because you did something stupid. God also gives us free will to make *gut* choices."

Jonas nodded toward the table. "*Danki* for the whoopie pies. The food isn't *gut* here."

"At least you have air conditioning." Irma Rose lifted an eyebrow before she moved toward the door. She knocked just as someone was pulling the door open.

"I told the kid to just pay the fine," the young man dressed in the black uniform said. "Seems weird to be holding one of your kind in the county jail."

Irma Rose lifted her chin and brushed past him, wondering how she was going to keep this secret without telling a lie. And when did it become her responsibility to clean up Jonas Miller's messes? But that's what she was going to do. By the time she returned to the Miller farm later that day, she had come up with a plan.

Elizabeth and Missy greeted her at the door, and even though there was a hint of lemon cleaner in the air, a pungent smell hit Irma Rose as she stepped over the threshold. "Elizabeth . . ." Irma Rose sniffed the air. "What is that smell?"

Missy ran to a pile of faceless dolls in the corner. She had them all sitting in a circle. Next to the dolls was a replica of a Captain Kangaroo Tasket Basket, a box filled with different-shaped blocks that fit into the shaped holes. Irma Rose had seen the toy in an *Englisch* store display. Although this model didn't have the words *Captain Kangaroo* etched into the side of the box. She wondered if Jonas had made it for Missy.

But before she could mention it, Elizabeth motioned

for Irma Rose to follow her to the kitchen. "Missy, we'll be in the kitchen. You stay in here with your dolls."

"Missy had an accident," Elizabeth whispered. "That's never happened until this past week. It's happened four times since Jonas has been gone. I just cleaned her up. I didn't realize the smell was lingering." She walked to the open window in the kitchen and raised it even higher. "Sorry."

Irma Rose leaned against the kitchen counter. "I'm sure Missy is wondering about Jonas and also worrying about your mother."

"I've been taking Missy to the hospital when Mae and Annie are at Bible class. I thought it would help her to see *Mamm*, but sometimes they are drawing blood while we're there, or *Mamm* looks like she might be having some pain. On those days, Missy seems scared. I was trying not to disrupt Annie and Mae's schedule any more than I had to, but I guess I need one of them to stay home with Missy while I visit *Mamm*."

Irma Rose tapped a finger to her chin. "Okay. Here's what we will do. I will come over at eight o'clock each morning. I can tidy things up and do some baking while you go visit your mother. Unless it upsets Missy even more not to go to the hospital, she can stay here with me while you're gone."

Elizabeth gave her a blank stare. "Why are you doing this?"

Irma Rose was surprised that no one in their community had offered to help Elizabeth, but then, folks didn't know that Jonas was away. "Because I want to help your family."

"But you . . ." Elizabeth paused, biting her lip. "You don't really know us all that *gut*. I mean, we've grown up in the same place, but we haven't been around each other very much."

Irma Rose had been asking herself the same question. "You need help, and since I'm an only child, it doesn't take nearly as much work to run our household. *Mamm* will be fine if I'm gone part of each day."

"That's nice of you." Elizabeth smiled. "Jonas was right."

Irma Rose suddenly felt warm all over as she raised an eyebrow and tried to appear casual. "About what?"

"He said that you are loving and kind, that you are *gut* with children, and that you go out of your way to help others."

Irma Rose felt her face reddening as she shook her head. "*Ach*, I don't know how he knows all that."

"But he does!" Elizabeth stood taller, smiling. "Anytime he talks about you to others, he tells stories. One is about the time you went to Widow Zook's *haus* every Monday for six months to do her laundry." Elizabeth chuckled. "And we all know Widow Zook is a bit cranky." She lifted a finger. "*Ach*, and he also tells people about the baby bunnies you found, how you hand-fed each of them with a bottle. And . . ."

Irma Rose was hearing part of Elizabeth's recollections, but mostly she was thinking about Jonas. How irresponsible and reckless he could be, how he always smelled of cigars—how he just wasn't right for her.

Maybe she needed to give Jake another chance, though she really didn't want to. Or maybe Isaac? She focused on Elizabeth again when she heard her name.

"*Danki* again, Irma Rose."

"You're welcome. But there is one more thing." She paused. "We don't want to lie, but we don't want people around here to know about Jonas going to jail. We need to say something that is truthful, but also keeps his whereabouts a secret."

"What about 'Jonas is away on business'? I heard an *Englisch* man say that once." Elizabeth smiled from ear to ear. It was the first time Irma Rose noticed how much Elizabeth looked like her brother.

"Then that's what we will say. 'Jonas is away on business.'"

Irma Rose wasn't sure that was the best solution, especially since Jonas's "business" was farming, but she couldn't come up with anything better.

CHAPTER 6

Irma Rose's mother put a loaf of cinnamon-raisin bread in the bag that Irma Rose was taking to Elizabeth the following morning.

"It's nice what you are doing for the Millers, going there to babysit Missy and help tend to the house. I suspected it might be too large a job for Elizabeth and those younger girls. Is Jonas helping out inside while his mother is away?"

Irma Rose swallowed hard, putting the plan to the test. A plan that now seemed ridiculous. "Jonas is away on business."

Mamm scratched her forehead. "What kind of *business* would take him away?" She stuffed her hands in the pockets of her apron, frowning. "The Millers make a living working the land."

Irma Rose stared at her mother, determined not to lie. She snapped her finger. "Oops. I forgot something upstairs." She left the room and darted up the stairs, hoping that by the time she returned, her mother would have forgotten the question. *This is going to get tiresome.* She grabbed her small black pocketbook, thankful she really had forgotten something. She wasn't going to let Jonas's shenanigans shove her into a pit of lies.

"So, what kind of business?" *Mamm* asked the moment Irma Rose walked back into the kitchen.

"Just business. Bye!" She grabbed the bag, kissed her mother on the cheek, and didn't look back as the screen door closed behind her.

• • •

Jonas stared at the pale yellow blob on the plate in front of him. He'd never missed his mother's cooking more than right now. He pushed the food around with a plastic fork, afraid to taste it, but too hungry not to give it a try. It resembled eggs but didn't look like any he'd ever seen. Up until now, his breakfasts in the jailhouse had consisted of either half-frozen waffles or a bowl of mushy cereal. His mother made the best dippy eggs cooked over easy, but these were overcooked, bland, and tasted old. Jonas loved the eggs they had at home with dark-yellow yolks fresh from their hens.

He forced himself to swallow, then eyed the only other offering on his plate, a piece of toast that was burnt, no jam or butter. He wished he hadn't forgotten to grab the box of whoopie pies Irma Rose brought yesterday. The guard confessed that he and two other men ate them. After a few more bites, he set the plate on the floor beside one of the cots in his cell. He picked up the Bible he'd asked for when he first arrived, and he gave the next hour to God. He was closing the Good Book when he heard a commotion down the hall. Lots of screaming and carrying on. He stood up when the same guard, whom he now knew as Peter, stopped at Jonas's cell, toting a young man in handcuffs.

"Jonas Miller, meet Theodore Von Minden the third, your new roommate." Peter unlocked the cell and the man's cuffs, then gave him a gentle push before locking them both in. Jonas closed his Bible, stood up, and waited for the man to stop screaming and cursing at the guard. Finally, Theodore turned to face Jonas. He threw his hands up in the air.

"You have got to be kidding me!" He spun around, grabbed the metal rails, and shook them. "Hey! I can tell by this guy's stupid haircut that he's Amish. You can't leave me in here with this religious freak!"

Peter strolled back up to the cell, grinning. "Oh, I can, and I am. Now quit all the yelling and screaming. There's a price to pay for that, so shut your mouth. Even your rich daddy can't help you now."

Jonas didn't move. Theodore yelled a string of curse words as Peter walked away. After he appeared to have exhausted himself, he hung his head, then seemed to remember that Jonas was in the cell with him.

"What are you looking at?"

Swallowing hard, Jonas had a better understanding of why his people tried to stay away from the *Englisch*. Jonas had heard curse words before, but never so many of them strung together at one time. He shrugged, towering over Theodore. "Just wondering if anyone tended to your wound." Jonas pointed to a trail of blood running down the side of Theodore's face from his eyebrow.

His blond hair was cut short, parted to the side, and shone with a mixture of hair gel and dried blood. He was short and skinny and wore the same kind of orange slacks and pants as Jonas. Except Theodore was wearing a pair of fancy tan loafers.

Theodore reached up and touched his head, cringing and cursing again. Then he walked over to the only other cot in the room and sat down. "Do me a favor, will you?"

Jonas nodded. "*Ya.* How can I help?"

Theodore pulled a handkerchief out of his pocket and pressed it against his head. "Do me a *favor*," he repeated in a strained voice. "Just don't talk to me."

Jonas sat down on his cot, picked up his Bible, and started reading, seriously wishing he'd had enough money to pay his fine. He wasn't sleeping. The food was terrible. And using the toilet in the corner was humiliating. Now he'd have to share this space with an irritable young *Englisch* man. He buried his head in the Book, but he could feel Theodore's eyes blazing a hole through him.

"It amazes me how you people buy into that bunch of bull."

Jonas didn't look up until Theodore sprang from the bed and knocked the Bible from Jonas's hands, causing it to fly across the cell. Jonas stood up and clenched his fists at his sides, fighting the urge to smack the guy. It wasn't their way, but . . . *Give me strength, Lord.* He calmly went and picked up the Bible, returned to the cot, and flipped the pages to find where he'd left off, this time keeping a tighter grip on the book. Theodore stood in front of him, and Jonas braced himself. When Theodore's arm swept down in front of him again, this time Jonas latched onto his wrist.

"Don't do that." Jonas let his eyes slowly drift upward until they were locked with his new cell mate's.

"Or what? You gonna hit me?" Theodore grinned. "Your people don't do that. I grew up in Pennsylvania. There isn't much I don't know about your kind." He wiggled loose of Jonas's hold. "So, what are you going to do?"

Jonas's blood was boiling as he stood up, and once again he asked the Lord for strength. "You might have grown up here, but you don't know everything about our *kind*. And you don't know *me*." Jonas said it with just enough intent to hopefully confuse the guy, and he breathed a sigh of relief when Theodore went back to his cot and sat down. *Like dogs marking our territories,* Jonas thought briefly. He set the Bible on the floor, then lay down, not completely sure that Theodore wouldn't start pushing him for a fight again. Jonas had only been in a fight one time, and it had been with another Amish boy when they were both about ten years old. Amos King wouldn't stop pulling Mary's hair that day, and eventually Jonas had shoved him, which led to a full-blown fight on the playground. Jonas was pretty sure that's when Mary developed a crush on him. It had won Jonas a trip to the woodshed when he got home. He'd endure a hundred trips to the woodshed for spanking just to have his father back. He sighed, knowing *Daed* would be disappointed in him for being here. Like Irma Rose.

A few minutes later Theodore spoke again. "So, what

are you in for? It's not every day you see an Amish man in jail."

Jonas opened his eyes. "Drag racing and alcohol in the car."

Theodore burst out laughing. "Well, ain't that something."

Jonas closed his eyes again but finally asked, "What about you?"

"I robbed an old lady and stole her purse. She beat me over the head with her cane, thus the blood."

Jonas sat up and stared at Theodore, wondering how he was going to keep from hitting this guy. It must have shown on his face.

"Relax, fellow . . ." Theodore held up a palm toward Jonas. "I'm just joking." He shook his head, frowning. "Man, I have some issues, but I would never rob anyone, especially an old woman." He grunted. "Yet you believed me." He pointed a finger at Jonas. "And you know why? Because that's the way we are. Humans believe the worst about each other. People at their core are untrusting, selfish, and mean. Even if we really aren't like that, people will just assume it. So you're doomed from the start." He pressed the rag to his head again, scowling.

"I believed you because you said it was so." Jonas wasn't sure what to say as he recalled Jesus saying that the truth will set us free.

Theodore grinned but shook his head.

Jonas wasn't sure the truth was going to set this guy free, but he owed it to Theodore—and God—to try to educate Theodore. "But the fruit of the Spirit is love, joy, peace, patience, kindness, goodness, faithfulness, gentleness, and self-control. Scripture doesn't say anything about people being born untrusting, selfish, and mean."

For a few long moments, Theo just stared at him. Finally he spoke. "I know all that. I didn't say we were *born* that way. But if people drill it into our heads enough over the years, I guess it just becomes true." Theodore tossed the bloody handkerchief on the floor near his bed. "I hope my father rots in hell."

Jonas was quiet for a few moments. It wasn't his place to minister to this man, so he went back to his original question. "What did you do to get in here? Were you in a fight?"

Theodore chuckled, then flinched and reached for the bloody rag nearby on the floor, placing it to his eyebrow again. "I guess you could say that. My pop was beating the snot out of me, and it's taken me seventeen years to fight back, but today I finally did." He shrugged. "And here I am."

Jonas ran his hand the length of what was becoming a beard. "That doesn't seem fair, that you're in jail for defending yourself against an abusive father."

"Bingo, Jonas Miller! You're the grand-prize winner today!" Theodore clapped his hands hard and loud. "You just hit the nail on the head. Life isn't *fair*! But when your father is Theodore Von Minden the second, the wealthiest and most powerful man in the state of Pennsylvania . . . well, let's just say you don't punch him in the face, no matter the circumstances. It can get you an assault-and-battery charge."

Wonderful memories flooded Jonas's mind, recollections of his father. He never would have struck Jonas in anger, and Jonas credited his father—and God—for helping to mold him into the man he was, or at least the man he hoped to be when he stopped doing dumb stuff. "I'm sorry for your troubles," he finally said.

"It's the hand I've been dealt." Theodore pulled back the rag, looked at it, then put it back against his head. "And this time, it was the hand with his college ring that met with my head."

Jonas was quiet.

"Your pop ever hit you?" Theodore locked eyes with Jonas.

"*Nee*. I mean no. Not like that. We got spankings, but . . ."

"Yeah, yeah. I know all about the perfect life of an Amish person."

Jonas thought for a moment. "I'm not so perfect since I'm in here."

Theodore laughed. "True. I guess even the Amish love a good race and having a few beers."

Jonas had never had a sip of alcohol in his life, but he let it go.

"So, how long you in for?" Theodore kicked off his loafers and tucked his legs underneath him on the small cot.

"Two weeks. I've already been here a week. What about you?"

He stretched his legs out and rested his socked feet on his shoes, grinning. "I'm here as long as my father thinks I need to be here. He'll convince the district attorney to drop the charges when he's good and ready. But I'll tell you this . . . the moment I'm out of here, I'm getting my hands on whatever money I can, and I'm leaving this godforsaken place. I hope my disappearance at least embarrasses him. He won't care if I'm gone, but he'll want to keep up appearances."

"Where will you go?" Jonas could understand Theodore wanting to run away from his father, but he suspected the guy was running from more than just that. "What about your mother?"

"I have no idea where I'll go. My mother's dead. Anything good left in me, I got from her."

"My father died three years ago. But my Father in heaven is always with me."

"See, that's the thing about you religious types. At the end of the day, it's always about God. He's responsible for everything." He pointed to his head. "Which means He is responsible for my father hitting me hard enough for me to see stars."

"Theodore, that's not how it works. Our Lord wants us to be healthy and happy, and He gives us free will to—"

"Stop." Theodore held up a palm again. "First of all, only my father calls me Theodore. My friends call me Theo. That's what my mother called me, too, and even though I highly doubt you and I will be friends, for the sake of our time stuck in here together, I'd appreciate you just calling me Theo." He paused, took a deep breath, and blew it out slowly. "And as for your rubbish about God and free will, do you really think that it was by choice that I was born into the life that was forced on me? No, sir. Not my choice. And if your God wanted me to be happy and healthy, He should have stepped up to the plate long before now."

Jonas sat quietly. *Not my job to minister to this man.*

Theo made a noise similar to a growl. "I'd do just about anything for a smoke."

"Me too."

Theo laughed. "Oh, stop the presses. Since when did the Amish start smoking?"

Jonas grinned. "I don't smoke. I just like to puff on a cigar every once in a while. I don't inhale. I like the way it smells and tastes though."

"Well, my good man, I must inform you. That is *still* a form of smoking."

They both turned their attention to the bars of the cell when they heard someone approaching.

"Well, I'm glad to see you two haven't killed each other," Peter said as he pulled keys from his pocket. "Jonas, your girlfriend is here again today."

"She's not my girlfriend." Jonas smiled. "Yet."

"Well, if she keeps bringing food every day, I'll be rooting for her to win the role. She always offers us some. Which, by the way, sorry we finished off your whoopie pies, but you left them in the interrogation room. Today she brought a shoofly pie. Not very original, but I've always been a fan of that Amish staple." He motioned with his hand for Jonas to step out of the cell, then he locked it behind him and led Jonas in the same direction as the day before. As much as Jonas wanted to see Irma Rose, he hated that it was under these circumstances, and he felt his stomach churn, hoping she wasn't bringing him bad news about his mother. Maybe *Mamm* was home from the hospital by now.

As he walked quietly alongside Peter, he fought the shame that was threatening to engulf him, promising God that he was going to work harder at being a better man.

CHAPTER 7

Irma Rose sliced the pie with the pocketknife the nice guard named Peter had given her. *They are very trusting in the jailhouse,* she thought as she handed the guard a slice, the same man as yesterday. In her mind, if she were extra sweet to the people who worked here, they would be nicer to Jonas. She owed that to Jonas's mother. Sarah Jane was still in the hospital, and she would want someone tending to her son. But when Jonas walked into the room, she admitted to herself that coming here wasn't just about doing the right thing for Sarah Jane Miller.

"I don't know if you should be coming here, Irma Rose," Jonas said after Peter left with his slice of pie. "Is my mother all right?"

"*Ya.* Elizabeth went to see her this morning, and I stayed with Missy and did a few things around the house while Mae and Annie went to Bible school."

Jonas put his hands flat on the table and hung his head. "I should have found a way to pay the fine. I thought *Mamm* would be home way before now." He looked up at Irma Rose. "I don't like you coming here," he repeated. "I love you for doing all this, but this is not a *gut* place for you."

Love? It should have rattled her, but instead, she was pretty sure she heard angels singing somewhere in the heavens. Whatever this infatuation was for Jonas, she needed to move past it. She'd thought that if she forced herself to be around him, maybe the clammy hands and pounding heart would go away. Now she was hearing choirs of angels.

"These are all things you should have thought about." She smirked as she handed him a plate with pie on it. He set it back down on the table.

"I told you, I will make it up to you somehow."

"I won't be by tomorrow unless there is news about your mother. Even though it's Sunday, I'll visit Elizabeth tomorrow morning to make sure everything is okay. There's no church service so I'll offer to stay with Missy so Elizabeth can take Mae and Annie to visit your mother. But I have a lunch date after that."

"Date?" He folded his arms across his chest.

"*Ya.* With Jake. It's our second date. We went to the singing, remember? The one you were supposed to take Mary to." No need to tell Jonas how the first date with Jake had gone.

"How was the date?" He looked her in the eye. "Please tell me Jake didn't kiss you."

You had to ask, didn't you? "That's none of your business."

"Ugh." Jonas lowered his head and gently hit his palm on the table. "That means he did."

Irma Rose avoided his eyes as she re-covered the

shoofly pie with plastic wrap. "This is mostly for the guards. So they'll be nice to you."

"You're bribing the jailers, kissing Jake Ebersol, and . . . what else are you up to, Irma Rose?" The hint of a smile played across his face, but the mischievous sparkle in his eyes made Irma Rose go weak in the knees for a moment, and all she could focus on was Jonas's mouth as she wondered if kissing him would be more enjoyable than Jake's kiss had been.

"I'm going to lunch with Jake," she said in a snappy tone, as if to convince herself it was the right thing to do. Just because their first kiss hadn't been everything she'd expected, maybe the second one would be better. But as she wound around the table, Jonas stepped in front of her and leaned down.

"I almost kissed you once in the buggy."

"If you try to kiss me in here, they're going to keep you locked up and throw away the key." She hurried toward the door and knocked hard until the guard came and let her out. She didn't look back as she hurried to where her driver was parked, with a quivering lower lip, clammy hands, and a swirling in her stomach that she loved and hated.

. . .

Despite his circumstances, Jonas had a bounce in his step as he walked with Peter back to his cell. He wasn't happy that Irma Rose would be having lunch with Jake, but he'd seen a playful fire in her eyes today, and he knew she wasn't just coming here to bring sweets and give him updates about things at home. At least he hoped he'd read her expression correctly. He needed that hopefulness to get through the next few days. Especially now that he had such a cranky cell mate. This time, he'd remembered to grab what was left of his pie.

"She seems like a sweet girl," Peter said as he unlocked the cell and let Jonas back in. Jonas nodded, then tiptoed to his side of the small room and sat on the cot, thankful that Theo was curled up on his cot, facing the wall. Surely the noise from the gate would have prevented Theo from sleeping, but Jonas was just glad that he was quiet. He felt badly for Theo, for the life he'd lived, and he made a mental note to pray for his cell mate.

"How was your conjugal visit?" Theo rolled over and faced Jonas.

"My *what*?"

"Never mind. How was your visit with your girl-friend?" Theo sat up and rubbed his eyes.

"I already said, she's not my girlfriend. But I hope she will be one day. I hope she's my wife someday."

"Wow. You've got everything all planned out."

Jonas shrugged. "*Nee*, not everything. But I know I want Irma Rose in my life." He paused, nodding at the covered pie dish he'd set on the bed beside him. "There's three slices of shoofly pie left if you want a piece."

"Not a fan of molasses, but thanks." Theo scratched his cheek. "Is Irma Rose a common name among your people?"

"*Nee*. Not really. There are a few women named Irma,

and even more named Rose or Rosie, but there's only one Irma Rose that I know of." He smiled. *My Irma Rose.*

"Hmm . . ." Theo continued to stare at Jonas. "I once knew a girl named Irma Rose. It was before we moved to Lancaster. I met her when we lived in Hershey, around three years ago. Maybe a little longer. She was a year or two younger than me, but wise beyond her years." He paused as he leaned against the cement wall that his cot was pushed against. "I was fourteen at the time, but I'll never forget her."

Theo seemed to drift away for a few minutes, just staring into space. Jonas was glad they were having a normal conversation without yelling and cursing.

"The first time I ever saw Irma Rose was when she was sitting under a tree at her house," Jonas said, recalling his own memories. "She was reading a book, and I was running an errand for my mother, returning a casserole dish. I knew Irma Rose was too young for me at the time, but I waited three years for her. I never dated anyone else. I watched her grow from a pretty girl into a beautiful young woman. And not just on the outside."

"She must be pretty special to come visit you in a place like this. Especially since she's Amish. Most Amish girls I've known wouldn't be caught dead here." Theo chuckled. "Maybe she just comes for the air conditioning since you backward people don't have that luxury."

"How is it that you are so familiar with the Amish?"

"I told you. I've lived in Pennsylvania my whole life. You people are everywhere." Theo grinned. "Before my father reached the level of success he has now, he and my mother ran several small inns in Hershey. We had a few Amish gals who came and cleaned the rooms. After my mother died, Pop sold his businesses and we moved to the city of Lancaster. He built hotels, ultimately making him worth more than most people could spend in a lifetime." He paused, slapping his hands to his knees. "But I'm here to tell you, money isn't worth the paper it's printed on if it can't buy you happiness, and I assure you . . . happiness costs more than I've got. But it'll be enough to get me out of Lancaster County."

Jonas scratched his scruffy chin again as his pulse picked up. "This might sound far-fetched, but . . ." Jonas waited for Theo to look at him before he went on. "Irma Rose lived in Hershey before she moved to Paradise, which is where I live. She was twelve or thirteen when they came to Lancaster County."

Theo sat taller as his jaw dropped. "Your Irma Rose is *my* Irma Rose?"

Your Irma Rose? Jonas frowned. "I don't know about that. Maybe it's just a coincidence."

"Wow." Theo spoke so softly that Jonas barely heard him. "Wouldn't that be something. I didn't think I'd ever see that girl again, but even at fourteen, I knew I'd never forget her." He smiled, and Jonas thought Theo's eyes looked a little misty. "I never knew her last name."

Jonas shook his head. "I doubt it's the same girl, but Irma Rose's last name is Kauffman."

"Only one way to find out."

Jonas raised an eyebrow and waited.

"Ask her if she remembers Theo from Hershey. If she does . . . that's her."

Jonas was having a hard time picturing Irma Rose with the likes of Theo, even as friends, but he nodded. "I will."

. . .

The next day, Irma Rose stayed with Missy while Elizabeth took Annie and Mae with her to the hospital. A couple of hours later, Irma Rose was sweeping the living room floor when she heard a car coming up the driveway. She stowed the broom and looked out the window, glad Elizabeth was returning in plenty of time for Irma Rose to meet Jake for lunch. But she was surprised when Sarah Jane stepped out of the backseat of the car at the same time all three girls did.

"Your *mamm* is home!" Irma Rose scooped up Missy from the couch. "Let's go greet her."

Irma Rose pushed the screen door open with her foot, and once on the porch, she set Missy down. The little girl took off barefoot toward her mother, only to be stopped by Elizabeth.

"Easy does it, Missy," Elizabeth said as she kept her hand in between Missy and their mother. "*Mamm* is sore."

Irma Rose listened and watched from the porch, waving to all of them. Elizabeth paid the driver as Sarah Jane spoke softly to Missy while rubbing her head.

"What a wonderful surprise," Irma Rose said as Elizabeth and Annie helped Sarah Jane up the porch steps while Mae lagged behind carrying a small red suitcase. Missy clung to her mother's dress. "How are you feeling?"

"*Wie bischt*, Irma Rose?" Sarah Jane took each step slowly. "I'm doing *gut*."

Irma Rose held the screen door as they all crossed over the threshold. Elizabeth hung behind, whispering to Irma Rose before she went inside. "I told her Jonas was away on business, but she wanted to know where he was, and eventually I had to tell her where he was. But I whispered it so Annie and Mae wouldn't hear."

Elizabeth walked inside and Irma Rose followed her. Sarah Jane sat down on the couch, Missy beside her. "Annie and Mae, take Missy upstairs with you. I need to talk to Elizabeth and Irma Rose alone. In a little while, I want to hear all about your Bible learning and anything I've missed while I was away, *ya*?"

Sarah Jane waited until the girls were upstairs before she spoke. "Irma Rose, Elizabeth tells me how much you have helped her and the girls the past couple of days, and I'm so appreciative." She paused, frowning. "She also told me that Jonas is in jail." She reached into her purse and pulled out a wad of money. "I can't stand to think of him in such a place, and I stopped at the bank on the way home." She looked up at Irma Rose. "I'm so sorry to ask this, but can you go get my *sohn* out of jail? I'm just not up to the task, and I'd rather as few people as possible know his circumstances. It's an awful thing to ask you to do, but Elizabeth said you've been to see him a couple of times." She raised her shoulders and dropped them slowly. "I can ask someone else if you'd like."

"*Nee*. Of course I'll do it." Irma Rose took the money.

"We are all in your debt. Elizabeth said she didn't know what she would have done without your help."

Irma Rose felt herself blushing. "It was no problem for me." She wondered how she would get word to Jake that she wasn't going to be able to go to lunch with him. And how was she going to get out of lunch without lying? She didn't want Jake to know she'd been visiting Jonas at the jailhouse.

. . .

Jonas grinned as Theo eyed his breakfast. "It won't kill you," Jonas said as he shoveled a nasty forkful of eggs into his mouth.

Theo continued to stare at the plate, then finally looked up at Jonas. "You got any of that shoofly pie left?"

Jonas nodded to the pie plate on the floor by his bed. "One piece. But I thought you didn't like molasses."

"I'll take it over this mess." Theo tossed the plate in a nearby trash can and picked up the pie plate. After peeling back the plastic wrap, he picked up the last slice and took a giant bite. When he was all done, he surprised Jonas by thanking him.

"You're welcome." Jonas bit into his toast, not quite as burnt as the day before. From the moment he'd woken up this morning, all he could think about was Irma Rose going on a lunch date with Jake today.

After breakfast, Jonas was glad that Theo fell back asleep for a while. Although, in the silence, he couldn't shake loose the vision of Jake and Irma Rose together. Maybe Irma Rose deserved someone like Jake, a man who was well respected in the community. A man who hadn't gone to jail. He bowed his head in prayer, vowing to stay away from fast cars and other *Englisch* hobbies that might get him in trouble again. Jonas accepted that this life lesson was part of the Lord's plan for him, but he didn't see how any good could come out of this experience.

He looked up when he heard footsteps. It was Peter. He unlocked the cell, smiled, and said, "Jonas Miller, you just got sprung."

CHAPTER 8

Irma Rose was hoping to quell the butterflies dancing in her tummy as she and Jonas rode home from the jailhouse. Sarah Jane had insisted on paying for a driver there and back. Jonas was as quiet as Irma Rose had ever seen, but he could also barely keep his eyes open, nodding in and out. Finally, he laid his head back against the seat and lightly snored. She latched onto the opportunity and watched him. Even during his sleep, she could see the hint of a smile. He didn't nap long, though, and when he opened his eyes, he turned to her and grinned.

"Sorry you missed your date with Jake."

"*Nee*, you're not." She folded her hands in her lap as she cut her eyes in his direction. She'd left a note on Jake's mailbox, just saying that she couldn't go to lunch today.

Jonas grinned. "*Nee*, I'm not." He squinted as he looked at her, and his expression stilled into a look of distress. "Irma Rose . . ."

She held her breath and waited.

"I'm so hungry, I feel like I might die without some food. Do you care if we stop and eat somewhere?"

Relief washed over her, and she laughed. "I'm quite

sure you won't die, but that's fine." She put a hand on the seat in front of her and leaned forward. "Sir, would it be possible for you to take us somewhere to eat? I'd be happy to pay for your meal as well."

"I've already eaten, but thanks," the driver said before he glanced over his shoulder. "I hear the Burger King has something new. It's called a Whopper. How does that sound?"

Burger King had come to their town about three years ago, and it was always a treat to go there. Irma Rose nodded, and a few minutes later, they were pulling in the parking lot off the main highway. The driver dropped them off, saying he had an errand to run and that he would return in forty-five minutes.

As they walked to the entrance of the burger place, Irma Rose noticed a sign advertising a movie that would be played in the *Englisch* theaters in November. *Jailhouse Rock* starring Elvis Presley. Giggling, she nudged Jonas.

"Very funny," he said, grinning.

Irma Rose couldn't stop her smile from spreading, but as they neared the sign, she stared at it for a few moments. She'd never been to a movie. She was barely into her *rumschpringe* and hoped one day to be able to. But it wouldn't be anything with Elvis Presley. *Mamm* said he wasn't fit for young girls to watch, and that some television stations only filmed him from the waist up because of the inappropriate way he danced.

Glancing at Jonas, she wondered if he'd ever been to a movie. Probably, she decided. She couldn't imagine seeing *Jailhouse Rock* with him. *I'd be so embarrassed.*

Cool air met them when they entered the restaurant,

and after they ordered and sat down, Jonas thanked her repeatedly for everything she'd done for him and his family.

"I would have found a way to come up with the money if I'd known *Mamm* would be in the hospital so long." He paused. "How did she look? How mad was she when she found out I was in jail?"

"She looked tired, but otherwise okay. And I don't think she was mad, more worried, it seemed."

Jonas just stared at her, which only fueled the dancing butterflies in her stomach.

"Why are you staring at me?"

He smiled. "Because you're so pretty. The prettiest woman I've ever seen."

She covered her face with her hands for a couple of seconds. "You're embarrassing me."

He gently lowered her hands from her face. "It's true, Irma Rose."

She thought about what Elizabeth had said, how Jonas always talked about her and told stories. Maybe the warmth she felt around him wasn't to be feared, but embraced. Maybe what made her uncomfortable was that he looked at her with such stark admiration. She wasn't used to being the center of attention, nor had anyone made mention of her outer beauty. It wasn't their way.

They were quiet as they unwrapped their burgers.

Jonas wasted no time biting into the burger. Irma Rose took a small bite, feeling self-conscious about eating in front of him.

"Do you like it?"

She was relieved he'd changed the subject. She finished chewing and swallowed. "I think it's very good. I'm not sure if thirty-seven cents isn't a bit much, though."

"You're worth it, Irma Rose." He grinned, but his expression quickly shifted. "I need to ask you something." He leaned back, his eyes locked with hers.

"Okay." She sipped her Coca-Cola from the straw.

"Before you came here, you lived in Hershey, right?"

She nodded. "*Ya*. I was thirteen when we moved here. Why?"

"Did you ever know a boy named Theo? It's probably a coincidence that my cell mate . . ." He paused, hung his head for a moment. "I hate the way that sounds, cell mate. Anyway, the *Englisch* man that was in my cell said he knew a girl named Irma Rose while he lived in Hershey. I think this guy is seventeen. Is that a coincidence, or did you know someone named Theodore? His parents owned some type of hotels there."

Irma Rose's breath hitched in her chest. She'd always wondered what happened to Theodore.

. . .

Jonas waited for Irma Rose to answer, but every time she opened her mouth to say something, she couldn't seem to get her words in order.

"I-I, um . . ." She took several gulps of her soda, then looked up at him. Then more soda.

"You *did* know him, didn't you?"

She stared back at him with a blank expression.

"It wonders me why you look like you've seen a ghost."

Blinking her eyes a few times, she opened her mouth, but still nothing came out. As badly as he wanted to know the connection between the woman he loved and his crazy cell mate, he could see that the conversation was bothering her. "We don't have to talk about it, if it makes you uncomfortable."

"Okay. *Gut. Danki.*" She took another sip of her soda.

"I told you that I'd make it up to you, remember? What can I do to show my thanks?"

She swallowed as she shook her head. "Jonas, you've told me *danki* a dozen times. That's enough."

"Let me take you on a proper date to a fancy restaurant." He didn't know how he'd get the money for that, but he'd figure out a way if she would agree to go with him. Lots of the fellows in their district had side jobs, but it took all of Jonas's time to take care of the farm. He didn't have time for anything extra. Even when it wasn't planting season or harvesttime, there were always outdoor chores. Repairing fences, tending to the animals, painting, and most recently leveling gravel across the driveway in an area that held water when it rained.

"*Nee.* That's not necessary." She dabbed her mouth with the napkin from her lap before she lifted a French fry to her mouth.

"Is it Jake? Is he courting you now?" Jonas held his breath, willing it not to be so. "Or you just don't want to date a *convict*?" He grinned, thinking how that sounded.

Irma Rose giggled, which was nice to hear. "I think you like hearing that word roll off your tongue," she said in a whisper.

"And I think that Jake Ebersol will never be exciting enough for you, Irma Rose. You have a fire in your belly, a sense of adventure."

She laughed again. "And Jonas Miller, you have way too much adventure to suit my liking."

"Then I'll change." He gazed into her eyes. "Who do you want me to be? Tell me three things you'd change about me if you could." Chuckling, he added, "then I'll tell you three things that I'd change about you."

"*Ach*, really?" She smiled. "And what makes you think I'd like to hear what you'd change about me?"

He shrugged. "You go first."

She tapped a finger to her chin. "I wish you didn't smoke cigars."

Jonas chewed on a French fry, nodding. That didn't seem too hard. "That's one," he said after he swallowed, "I'll try to change," he added, winking at her.

"Actually, I don't think a person should change for another person. That doesn't seem right."

Jonas pointed a finger at her. "You can't think of anything else that you'd like for me to change."

"That's not what I said. I said that any changes a person makes should be for himself . . . or for God."

He sighed. "Okay. But I had a really long list of things you need to change."

Her eyes rounded as she halted a French fry between her mouth and her tray. After she put it back down, she scowled at him. "Then let's hear your list." She was so cute when she pouted.

"First and foremost, you need to change your dating circumstances and not date anyone but me."

"That's not changing something about *me*. That's just doing something you want me to do." She leaned against the seat of the booth. "What else?"

"You need to sell your baked goods at the market. That shoofly pie was the best I've ever had." He was telling her the truth. The woman could cook. "You could make money from the tourists."

"I'm listening." She straightened, raising that cute little chin of hers.

"I've heard folks talking. More and more *Englisch* people are coming here to visit and shop. The local vendors are talking about forming something called the Pennsylvania Dutch Tourist Bureau. All the shop owners would work together to attract people to Lancaster County."

"Don't you think it's touristy enough here?"

Jonas shrugged. "I think that Lancaster County is going to become a place that people all over the United States will know about. The *Englisch* seem real interested in the way we live, and I don't think there's any gettin' away from them. You've heard the saying, 'If you can't beat them, join them.'" He smiled at her. "And you're a real *gut* cook, Irma Rose. You could even have a bakery in the heart of Paradise, maybe even right off Lincoln Highway."

"I think I'd rather be married, stay home and have *kinner*, and tend to *mei* family."

That was music to Jonas's ears. "If you were my *fraa*, I'd want you to do whatever made your heart sing."

. . .

Irma Rose was speechless as her entire being filled with
warmth. She folded her hands atop her napkin, surprised
they weren't clammy. And as they eyed each other across
the table, she had to rethink why she kept fighting the
attraction she felt for Jonas. She'd thought it had been
simple, that he just wasn't right for her. Anyone who
unnerved her in such a way couldn't possibly be the person God intended her to be with.

She thought about how comfortable she was around
Jake. But then she thought about their kiss and wondered if safe and comfortable would ever be enough.
What would walking a little bit on the wild side with
Jonas Miller be like? Would life be filled with his desire
to live more adventurously than Irma Rose would like?
Or would she saddle up next to him, love the ride, and
not worry about the destination? And all these thoughts
were reasons why Jonas upset her stomach. He con-
stantly tipped the balance of her applecart, tempting
her with a life she hadn't planned. "What else would you
change about me?" she finally asked.

"Irma Rose, if the truth be told, you are perfect in
every way. I wouldn't change one thing about you. I've
loved you since the day I saw you sitting under that tree.
I could tell you were nervous, and you were real young.
But I've watched you become a woman, and there isn't
anyone else I'd rather spend my life with. And I feel like
I need to tell you this because life is short. *Mei daed* is
gone, and *mei mamm* gave us all a real scare." He paused,
and Irma Rose could feel herself trembling. "And I know
in my heart that you feel something for me too."

Irma Rose swallowed back the knot in her throat,

and in the distance, she was sure she heard angelic singing again. It wasn't real. It couldn't be. "I-I think we need
to go."

Jonas's expression dropped instantly, and Irma Rose
had a strong urge to reach for his hand across the table.
But until she could corral her feelings, she couldn't tell
him how she felt.

Jonas picked up their trays and deposited them in
the designated area, and Irma Rose offered again to
pay for her half of the meal. Jonas shook his head, and
they were quiet as they walked outside. The driver was
waiting curbside, and Jonas opened the door for her.
They rode silently to Irma Rose's house, then politely
said good-bye. She stood in the grass, the afternoon
sun blazing down on her, and watched the car until it
was out of sight, tears filling her eyes.

God, I need a sign from You. What should I do?

CHAPTER 9

Irma Rose stayed to herself for the next couple of weeks. When she wasn't busy cooking, sewing, or tending to the farm animals, she read books her mother had approved for her. She craved anything that would take her away from her own thoughts. She'd waited a long time to be old enough to date, but now the prospect of marriage and making lifelong decisions overwhelmed her. What if she didn't choose correctly? Would the wrong choice land her on a path that wasn't the one God intended for her? People married young in her community. *But I'm only sixteen years old.*

She was sitting on the couch reading a book, the warm breeze wafting into the living room and mingling with the aroma of oatmeal cookies baking in the oven. Not even the battery-operated fan on the coffee table did much to counter the August heat that had settled upon them like a dense fog. She tried to focus on the book she was reading, but her mind kept drifting.

"Are you okay, *mei maedel*?" Her mother walked into the living room, a kitchen towel draped over her shoulder and an oatmeal cookie in one hand. She smiled.

"Because I don't think there is anything an oatmeal cookie can't cure."

Irma Rose closed the book. She'd considered talking to her mother about the confusion swirling around in her head, but she felt like even the decisions she might make at sixteen years old should be based on her own thoughts and feelings. Once she got them figured out. "I'm fine, *Mamm*. Do you need me to do anything this afternoon?"

Her mother shook her head. "*Nee*. It's too hot to do more than get by today. I shouldn't have baked in the middle of the day, but I couldn't stop thinking about *Mammi's* recipe." She handed the cookie to Irma Rose, and the moist, warm treat melted on her tongue. Her grandmother on her mother's side had been the best cook Irma Rose had ever known, a thought that made her think of her conversation with Jonas a couple of weeks ago.

Mamm sat down on the couch next to her. "I ran into Mary's mother at the market yesterday. She asked me if you were all right. She said you haven't been to the malt shop with Mary and Hannah in two weeks." Her mother nudged her gently with her shoulder. "And I know how you feel about strawberry shakes. And you didn't feel up to church service last weekend either."

Irma Rose again considered talking to her mother, but decided against it. Again. "It's so hot outside. I guess I'm just being lazy after I get my chores done. But I really didn't feel very well the day of worship." It was a partial version of the truth. Mary and Hannah would ask about Jake, if they were going steady, as the *Englisch* would say.

Irma Rose was afraid of getting pulled into a conversation about Jonas, and she didn't want to lie to her friends. She'd avoided Jake too.

Mamm patted her on the leg. "Since we're ahead this week on some of our chores, I think I'm going to take a nap." *Mamm* stood up, yawned, and headed toward her downstairs bedroom, but she stopped and faced Irma Rose. "*Ach*, next time you go outside, can you fetch the mail?"

Irma Rose nodded. "Have a *gut* nap." She thought about Sarah Jane Miller and wondered how she was doing, if she was fully recovered from her time in the hospital.

She opened her book, a sweet tale about two childhood friends who reconnected after years apart. She'd read the book before—it was a favorite of hers—but try as she might, she just couldn't keep her mind on the story. Setting the book aside, she decided to face the heat and get the mail.

It was a fair hike down their long driveway to the mailbox, and by the time she got there, she was dripping with sweat. She reached into the box for the mail. A flyer, one regular-sized envelope, and one larger package stuffed so tight she had to yank on it a couple of times to get it out. The flyer was an advertisement for a new Kenmore twelve-speed mixer that was on sale for thirty-two dollars and ninety-five cents. She eyed the special features, wondering what it would be like to use such a fine electric appliance. *The Englisch spend lavishly,* she thought as she walked back to the house.

The second envelope was addressed to her father, and Irma Rose recognized the return address as a cousin's from Ohio. The large envelope was addressed to Irma Rose, and at first glance she assumed it must be from a relative also, but she stopped abruptly when she read the return address:

Theodore Von Minden III
32 East Willow Road
Chicago, IL 60004

She'd thought about Theo ever since Jonas said he'd shared a jail cell with him. But she'd also promised never to speak about what happened. She'd kept her word.

She opened the envelope and pulled out a white sheet of paper, along with a book. A Bible. Her heart flipped in her chest, and with shaky hands, she read the letter.

Dear Irma Rose,

Once I found out what your last name was, and that you lived in Paradise, it was easy to track you down. You probably know that I spent some time in jail with your Amish boyfriend, Jonas. He said he wasn't your beau, but I know he sure wants to be. I've thought about you often over the past three years, and your words on that day stayed with me. Jonas told me something that reminded me of something you'd said. It seems like more than a coincidence, and I hope that you'll consider what I'm saying as both appreciation and hope for a bright future for you.

Irma Rose paused as she recalled the three hours she spent with Theo, both of them hiding in a broom closet in one of his father's small hotels—"inns," he'd called them. She'd just finished changing sheets in one of the rooms when she set out to find a mop and broom. She'd opened the closet to find Theo crouched in the corner, crying. They'd both heard footsteps approaching, and Theo had begged her to hurry inside and to stay quiet as a church mouse. So she'd done what he asked since he was so upset . . . and bleeding. She pulled herself from the memory, a recollection that was painful and life-changing at the same time.

Jonas said the fruit of the Spirit is love, joy, peace, patience, kindness, goodness, faithfulness, gentleness, and self-control. Do you remember telling me that, Irma Rose? Do you remember what else you said that day? You told me that one life could make the difference in a thousand lives and that I had a purpose. Holding hands, we whispered a prayer together, fearful that my father might hear us. You ripped the pocket from your apron and held it against my bleeding ear, and you cried along with me that day. You saved my life.

For the next week, I looked for you. When I finally tracked you down, it was to learn that you had moved away. No one would tell me where. But for the next year, I prayed, I secretly went to church with a neighbor kid, and I forgave my father . . . for a while. I had hope. But the abuse didn't stop, and over time . . . I fell back into the dark place I'd been before. By the time I landed myself in jail with your Jonas, I'd decided that I couldn't go on this way. I treated him rather badly. When you talk to him, please tell him that I'm sorry. I was lonely after he left, and I spent another week in that cell with nothing to do but read. The only reading material was the Bible that Jonas left behind. I read it cover to cover and took it with me when I left.

I'm sending it to you, knowing that life is filled with coincidences, but to me, the events that have unfolded aren't coincidences, and once again, I have hope. I left Lancaster where I was living with my father and made it to Chicago. I'm broke, working in a diner, and renting a fairly trashy room over the place. But I'm safe. I'm finally working toward happiness. And I'm going to turn my life around. Hearing about you from Jonas, reading the Bible, and remembering our time together has lifted me out of the darkness yet again.

I think you must be an angel. Maybe Jonas is your messenger, I don't know. But open this Bible to page forty-six. There's a letter folded between the pages that Jonas was writing you, but he didn't finish it. I hope you will let me know how the story ends.

Sending you thanks and blessings from Chicago.

Theo

Sweat was pouring down Irma Rose's face and mixing with her tears as she stood in the middle of her driveway, the searing sun blasting down on her. But her feet were rooted to the ground as she thumbed open the Bible and found the letter.

Dear Irma Rose,

What does the future hold for us? Will we be together or apart? I'm writing this from a jail cell, so that's probably not a *gut* start. But I know I have enough love for you in my heart to get me through any situation. I have time to think about things in here, and I want to be a better man.

Irma Rose paused. *You are a gut man, Jonas.* The thought breezed through her mind easily and without hesitation.

I want to raise a family with you. I want to love you for the rest of our lives. I want to hold and protect you. I want to cherish you. And most of all, I want

The words stopped, and Irma Rose stiffened. *And most of all you want what? No, no, no!* It couldn't just end like that. What did Jonas want most of all? She sat down in the middle of the driveway, reread Theo's letter, then reread Jonas's letter three more times. She stood up, hugged everything to her chest, and started running as fast as she could.

· · ·

Jonas pressed his heel on the auger, then threw his weight onto it, struggling to break the dry dirt to put in a new fence post. He'd waited until after the supper hour, but the setting sun to his west was having no mercy on him. There were still six posts he needed to get into the ground, so he forged ahead, hoping to finish before dark.

He hadn't seen Irma Rose since their burger, and he was trying to imagine a life without her since she didn't have much of a response to his laying out his soul to her. But he was wise enough to know that he couldn't force her to love him, so he'd been working on readjusting his thinking about his future. If it were God's plan for them to pursue a future, He would lead them to each other. Jonas couldn't continue to lay all of his hopes on a dream that might not ever turn to reality.

After several more attempts, he'd dug deep enough for the post, so he set the hole digger aside, hoisted up the piece of redwood, and dropped it into the hole. Breathing heavily, he used his handkerchief to swipe sweat from his forehead, wishing for the umpteenth time that the Lord could have seen fit to give him a brother or two for times like this. If nothing else, maybe He could just send some rain to cool him off.

After he gulped from his thermos of water, he glanced at the setting sun, knowing he didn't have time to dillydally if he planned to finish tonight. He picked up the auger again and moved a few feet to his left. Distracted by a movement in the distance, he noticed someone running up his driveway. A woman. He put down the tool and starting moving in that direction. The closer she got to him, the faster he made his own stride, until he was running toward the girl who had his heart.

"What's wrong?" He grabbed both her shoulders to

hold her up since she was completely out of breath. "What is it? One of your parents? What's wrong?"

She shook her head repeatedly and finally caught her breath. She handed him the Bible and the letter he'd written. Jonas reread what he'd written that day. He'd left the jail so fast, he'd forgotten about the letter. He never would have had the nerve to give it to her. He was just writing down his thoughts, mostly for his own benefit.

"Theo read your Bible," she said, still breathing hard. "It's a long story about Theo, but I think he'd want me to tell you about it." She wiggled out of his hold. "But first . . ." She pointed to the letter in Jonas's hands. "I need to know what you were going to write, what it is that you want most."

Jonas was sure his blood pressure was dropping and he might pass out. If ever there was a time he wanted to lie, it was now. He remembered exactly what he was thinking at that moment, and since he'd had no plans to give her the letter, he remembered even chuckling about what he was going to write next. Then the guard came, and his time in jail was done.

"Tell me, Jonas. What is it you were writing? What did you want the most?"

Jonas was sure she was waiting for him to say something that would make the earth move beneath their feet. But he was still trying to understand why she was here.

"Why are you here, Irma Rose?"

Her eyes filled with tears. "I want to be with you, Jonas. I want us to date."

He cupped her face, but she took a step backward.

"I'm only sixteen years old though. I'm not ready to decide my entire future today, next week, next month, or maybe not even next year. But I know that I feel different with you than I do with anyone else. And I think there is something to that, but it scares me. I think I love you, and I'm so confused." She covered her face, and Jonas wrapped his arms around her.

"Oh, Irma Rose . . . I'm not scared at all, and someday you won't be either." He kissed the top of her head. Then when she looked up at him, his lips met hers. The earth definitely moved beneath them.

• • •

Irma Rose lingered in the kiss, and before Jonas even pulled away, she was certain she would spend the rest of her life with this man. *So this is what kissing is all about.* She let him kiss her two more times, each time better than the last, and somehow she knew that if she was with Jonas, that's how it would always be . . . each day better than the last. She forced some distance between them and asked, "What was it in the letter that you wanted the most?"

"I'm going to assume that I need to tell the truth."

Irma Rose squinted at him. "*Ya.* The truth would be *gut.*"

"I, uh . . ." He paused, stood taller, and looped his thumbs beneath his suspenders. "I wasn't going to give you the letter. I was just writing my thoughts."

She smiled the sweetest smile Jonas had ever seen.

"That's okay. What you wrote is beautiful, and I can't wait to hear what you wanted the most at that very moment."

He hung his head and sighed, then looked back up at her and grinned. "I wanted a cigar."

Irma Rose's lips parted. "Are you teasing me, Jonas Miller?"

He wrapped an arm around her. "Now, now, Irma Rose . . . let's walk over to the bench near the garden." Moving slowly with his arm around her, he added, "I probably need to tell you about a certain situation that involved some bullet holes in my buggy . . ."

Irma Rose laughed. Being married to Jonas was going to be one adventure after another, but she was excited to see what God had in store for them both.

EPILOGUE

*M*any years later, Jonas and Irma Rose had a daughter named Sarah Jane and a granddaughter named Lillian. Jonas's love for speed never dwindled, even after forty-eight years of marriage. Nor did his love of cigars.

"Let's kick up some dirt, Lilly! Let ol' Jessie stretch his legs. Give a gentle flick with the reins. Jessie will do the rest."

Doing as her grandpa suggested, Lillian carefully maneuvered the buggy down the dirt lane to the main road. Then she looked at Grandpa again. He grinned and nodded.

"*Ya!*" she yelled, which thrust Jessie forward so fast Grandma fell backward against the seat.

"Thata girl, Lilly! A *wunderbaar* day to feel the wind in our face," Grandpa said as Jessie got comfortable in a quick gallop.

"Jonas, the Good Lord will still be there when we arrive!" Grandma yelled, regaining her composure as she adjusted her *kapp*. "This is Lillian's first time to drive the buggy. She might not feel comfortable moving along so fast."

"Sure she does. Pick it up, Lilly! Another gentle flick of the reins."

Lillian glanced at her grandma, who was preparing herself for another increase in speed. But when she smiled in Lillian's direction, Lillian took that as the go-ahead and did indeed pick up the pace.

"Yee-ha!" Grandpa wailed.

. . .

Suddenly his face took on a fearful expression and he stuffed the cigar into the coffee cup. "Quick! Start fanning the room! Dump this out!" He handed Lilly the coffee cup. "My hearing must be off too! I usually hear Jessie's hooves before he hits the dirt drive. Look at that! They're already in the yard!"

She grabbed the coffee cup and dumped the contents as instructed. Grandpa moved faster than she'd seen him since she arrived, waving his arms about, pushing the smoke toward the open windows. She watched with amusement at his wholehearted effort to keep his secret. Then, shaking her head, she said, "I'll go outside and try to stall Grandma. I'll show her the flowers I'm going to plant today."

With her grandpa still flailing his arms wildly around the room, she moved toward the open screen door. "I still think you shouldn't smoke," she whispered before she walked onto the porch.

"Hurry, child! Or Irma Rose will have my hide!"

—FROM *PLAIN PERFECT*, BOOK ONE IN THE
DAUGHTERS OF THE PROMISE SERIES

• • •

The complete story of Jonas, Irma Rose, and their family and friends can be found in the Daughters of the Promise series:

Plain Perfect
Plain Pursuit
Plain Promise
Plain Paradise
Plain Proposal
Plain Peace

DISCUSSION QUESTIONS

1. Irma Rose is interested in Jake because she thinks he is "right" for her. We all know it takes more than logic to attain true love. Do you think that Irma Rose could have been happy with Jake if Jonas hadn't made his intentions known? Or would she have always longed for more?

2. Irma Rose thinks Jonas is wild and reckless, but what are some of the qualities in Jonas that Irma Rose overlooks early on, and which parts of Jonas's character shine toward the end of the story?

3. My mother was the same age as Irma Rose when she married my father. My parents were married fifty-four years, and Irma Rose and Jonas were married almost that long. Do you think marriages back then were more apt to last, especially when marrying so young? Or are young people today just as likely to have a long-lasting marriage when they commit at such an early age?

4. If you could have written Irma Rose and Jonas's love story, would you have done it differently? If so, discuss with the group.

ACKNOWLEDGMENTS

God continues to bless me with stories to tell, and I loved writing this novella about Jonas and Irma Rose. All of the characters in the Daughters of the Promise series are special to me, so it was like revisiting old friends.

Many thanks to Larry Knopick for his friendship and continued support along this amazing journey. Larry, you've been an ambassador of the Amish genre, and it's an honor to dedicate this very special story to you. Peace be with you and Jolene, my friend. ☺

To my family and friends—I couldn't do this without you. And I have a fabulous publishing team at HarperCollins Christian Publishing.

Thank you, Natasha, for all you do to guide my career and for your friendship.

WHERE HEALING BLOOMS

VANNETTA CHAPMAN

For Uncle Joe, who still keeps a garden

There is a time for everything, and a season for every activity under the heavens.

—ECCLESIASTES 3:1

GLOSSARY OF SHIPSHEWANA AMISH WORDS

ach—oh
boppli—baby
daed—father
dat—dad, father
danki—thank you
Englischer—non-Amish person
freind—friend
gem gschehne—you're welcome
Gotte's wille—God's will
grandkinner—grandchildren
gut—good
haus—house
kaffi—coffee
kapp—prayer covering
kinner—children
mamm—mom
mammi—grandma
nein—no
Rumspringa—running around; time before an Amish young person has officially joined the church; provides a bridge between childhood and adulthood.
schweschder—sister

Was iss letz?—What's wrong?
wilkumm—welcome
wunderbaar—wonderful
ya—yes

CHAPTER 1

Emma Hochstetter stepped onto the back porch and pulled in a deep, cleansing breath. The colors of the May afternoon were so bright they almost hurt her eyes. Blue sky spread like an umbrella over her family's tidy homestead, which was dotted with green grass, three tall red maples, and an entire row of bur oak trees. And the garden—Mary Ann's garden.

Her mother-in-law could be found out among the garden's rows every morning and every afternoon. The place was a work of beauty. Emma would be the first to admit it. It was also a lot of work, especially for two old ladies living on their own. Emma wasn't in denial that she was now officially old. The popping in her knees each time she stood attested to that. Turning fifty the past winter had seemed like a milestone. She now woke each morning grateful to see another day, which might have seemed like an overreaction, but they'd had a hard year.

"Done with the laundry?" Mary Ann called out to

Emma from her bench in the garden. She'd recently turned eighty-four, and some days it seemed to Emma that her mother-in-law was shrinking before her eyes. She was now a mere five-one, which meant she reached past Emma's chin, but barely. Her white hair reminded Emma of the white boneset that bloomed in the fall, and her eyes reflected the blue, bell-shaped flowers of the Jacob's ladder plant.

"*Ya.* Just folded and hung the last of it." Emma walked down the steps and out into the garden.

"Gardens will bless your soul, Emma."

"I suppose so."

"They are a place to rest, to draw near, and to heal."

"At the moment this garden looks like a place to work." Emma scanned the rows of snap beans, cabbage, and spinach. The weeds seemed to be gaining ground on the vegetables.

"Remember when the children used to follow behind me, carrying a basket and picking up the weeds I'd pulled?"

"I do." Emma squatted, knees popping, and began to pull at the crabgrass.

"The girls were cute as baby chicks. Edna leading the way with Esther and Eunice following in her steps."

"All grown now, *Mamm.*"

"Indeed."

"We should probably think of cutting back on the size of this garden."

Mary Ann fell silent as Emma struggled with a particularly well-rooted dandelion. The weed pulled free and dirt splayed from its roots. They both started laughing when two fat worms dropped from the ball of dirt and crawled back toward the warm, moist hole.

"I guess we know what Harold and Henry would do with those."

"My boys always did prefer fishing to gardening." Emma brushed at the sweat that was beading on her brow and resumed weeding. The temperature was warm for mid-May, nearly eighty. With the sun making its way west and a slight northern breeze, the late afternoon was a bit more pleasant. Perhaps the heat was why everything in the garden was growing with such enthusiasm.

Summer had barely begun, and already their vegetable plot had become a place of riotous chaos. The flowers tangled into one another in an unruly blend of scents and colors—reds, blues, yellows, oranges, and pinks. Shipshewana had experienced an early spring, bountiful rains, and mild temperatures. Emma struggled to keep up, and the garden became more a place of labor than of healing.

Still, she continued to work on the row of snap beans.

Mary Ann sat on her bench and watched.

"Gardens are a reflection of God's love for us," Mary Ann said.

"*Ya*, indeed they are."

"You missed a weed, dear. Back near the bean plant." Mary Ann pointed at the bunch of quack grass with her cane.

Emma smiled and reached for the grass. She no longer thought of Mary Ann as Ben's mother. After living on the same property for over thirty years, she was just *Mamm*. Sweet, dear, and at times, more work than an infant.

Emma prayed nightly that she would live forever, that she wouldn't leave her alone.

"The weeds aren't easy to find because the plants have grown so large." She used her apron to wipe the sweat from her forehead. "Everything is running together."

"Evil can overtake good—"

"I'd hardly call a weed evil."

"Especially when you don't spend a little time each day tending to what is important." Mary Ann's eyes twinkled in the afternoon sunlight. She might have been referring to Emma's recent absence.

"I'm glad I went to Middlebury and spent the week with Edna. All three of her children suffering with the flu at the same time? *Ach!* We had our hands full with laundry and cooking and nursing."

Mary Ann moved her cane left and then right. She gazed off past the barn, and her voice softened. "Do you remember the year Harold came down with a bad case of the influenza?"

"He was nine."

"While you were tending him, I spent many an hour out here, praying for that child's soul and body—that the Lord would see fit to leave him with us a bit longer."

"Harold would call out, and his blue eyes, they'd stare up at me and nearly break my heart. The fever was dangerously high. I can still recall how hot his skin was to my touch."

"Difficult times."

Emma had reached the end of the row. She turned to

the next and stifled a sigh. Most afternoons she enjoyed
her time in the garden, with Mary Ann sitting on the
bench and sometimes dozing in the sun. But today weari-
ness was winning, that and a restlessness that resembled
an itch she couldn't reach. Perhaps her impatience came
from comparing her own life to her daughter's.

The trip to Middlebury should have been a nice
reprieve from the work of the farm, but she came back
nearly as tired as when she left.

Certainly it had been a delight to spend time with
Edna, her husband, and the grandchildren while a neighbor had stayed with Mary Ann. But looking around her
daughter's tidy farm and newer house, she found herself
wondering if they should sell the old place. Perhaps it was
too much for two old women to maintain. Something
smaller would be good. Her daughter's place was half the
size and much more manageable.

"*Mamm*, this garden is too big."

"No garden is too big, dear."

"We can't possibly eat all of this food."

"Which is why we share with those in need."

They'd joined a co-op several years ago. In exchange
for the vegetables, they received fresh milk, eggs, and
occasionally cheese. Both Emma and Mary Ann were
relieved that they didn't have to look after a cow—
Emma had never been good at milking, though she'd
done it enough times as a child. And chickens required
constant tending. She also didn't favor the idea of pur-
chasing their dairy products from the local grocer.
Fresh was best. Still, what they put into the co-op far
exceeded what they received.

"Maybe it's grown past what we can manage. Instead of adding a little every year, maybe we should hack something back." Emma stood and scanned right, then left. The garden, which had once been a small vegetable patch, now took up one entire side of the yard. "We could plow up that row of flowers over there, maybe plant some grass instead. And we do not need ten tomato plants."

"Help arrives when you call."

"Yes, but—"

"Hello, Danny."

Emma had turned her attention back to the row of blooming plants and was reaching up to trim back the joe-pye weed, which threatened to take over the Virginia bluebells that were already in bloom. Her hand froze at Danny's name. Slowly, she brushed the dirt from her fingertips by running her hands across her apron, inadvertently leaving a stain of brown slanting from right to left against the light gray material. She swiped at the hair that had escaped from her *kapp*, tugged her apron into place, and turned to face the man who had first courted her.

CHAPTER 2

Danny enjoyed the sound of Emma's voice, even when it was only two words. There was something about seeing her in the garden that set his day on a solid foundation.

Emma.

He'd loved her so many years ago, when he was only a boy. Then he'd gone away, and she had married. Her life with Ben had been a good one, by the looks of things, and he understood fully how much she must miss her recently deceased husband. Danny's own life was solitary, though he was grateful to be surrounded by a good community.

On various occasions, he'd heard Mary Ann insist that he was one of God's many blessings, that the Lord Himself had sent Danny home to Shipshewana to be their help and neighbor.

Emma didn't seem as sure.

They'd had a hard year. Emma's father-in-law, Eldon, and husband, Ben, had both passed within a few weeks of each other as winter turned to spring the year before. Danny was glad he'd returned when he had, in the middle of the winter, when the snow was still falling and the land lay fallow. He'd thanked the Lord more than once that he'd had a few months to spend with Ben before he'd died. Long enough to know there were no ill feelings between them.

"Gardening, I see."

Emma glanced up after she'd pushed some stray hairs back into her *kapp*. He'd only glimpsed the brunette curls that were now mostly gray. But Emma's caramel-colored eyes looked the same as when she was sixteen.

She must have stopped growing about that age, because she still only reached his shoulder. And though she'd put on a little weight over the years—what woman didn't after five children—she carried it well. Emma looked healthy, and in brief moments, she looked happy.

When she glanced his way, the dismay in her eyes amused Danny, and it also kicked his pulse up a notch. He wasn't a young man and wasn't sure why he reacted this way when he was around Emma.

"Indeed." She smiled tightly. "Every afternoon, as the sun creeps toward the horizon, you're bound to find us here."

"We love our time in the garden," Mary Ann said.

Danny raised an eyebrow, but Emma only shook her head and threw an endearing look at Mary Ann. The garden was her passion, not Emma's. Mary Ann obviously did enjoy her time in the garden. Then again, she was sitting on a bench, not sweating over a vegetable patch.

Emma had confessed one night that she was grateful

she could still work in the garden. And she was grateful Mary Ann was still sitting on the bench.

Since Danny didn't know how to respond to either of them, he placed his walking stick next to Mary Ann's bench and turned back to the task at hand. Without asking what she needed, Danny moved to the other side of the row Emma was working on and held back the plants she was trimming.

They worked in silence for another ten minutes. When they'd reached the end of the row, he wiggled both eyebrows and asked, "Where to next? Carrots and onions, or another floweredy row?"

Danny knew the name of every bloom in their garden, but sometimes he felt self-conscious about the years and years of knowledge stored in his mind. Like the stack of notebooks in his office, he didn't think what he'd learned and seen should be displayed in every conversation. Sometimes it was good to be the clueless old guy who lived next door.

Emma wasn't buying it. She snorted and said, "Don't play ignorant, Danny. I saw your piece in *The Budget* on using indigenous plants throughout your yard."

"*Ya?*"

"I'm pretty sure you have an encyclopedic knowledge of gardening, among other things."

When Danny only blinked, Emma dusted her hands on her apron and turned in a circle. "I need to work the ground around the carrots and add a bit of fertilizer."

"Want me to bring some from the barn?"

"*Nein.* I have some in the bucket at the end of the row, but there's no need for you to—"

"I'll fetch the bucket and meet you at the carrot patch."

Emma glanced at Mary Ann, but she appeared to be ignoring them. Her cane was raised, and she'd plunged it into a boisterous stand of flowering mint. She was attempting to coax a butterfly into settling on the polished oak walking stick.

So they turned to the vegetable section, and that was when Emma froze. She pressed her fingers to her lips. Danny followed her gaze and saw a young lad, probably fifteen. He was sneaking out from the back of Emma's barn. As his scrawny frame came around the corner, he looked right at them.

For a moment, their eyes connected, and then he sprinted away, like a young buck in flight.

Emma dropped the gardening tools and rushed after him.

Danny caught up with her when she was halfway to the road. "We'll never catch him."

"Probably not."

"Amish?"

"*Ya.*"

"Any idea what he was doing there?"

"*Nein*, and I don't need this right now."

"Best go see if he took anything."

They reversed direction and headed to the barn.

"The door isn't latched, and I always make sure to fasten it."

"He probably doesn't know you bring in the horses every evening. In some counties, they're left in the pasture."

"This early in the year? *Ach!* It's still too cold in the evenings."

As he walked into the darkness of the barn, Danny's mind was flooded with memories of Ben, Eldon, and his own father. For so many years, their families had been intertwined like the mint mixed with the tomatoes in Emma's garden. The barn smelled like the memories of those he'd loved—wood chips, hay, oats, and leather.

"Do you keep any money in here?"

"*Nein.*"

"What's in the office?"

"Old files. Ben's things. Nothing anyone would want to steal."

"He was here for something."

"Maybe he was hiding out."

"Maybe." Danny crouched down near a bit of stray hay.

Emma shrugged, but Danny pointed toward the farthest stall. The door was cracked open a hair's width. Danny held up his hand for her to stay put.

Instead, she strode in front of him, across the barn, and to the stall. When Emma saw the bedroll, camp stove, and extra set of clothes, she backed up until she'd reached the opposite wall and stood against it, as if for support.

"Do we have an Amish runaway living in our barn?"

"Or he could be a hobo."

"Whatever he is, what are *Mamm* and I going to do about it?"

CHAPTER 3

The boy had upended one of the pails she used to carry horse feed. Apparently he was using it as a table. Her stomach tumbling, Emma walked back into the stall, sat down on the pail, and looked around in disbelief.

"What are you going to do?"

"Do? I suppose I'll call Bishop Simon, and he'll decide whether to call the police."

Danny leaned against the stall wall, crossed his arms, and rubbed at his clean-shaven jaw with his right hand. "Or . . ."

"Or? We have an *or* here?"

"Just saying." He spread his hands out in front of him. Big hands.

Danny brushed at straw that clung to his dark pants. Suspenders draped over his pale-green shirt. He pushed back the straw hat covering his mahogany brown hair sprinkled with gray. When he did so, Emma noticed his bangs flopped close to his chocolate-colored eyes. The gesture made Emma think of the boy he had been. Perhaps that was the problem. She suffered from memory misplacement.

He was a big guy—over six feet and trim. It was one of the reasons folks were surprised when he decided to be a writer. Danny would have made a great farmer, or a farrier, or even a cabinetmaker. All of those occupations would have made sense. But a writer? An Amish writer?

She sighed and returned her attention to the horse stall. "You haven't said anything."

"I wouldn't want to put my opinion where it has no place."

"Out with it." The words escaped as a growl. She sounded moody, even to her own ears. It occurred to her that she never used to snarl at folks, unless they were tracking mud through the kitchen.

"What if you left him some food instead?"

"Why would I do that?"

"Because he's obviously living here, and he must be hungry."

"But I don't want him to live here. I want him to leave. My barn is for my horses."

"You're right."

"People don't live in barns."

"Most don't."

"And he must have a home. His parents are probably worried sick."

"Maybe."

Emma closed her eyes and pulled in a deep breath. When she'd spoken to her daughter Edna about her moodiness, Edna had smiled and reminded her of *the change*. She had thought she was through with that. Maybe not.

"I don't want him to stay. I want him out of my barn and off my property."

Danny pulled down on his hat. He looked Amish, but there were times Emma wondered. All that traveling must have affected his way of thinking.

She stood and swiped some hay off the back of her dress.

"Seems as if he was careful with the cookstove," she admitted. The boy had placed it inside one of the mid-sized tin troughs.

"Indeed."

"Don't know what he could have been cooking."

"He probably caught a rabbit."

She brushed past him into the main portion of the barn. A young boy, a boy her own *grandkinner*'s age, eating rabbit he'd caught from the field? And nothing else?

"I'll bring him some leftover ham and bread from last night's dinner, leave it in his stall, but only this once."

"It would be a kind thing to do."

"And he can reciprocate by moving on."

"Maybe he'll see the food and trust you, tell you what's happening and why he's here."

She humphed as they stepped out into the late-afternoon sunlight. Old people made that sound, and she was not that old.

Danny touched a hand to her shoulder, and Emma froze. Her feet became like cattails in an iced-over pond. Her heart thudded in her chest. She refused to look at him as he leaned close and whispered, "Perhaps *Gotte* has sent him to you, Emma. Perhaps *Gotte* has sent this child to us."

Against her better judgment, she turned and looked up into Danny's eyes. His expression was a curious mixture of intensity, hope, and amusement.

What was she to say to that?

How was she supposed to respond?

Emma had no idea, so she turned and trudged off toward the garden.

. . .

"I think Danny was right." *Mamm* squinted her eyes as she glanced across the room and out the window. "We should try to help this one who is lost."

"We don't know that he's lost. Maybe he's lazy."

"Few children are actually lazy, though they are often confused. Sometimes one looks like the other."

Emma stood to gather their dinner dishes. With only the two of them, cleaning up had become much easier. She checked the large kitchen table to be sure she had all the dishes, and the memories almost overwhelmed her. She could see their brood of five, plus Ben's parents, crowding around the table. The children often jostled one another as they made room on the long bench or in the chairs. As if they were still there, she could see—actually see—them settle for prayer. The boys bareheaded, the girls with their *kapp* strings pushed back and stray locks peeking out. The deep baritone of her husband's voice when he'd ask who was hungry.

Mary Ann reached out and covered Emma's hand with her own.

It startled her from the past.

"It's okay to feel what you're feeling, *dochder*."

About the past?

About the vagrant in her barn?

About Danny?

"I don't know what you mean, *Mamm*. Unless you're referring to my feeling tired. I'm not as young as—"

"*Gotte* isn't done with you yet."

"I suppose not, since I'm still here."

"He has plans, Emma."

"*Ya?* Has He let you in on any of them?" She couldn't help smiling as she added dish soap to the warm water and plunged the first plate into the suds.

"You're laughing, but He has. I believe He has." Mary Ann stood and carried her glass to the sink. At a time in life when most folks slowed down, she was still quite spry. Too thin. Emma remarked occasionally that she'd like to give some of her extra girth to Mary Ann, if that were possible. It seemed no matter how she changed their meals, Mary Ann became a little smaller each year, and she became a pound or two heavier.

"Share with me, then. I'm interested to know what my future holds."

"No one knows that, dear." *Mamm* picked up a dishcloth and began to dry.

There was something about her tone that caught Emma's attention. All this talk of the future and God's plans. It was different from their normal evening banter.

"Danny says perhaps *Gotte* brought this boy to us. That maybe that's why he's here or why we found him."

"The boy could have gone anywhere," Mary Ann said.

"There's no telling how long he's been hiding in there. I don't look in that back stall often."

"But today you saw him."

"I did, which is strange, *Mamm*. If he were hiding, it seems he would have been more careful."

"Maybe he wanted you to see him."

"That doesn't make sense. He ran the moment our eyes met." Emma let her hands soak in the warm water. All that was left to wash was the pan she had used to stew the chicken and potatoes. She wanted to enjoy the dishwater before it grew cold and soiled.

How long had it been since the boy had enjoyed a warm bath?

She closed her eyes against the question. It wasn't her responsibility to worry about the well-being of this boy.

And yet the Scriptures spoke often about strangers. Didn't they? Something about the welfare of strangers and angels unaware?

Mary Ann hung up her dish towel, then stretched to kiss Emma on the cheek. She'd always been affectionate, but in the last few years, she'd become more so. Maybe she realized the importance of expressing her feelings while there was still time.

"Pray on it, my dear."

With those words of wisdom, Mary Ann turned and left the room.

CHAPTER 4

The next day proceeded as most Tuesdays had since the children moved away. Emma and Mary Ann ate their breakfasts, cleaned two of the downstairs rooms, and then donned their shawls for the Stitch Club, which took place at a neighbor's home.

Laura's home was on the other side of town. It wasn't a far drive, and though the day was cloudy, it felt good to be out and about. Emma guided their buggy through Shipshewana, past the Blue Gate where Edna had worked her first job as a waitress. They stopped at the light, and she glanced over at the Davis Mercantile. While she didn't need any more fabric, it was always nice to drop in and say hello. The light changed, and she resisted the temptation to stop, directing her sorrel mare past Yoder's and onto Laura's street.

The group was working on a quilt for the June auction. The women numbered a baker's dozen, and they were all excited to be in the last stages of the project. Stretched on the quilt stand, which took up a good portion of Laura's sitting room, was a large double-wedding-ring quilt. As they stitched it together, Emma wondered about who would purchase it. Newlyweds?

Or a couple who had already spent a lifetime together? Amish? Or *Englisch*? Would someone buy it for themselves or for a loved one?

The Lord knew. Before they began stitching each week, Laura reminded them to pray for the recipient. As soon as they had silently done so, the room became a bevy of activity.

Emma's daughters had not been able to attend, since school was now out of session and they were busy with their children. Instead, she and Mary Ann would stop by Eunice's house on the way home. Her eldest daughter, Eunice, lived next door to Esther, her youngest, which made for easy visiting.

They'd finished piecing the quilt together and were now ready to begin the actual quilting, as they'd basted the top to the back the week before. Once the quilting was finished, they'd bind the edges and be done! Perhaps three more weeks.

The conversation around the quilt fluctuated from letters folks had received, to items read in *The Budget*, to the occasional phone call shared with a loved one. Finally, they descended into gossip.

Emma wasn't proud of this, though it probably wasn't the type of gossip a bishop might frown upon. She thought of it as gossip because the conversation was based on what had been heard and tidbits passed along the grapevine, versus cold hard facts.

She only listened, though she'd been known to participate. Her thoughts kept wandering to Danny and the boy in her barn. Suddenly Emma realized someone might know something about the boy, so she focused her attention on the conversations swirling around her.

Nothing related popped up. Certainly this group would know if the boy was a runaway from any of their families.

There was a lull in the conversation. Laura cleared her throat and asked if anyone had seen or heard from Nancy Schlabach. An uncomfortable silence filled the room.

"I sent my youngest girl to take them some fresh eggs." Verna pulled off her glasses and pinched the bridge of her nose. "She told me Nancy was sporting a black eye. Didn't offer any explanation about it."

"Like before, I'm sure she would give some illogical account of what happened." Laura shifted her chair to the right and bent over her row of stitches.

"I know the bishop has been by to see Nancy and Owen." Emma ran her fingers down the strings of her prayer *kapp* as the group stopped what they were doing and stared at her, waiting for more details. "I asked Bishop Simon because I was worried, and I thought maybe there was something we could do."

"And? What did Simon say?"

"That the church leadership was meeting with Owen, trying to convince him to enter a rehab program. He hadn't agreed to it, and Simon suggested it might be necessary to move Nancy and the boys."

Verna spoke up. "The problem is that they've no family here. When they moved from Ohio, they thought the land they were buying would be forty-five acres of heaven. But farming is hard work, and their property was a mess when they bought it." Verna replaced her glasses and picked up her quilting needle. "I've spoken to her about staying at our place, but she won't. She knows we have children to the roof rafters. Still, we would make room for her."

"*Ya*, we all would," Laura murmured.

Each woman in the circle nodded in agreement. Each of them would gladly offer shelter to Nancy and her two small boys.

Mary Ann had barely said a word since they arrived. She glanced up from her stitching. "Nancy needs a sanctuary."

"Sanctuary? What type of sanctuary?" Laura stowed her needle and sat back in the chair.

"A place of healing. A safe place."

"*Ya*, we could use that in our community. Oaklawn has been a real benefit to Goshen, Elkhart, and South Bend. Perhaps they will build a facility here."

Verna sighed and bent even closer to her stitching. "Supposing the Mennonite Alliance did plan a facility like that here, it would take a year or more to complete. Nancy needs help now."

"God provides sanctuary," Mary Ann reminded them.

Emma remembered what she'd said the day before, about gardens being a place of blessing. Where a person could rest, draw closer to God, and heal. That was the sort of place Nancy needed. A garden of God's design.

So many people were hurting in the world. Emma felt rather ashamed that her thoughts had been ungrateful of late. Mary Ann was right. More time in prayer and no doubt she would have a better perspective.

• • •

"Let me hold that little man." Mary Ann settled into the rocker, and Eunice placed the baby in his *mammi*'s arms.

Emma didn't know who looked more content, the child or Mary Ann.

"Where's Esther today?"

"The boys wanted to go into town and do some shopping with the money they earned from helping tend to Doc's garden."

"It's a wonder he has one at all, as much time as he spends in his office."

"Georgia loves the fresh vegetables, but the arthritis in her hands makes gardening nearly impossible. It must be hard for the doctor to see his own wife suffering so. The boys were only too happy to make a little spending money."

"Only eight years old and already the twins are hard workers." Emma pulled Miriam into her arms when she skipped over to show the women the horse she was playing with. Even at her young age, she already had a real preference for anything to do with animals.

"So tell me about this boy in your barn."

Emma wasn't surprised she'd heard. It was the way of life in their small community. She told Eunice all she knew, and then added, "The food I left last night was gone when I checked on him this morning."

"But he wasn't there?"

"*Nein*. His stuff still was—a small duffel bag too small to hold more than a change of clothes."

"It is strange that he'd pick your barn."

"Have you checked yours lately? Could be that we all have Amish teens stowing away, and we just don't know about it."

Eunice laughed but then grew somber. "Just be careful, okay, *Mamm*? And tell Danny if you need anything."

That was the way of things too. Her family now accepted Danny, counted on him, as if he'd never walked away from their community. She'd asked Danny about that once, about how he could bear to leave. He'd told her that at the time it had seemed what he ought to do, what he had to do, but that now he couldn't imagine being anywhere else.

As they were walking back toward their buggy, Eunice tucked her arm into the crook of her mother's. "I saw Danny's piece in *The Budget*. So he is still writing."

"*Ya*. I suppose."

"Do you ever talk to him about it?"

"*Nein*. What's to say?"

"You could ask where he's been, what things he's seen. Maybe he wants to share his experiences with someone."

"I believe he shares them with his notebooks, piled high around his desk."

"Well, we're all relieved that he decided to come home, that he changed his mind about selling his parents' land. It's *gut* to have an Amish man living next door to you. Someone we trust."

"Must have been a hard decision for him."

"Why do you say that?" Eunice had helped her *mammi* into the buggy. Now she stood in the afternoon sun, studying her mother.

"He didn't stay when his folks passed. Only came home for a week or so."

"I'm sure he had his reasons."

"*Ya*. Then a year later he shows up, pulls the For Sale sign out of the yard, and settles in. I guess he had a hard time deciding whether he wanted to continue with his travels, with his studies, or move home."

"What's important is that he's here now, and you can depend on him if you need someone."

"I can depend on my *kinner* too."

"*Ya, Mamm*. But Danny is right next door. Don't be proud. Let him know if you need something. And call me from the phone shack if you want Aaron to come over and speak with the teen in your barn."

"Your husband has plenty to do without worrying over a teenage boy."

Eunice stared down at the baby in her arms. "He'll be that age before I know it. And I would not want him sleeping in a barn, but if he was . . ." She stepped closer and kissed Emma on the cheek. "I'd want him in yours."

. . .

She didn't want to ask what it was. Somehow it seemed rude unless he brought up the subject.

Besides, if he wanted her to know, he would tell her. Wouldn't he?

They finished pulling carpetweed and prickly lettuce from around the mint, then moved on to care for the butterfly weed. Though its name indicated it was a weed, it was far from it. The plant's orange blossoms hadn't made an appearance yet, but they would soon—before July. Once they did, the butterflies would descend on it, and what a sight that was.

Working in the flowers did much to ease Emma's worries. She was even considering inviting Danny to dinner when he straightened up, stretched his back, and motioned toward the barn.

"Any sign of your guest?"

"*Nein*, but the food was gone this morning."

"Bedroll still there?"

"It is. I'm wondering if I should sneak up on him in the middle of the night so we can have a talk."

"If he's ready, that would work. If he's not, he'd run, and this time you might not see him again."

"I'm not sure I want to see him again. This mission of mercy is your idea."

"We are to be peacemakers," Mary Ann chimed in. "Full of mercy and good fruits."

"Yes, *Mamm*. But—"

"I've been thinking." Danny ran his fingers through his hair. He'd be needing another cut soon. Who did that for him? Most Amish men had their hair cut by their mother or sister or wife. Danny was that rare occurrence—an only child in an Amish home. He had none of those people in his life. He'd have to go to a barber and pay good money for what family would normally do. "It's supposed to dip into the forties again tonight. Our lad didn't have much of a bedroll."

"He's not our lad."

"I have a nice sleeping bag at home. Never use it anymore."

"You could offer him a room in your house." She said the words in jest before she considered how they might sound.

Danny crossed his arms and stared at her. "You're right. I do have an extra room."

"I didn't mean—"

"Still need to catch him first."

"He's not a fish, Danny. He's a boy with a family and some sort of past he needs to deal with."

"I'll go and fetch the sleeping bag. It's a *gut Englisch* one, rated to zero degrees. He'll be snug and warm in it." The smile that covered his face was tough to interpret.

Emma wasn't heartless.

She wanted to help the boy as much as anyone.

But why did Danny find such joy in it?

"Back in a few."

He ambled off toward his house. Emma turned and spoke to Mary Ann. When she was confident that her *mamm* would be fine alone, she took off after him.

Danny looked mildly surprised when she called out to him. He stopped and waited for her to catch up.

"No need for you to walk all the way back," she said, quickly nixing the idea of inviting him to dinner. It was nearly time to eat already, and she would be feeding three again since the boy in the barn would need dinner.

The boy in the barn. It sounded like a child's story.

Why was Danny so focused on helping him?

Why was he convinced the boy needed more than a place to hide?

And what did he expect to happen next?

They were met at the porch by a large black Labrador.

"Emma, meet Shadow."

Danny must have been training the pup, because he settled flat on the porch, raising his warm, dark eyes to study both of them.

"He won't jump, but he will shake with you."

"Shake?"

Shadow jumped to a sitting position, tail thumping a happy beat against the porch floor, and raised one paw, which Emma readily shook. She'd wanted a dog, had thought about it often in the last few months. The last one they'd had, Cocoa, had passed when the boys were in their teens. In the end she had decided it was too much work, and she didn't want a dog knocking Mary Ann down.

"He's so well trained."

"We're working on it. He still chews up the occasional shoe, but he's coming along."

"You did the training yourself?"

"*Ya.*"

"Where'd you learn how?"

He raised his eyes to the corner of the roof as he tried to remember. "Wisconsin. I was in a community called Pebble Creek, and the gentleman I stayed with trained hunting dogs. I learned a lot from him, though I had no need for it until I saw Shadow at the feed store a few weeks ago."

Danny Eicher knew how to train dogs? She wondered what other things he had learned on his travels. As always, her thoughts circled back to the main question—could he be satisfied living in their little town?

Then Emma stepped into Danny's house, the home that had been in his family for two generations, and she promptly forgot all of her questions.

CHAPTER 5

Emma had been in Danny's home before, when he'd first come back.

She and Ben had gone over to welcome him, and she'd carried with her a plate of oatmeal cookies. That was over a year ago. She'd had no need to stop by since. Most days he found a reason to come to their house, though she still hadn't figured the *why* that was tied to that.

"I guess you spend the majority of your day at your desk?" Emma worried her *kapp* strings. The thought of all those words, all the places that Danny had visited, overwhelmed her. Did he write about Shipshe? Did he include *them* in his articles?

"A good bit, yes."

"Going through the notebooks?"

"*Ya*, I have a *gut* memory, but checking against my notes I find that I sometimes remember things differently than they actually happened. Reading what I wrote while I was there, it brings people and places into focus."

The house was small since his parents only had the one child. Many Amish couples start with a home big enough for three or four and add on rooms as the family grows. Danny's parents never had a need to add on, and the last time Emma had been in the house, it had needed updating.

She now stood in a home that looked as if it was recently built.

The paint was fresh, white trim and a light-beige color on the walls. Danny had taken out half of the furniture, so the rooms appeared larger. He'd also spent some time scrubbing and shining the wooden floors.

"I didn't realize you'd been remodeling over here."

Danny laughed as he put his hands on his hips and looked left, then right. "Let me show you the kitchen."

She could see some of the kitchen from where they stood in the sitting room, but she followed him eagerly.

"What would your *mamm* say?" Emma walked over to the new stove and ran her hand across the front panel. "Still gas, *ya*?"

"Sure. Of course. So is the fridge, but it's one of the newer models."

The appliances weren't over-the-top. They were what a bachelor would need. He'd chosen well. Emma had looked at a refrigerator like his, but decided it was a bad use of their money since the one they had still worked.

"Writing must be paying well!" The words popped out of her mouth, and she immediately wished she could yank them back. It was none of her business how Danny Eicher managed to afford his home improvements.

"It pays all right, probably as well as farming. *Mamm*

and *Daed* didn't leave much as far as money in the bank, but they left the land, and it's a good source of income."

"You're still leasing it to the Byler boy?"

"I am, though he's hardly a boy. He turned twenty-two this year, and he's a hard worker. I think he'll do well farming. I know he'll do better than I would. Never did have much experience planting or rotating crops, though I've learned enough about both in my travels. I do think I'm somewhat handy with a family vegetable garden." He said the last with a wink.

Emma didn't know what to think of that, but she suddenly wondered if it would look proper for her to be alone in Danny's house with him. Her cheeks flushed at the thought, because it was ridiculous. They were well past the age when they needed to worry about chaperones.

"Well, you've done a *gut* job here. I think your parents would be proud."

"I wish I'd come home and made improvements while they were both still alive."

He'd crossed the room to stand next to her. Emma couldn't resist. She reached out and rested her hand on his arm. "Your *mamm* wouldn't have allowed new appliances in her kitchen. Like Mary Ann, she was always a bit stubborn."

The worry lines between his eyes vanished. "*Ya*. One Christmas I offered to paint the hall. You would have thought I'd suggested knocking a wall out. She informed me the hall was fine as it was, and if I was lacking for things to do, I could help her wash the baseboards."

Emma walked to the doorway between the kitchen

and the sitting room. The desk was neater than the last time she'd visited. Now the spiral notebooks were organized on a bookshelf, and the top of the desk was clean except for a gas lantern, a pad of paper, and a pen. Her curiosity was winning over her vow to not ask.

. . .

He'd known Emma so long, she seemed like an extension of himself. Now that he was home, he couldn't quite understand how he'd survived without her all the years he'd spent traveling. Danny had left, with his father's blessing, when he was seventeen. It had hurt him to leave Emma, but he'd known it was the right thing to do—for her sake. She deserved a normal Amish life, with a husband who stayed in one place. When he'd tried to explain that to her, after they'd been attending singings together for over a year, she'd listened with tears running down her face. He'd returned home occasionally for a holiday or because he was in the area researching, but he'd spent the majority of the past thirty-three years away. It seemed like a lifetime. He had never regretted that decision, but watching Emma, seeing her in his home, he also knew it had been the right time to return home.

"Do you still write every day?"

"*Ya.*"

"What do you plan to do with it?" She turned and studied him. She wasn't being nosy. She wanted to know. "Do you expect to receive an *Englisch* contract to write a book?"

"Haven't thought much on that."

"If you did, would you—" The words died on her lips, and the vulnerable look in her eyes tore at his heart.

"I won't be leaving again, Emma. I'm here to stay. This is home now."

She nodded but didn't respond.

"Right now I'm working with the Menno-Hoff. They offered me a grant to share some of the things I observed in my travels. It's important that we record our history. I believe I can offer an accurate telling from the inside."

"Why?"

"Perhaps it will help the next generation." He shrugged. "I'm not sure I know why. I only know that I'm supposed to be doing it."

She nodded as if she understood.

"Let me fetch that sleeping bag."

He found it, then walked her back out to the porch.

"I wasn't meaning to be nosy."

"Of course not. Emma,"—he waited until she turned toward him—"you can ask me anything you want to know."

Now the smile he was so accustomed to broke through. "You always knew what you wanted to do, Danny. Even at seventeen—all you were interested in was jotting down things in your notebook."

"I was interested in you." His pulse raced as that memory came back to him full force.

"When you were sixteen. At seventeen, you only had eyes for your books."

"I suppose so." The memory of what was lost, what

they'd almost had together, sank between them, drawing some of the color from the day.

"Remember the time you were supposed to be checking on the goats your *dat* had? You were moving them from one pasture to the other—"

"And I left the gate open, the side gate, while I was writing a piece about a typical day in the life of an Amish lad."

"The goats were in Mary Ann's garden before we saw them."

"*Dat* gave me extra chores for a week."

Emma reached out and touched his arm, as she had in the kitchen. "You were doing what you were called to do. Your *dat* understood, and your *mamm* too."

"Did you understand, Emma?"

She tore her gaze away, studying the setting sun and their two properties. "After a while I did. I led the life I was supposed to live, and so did you."

Danny nodded, but he didn't like the period she put on that observation.

There was still plenty of light to see the area between his place and hers. In truth, the Eicher property had always been the better of the two lots. His house was set back from the road a good space. The northwest section had a small pond where her boys had spent many an evening fishing. It was shielded from the street by a stand of white elms. They were seven, maybe eight feet tall. Beyond the pond was a low spot that ran the length of their property line. An optimist would call it a creek, but water ran in it only once or twice a year. Even with all the rain they'd had, it was muddy but not wet. Long ago his parents had put a wooden walk across a four-foot portion, which provided easy passing from one place to the other.

What he could see now, what he hadn't realized but had been suspecting, was that Mary Ann's garden had practically grown to the property line.

"Indiana evenings are a pretty sight." Danny's voice was low. Shadow's tale thumped against the porch floor, and Emma clasped her arms around the sleeping bag.

"Your neighbor is on the verge of encroaching upon your property."

His laughter filled the night, joined the songbirds, and caused Shadow to bound down the porch steps.

"I'd be happy to walk you back home."

"Don't be silly. There's no need."

Danny hadn't been thinking about whether she needed someone to walk her home. He'd simply wanted to prolong their time together. He stepped away, flustered and unable to remember what they had been talking about.

"Thanks for taking the sleeping bag to him. I wish he'd picked my barn instead of yours."

"Danny, we need to talk to this boy. I'll take your sleeping bag, and I'll leave it for him, but I'm going back out there later tonight. He's going to tell me what his situation is."

Instead of arguing with her, Danny reached down and patted the top of Shadow's head. The dog looked sublimely happy. Affection could do that.

"What time?"

"Thought I'd set my alarm for midnight."

"Okay." He nodded and rubbed the back of his neck. "I'll meet you on your back porch."

"Are you sure?"

"It's because of me you're providing lodging, and now food, to the boy. I don't blame you for wanting to call the bishop that first night. What with you and Mary Ann being over there alone—"

"This isn't about us being alone. It's about what's right for the boy. If he runs from us again tonight, I'll go straight to the bishop in the morning."

Danny's shoulders slumped, but a smile tugged at the corners of his mouth. "Mary Ann thinks we're supposed to minister to the boy."

"She told you that too?"

"While you were inside fetching her a glass of water."

"She brought the subject up at dinner as well. Seems she recognizes something special in this boy, or perhaps she thinks it would be a *gut* way for us to give back to the community. Either way, in a few hours we'll see if she's right. We'll see if he's willing to let us help him."

Without another word, Emma turned and walked back across Danny's property, skirted the pond, and stepped onto the small wooden walkway over the low point. Suddenly she stopped and clutched the sleeping bag to her chest. He was about to start after her, to make sure she was all right, when a flock of birds rose from the garden as one, flapping their wings and catching a draft to carry them out into the night. Danny's heart knocked against his ribs, and he chided himself for worrying over her. Emma Hochstetter was a capable woman, and she'd been taking care of herself all the years he'd been gone.

That wasn't quite right though. She'd had Ben and Eldon then. Last spring, as the green beans were climbing and twining through the trellis he'd helped Ben build, her father-in-law had died. He was nearly ninety, and he'd been sick for over a year. His passing was a great loss, but not unexpected. Six weeks later she found Ben in the barn, near the horses he loved so much. Her husband, and Danny's friend, had suffered a fatal heart attack.

Not to say the entire year had been all gloom and doom. God sprinkled in a few blessings as well, perhaps to assure Emma and Danny He had not turned away.

All of Emma's children—Edna, Esther, Eunice, Harold, and Henry—were happily married. And her oldest granddaughter, named Mary Ann after her two great-grandmothers, had been baptized into the church. Three more grandchildren had been born, which brought Emma's total to twelve. Each was a bright spot in her life, even little Thomas, who was quite the mischief-maker at age four. Danny enjoyed watching them at the Sunday socials. Having a grandchild was something he would never experience. These days, he understood more fully than ever what things he had sacrificed to follow his dream.

CHAPTER 6

Emma was lying on her side with her eyes wide open, waiting.

As she waited, she remembered things from the evening and prayed about the worries that weighed on her heart.

When she'd left Danny's, crossed the bridge, and walked through the garden, she'd looked up and seen Mary Ann in the kitchen, silhouetted against the window by the gas lantern on the table. Mary Ann might be old and increasingly frail, but Emma still considered her to be her parent in the faith. If she said they were to minister to the boy, then Emma would take her word that it was to be so. The fact that Mary Ann and Danny both felt that way confirmed that God had a purpose in what was happening.

But something more was flitting through her heart.

Emma thought of their garden, pictured it in her mind, and considered the idea of a sanctuary. What did that mean? Was it so complicated, or was it merely a place where people could rest? A place where they could heal?

Before she'd walked inside, Emma had turned and studied the garden. In the moonlight, it looked less like something that had grown out of control and more like something Mary Ann had planned over the years. A place she'd cared for patiently and tenderly and that was now coming into its real purpose.

But what was that?

And why did Nancy Schlabach and her two boys suddenly come to mind?

Shaking away the many questions, she'd wound her way back through the garden and to the barn. No sign of anyone, so she checked a final time on the horses and left the sleeping bag in the back stall.

Closing the barn door firmly, she'd made her way up the back porch steps and into the kitchen. She needed to go to bed early since she was going to set the alarm for midnight.

Now, watching the tiny hands of the battery-operated clock move, she knew that she wouldn't sleep until this thing was settled. So she waited, and she prayed, and she saw the moment the time switched from 11:58 to 11:59. She reached for the clock and turned off the alarm before it could sound.

It had seemed smarter to lie on top of her quilt in her dress. When she rose, she only had to fasten on her *kapp* and lace up her shoes. She was able to do both of those by the light of the moon spilling in her bedroom window.

Unlike Danny's home, Emma's was two stories. The extra bedrooms had been a blessing when all the children were home. Even now they were frequently filled with grandchildren, especially during summer break and weekends.

She crept downstairs, careful not to disturb Mary Ann, and snagged her shawl from the mudroom to ward off the night's coolness.

When she reached the back porch, Danny was already waiting.

"Any plans for how to do this?"

Emma shook her head in the darkness. "Can't be too hard."

"Coming from you, I'll believe that. You do have five *kinner* and twelve—"

"Soon to be thirteen. Don't forget that Esther is expecting again."

"Thirteen *grandkinner.*" Danny whistled softly. "You've had a full life, Emma."

"As have you, and let's not talk as if we're done yet."

They'd reached the back side of the barn. She knew when they opened the door, the hinges were going to squeak. If the child was a light sleeper, he'd be alerted by the noise.

"Don't let him scoot by you," Emma whispered.

They needn't have worried. A minute later they stood at the back stall, peering over the half door at the snoring adolescent. Even Danny's flashlight didn't waken him, but when Emma rang the bell she used to call in the horses, the lad jumped as if he'd been struck.

Seeing that his way out was blocked—they hadn't bothered to open the stall door—he sat up and pulled his jacket tighter around him. The thing was thread-bare and couldn't have provided much warmth, though he had been tucked deep into Danny's sleeping bag.

Danny repositioned the beam of the flashlight so

that it wouldn't be directly in the boy's eyes. It was clear he was a boy, though he might have been edging toward sixteen. He still had the look of Danny's pup, as if he hadn't quite grown into his hands and feet. Emma recognized the age. Her boys had gone through the same final growth spurt, and it seemed to take a few years before everything evened out.

His dark-brown hair hung in his eyes, which looked hazel to Emma in the dim light. He was much too skinny, she could see that well enough. Average height. Not much to tell the bishop as far as description.

"What's your name?" Emma opened the door and entered the stall. Danny remained in the doorway, still blocking the boy's escape path.

"Why should I tell you?" His voice was soft but somewhat ragged, as if he were aiming for belligerent but unable to pull it off.

"Because you're staying in my barn. Apparently you have been for a few days." When he didn't speak, she added, "And you've been eating my cooking. You can at least trust me with your name."

"Joseph."

He didn't provide a last name, but then, Emma hadn't expected he would. She'd coax it out of him before they were done.

"Joseph, we'd like to talk to you a minute." Danny picked up a wooden stool once used for milking and carried it into the stall. He sat on the upended oats bucket and left the stool for Emma.

"What about?" The panic in Joseph's eyes nearly broke Emma's heart. She'd been prepared to dislike him, to throw him out, to call the bishop and the police. As she studied him, she realized that Danny had been right. This way was better.

"Why are you here? Where's your family?"

He stood and began stuffing his things into a backpack. "Not going back there. You can't make me either. I'm nearly seventeen now. No use trying to make me go back."

"Son, we're not trying to make you do anything."

Joseph flinched at Danny's use of the word *son*.

"Would you mind sitting down so we can talk?"

Joseph didn't look any more at ease, but he zipped the backpack and sat.

Emma closed her eyes and prayed for wisdom and patience, then she cleared her throat. "Where are you from? I don't think you live in Shipshe, or I'd recognize you."

"Goshen."

"How did you get here?"

"Walked on the Pumpkinvine Trail."

Danny glanced at Emma, his eyes questioning. She nodded. It was a fair distance, but doable.

Since he was answering, Emma decided to dig for more information.

"My *dochder* lives in Middlebury. It's a nice town. Why didn't you stop there?"

"I did, but after a while I moved on. It's best not to stay in the same place too long. I should have left here last night." Dismay flooded his eyes, and Emma got the impression he was fighting back tears.

When he told them his last name was Lapp, a fairly

common name among Amish folk, Danny spoke up again. "Won't your parents be worried about you?"

"Why would they? I'm a burden to them. One more mouth to feed in a home that's already too crowded. They're probably glad I'm gone." Bitterness filled his voice, which cracked, accentuating the fact that he was teetering between boyhood and manhood. "I never did anything right anyway. You can't make me go back. You can't, and I won't."

Emma checked Danny's reaction. He shrugged.

She stood and straightened her dress. Her toes were nearly numb, as were her fingers. She'd learned enough so that she'd be able to sleep. Joseph wasn't sick, and he didn't seem to be planning to rob her blind during the night. Anything else could wait until morning.

"That's it? You're just going to let me . . . let me stay?"

"Breakfast is at six thirty. We'll talk tomorrow about how you can earn your keep until we figure out what to do."

Joseph's mouth fell open, but he didn't argue.

They were leaving when Danny paused and turned back. "You're welcome to come to my house. I live next door and have an extra bedroom."

"*Nein.* I'd rather stay here."

"Suit yourself." Emma put her hand in the crook of Danny's elbow and tugged him out of the stall. "Morning will be here soon. We best get to sleep."

Instead of talking outside the barn, she invited Danny into the house, set the kettle on the stove, and brewed them both a cup of decaffeinated herbal peppermint tea.

Danny was quiet as she moved around the kitchen,

gathering cups, saucers, and a slice of the leftover lemon cake.

"I believe your gift is feeding people, Emma." The words were said in jest, but the look in Danny's eyes was solid admiration.

It occurred to Emma that if you served a man a piece of cake, he would believe you could solve the problems of the world. Give him cake in the middle of the night, and he'd likely burrow in and refuse to leave.

Did she want Danny to leave?

He looked completely at home in her kitchen.

"I wasn't much of a cook when I first married Ben. It didn't take long for his mother to teach me, to ensure that I had the basic skills. That first year, I think *Mamm* was afraid that she'd be called home to heaven before the lessons were done. I suspect she was motivated by the fear that her son would be left here to starve with a well-meaning but unskilled cook for a wife."

"Were you that bad?"

"I burnt my share of casseroles, and bread was completely beyond me." She sat at the table, ignoring the cake—though she wanted some. She'd learned long ago that late-night snacking meant disaster for her waistline. Emma had heard an *Englisch* woman at the market commenting on how nice it would be to be Amish—to not worry about your figure or the gray in your hair. It was true that they believed vanity to be a sin, but most women she knew worried at least a little about their weight. Emma could stand to lose five or ten pounds. Hopefully that concern was for health reasons and not because of vanity.

Why was she even worrying about such things? Emma had enough on her plate at the moment without counting her sins at forty minutes past midnight.

"After a few years I understood that cooking was *Mamm*'s special talent, and she wanted to share it with me."

"I'm glad she did!"

They sat together in the near darkness. She had lit one of the gas lanterns but had turned it to low. No use disturbing Mary Ann, not that she could see a lantern in the kitchen. She had a way of sensing such things though, and Emma knew she needed her rest.

It surprised her that she was so comfortable with Danny. Around most folk, even Amish folk, she was often seized by the urge to make some sort of conversation. Danny appeared content to silently enjoy the tea and cake. Emma wanted a few moments to process what they'd learned in the barn.

Finally he carried his plate to the sink, rinsed it, and returned to the table.

"It's good of you to allow the boy to stay," Danny said as he sat back down.

"I'm only doing the Christian thing. I hardly deserve praise for it."

"But you do." He leaned forward, arms folded on the table, his eyes locked with hers. "Because you spoke to him with compassion, and you offered him kindness, which sometimes is as important as a place to sleep."

Danny's words flowed over her, settling some of the questions in her heart. "What do you think happened to Joseph? To cause him to leave his home?"

"Hard to say. I didn't notice any bruises on the boy, but sometimes abuse takes other forms. It's not something we see a lot in our communities. It is present though, same as any other group of folk."

"You saw things like this? While you were traveling?"

"*Ya*, and it's handled differently in each community it seems. Overall I'd say the bishops provide *gut* guidance, attempting to provide help for the families. Sometimes . . ." He stared down at the old oak table. "One place I stayed in for about a year had a case like this. The *dat* needed help for his moods, needed some of the *Englisch* medicine—truth be told. But they wouldn't hear of it, and the community decided to sweep the entire situation under the rug."

"And?"

"And it didn't work. Something like this, ignored, will always fester until it sickens the body of believers."

Emma thought about that, thought of the day last summer she'd caught a splinter in the palm of her hand. She had been in a hurry that afternoon, and then tired by the time she fell into bed. She had thought she could ignore it for a day. When she woke, the spot was swollen and warm to the touch. It had festered and was much more painful to treat than if she'd dealt with it immediately.

Ignoring things rarely worked.

"What if he's making it up?" Emma rubbed her forehead as she envisioned the boy sleeping soundly in the barn.

"That's possible. You know more about Joseph's age group than I do—"

"The fear in his eyes seemed real."

"It did indeed."

"Tomorrow we'll feed him properly and set him to work, and then I'll walk down to the phone shack and call the bishop."

"I can do that for you."

"You don't mind?"

"Shadow enjoys a morning walk." He reached across the table and squeezed her hand, sending sparks zipping like fireflies through her nervous system. "I want to help however I can."

She walked with him through the mudroom to the back porch.

Emma didn't know what caused her to utter her next words. Perhaps it was the feeling she'd had back at the table—when Danny had touched her hand. "I still miss him."

Danny turned and looked at her. "I'm sure you do."

"At times I still expect to see Ben walking across the field, carrying his water jug and raising a hand to wave when I come out onto the porch."

"His life was complete, Emma." Danny didn't move closer, didn't reach out to touch her this time, and she was grateful for that. At the moment, she felt as fragile as the specially carved glass figurines sold at the shops in town.

"Ben would be glad you're helping the boy." He added, almost as an afterthought, "He'd want you to be happy. You know that, right?"

Emma nodded, then whispered a good night.

As she watched Danny make his way home under

the May moon, she thought about the deep ache she'd endured since Ben's death. For the first six months, it had seemed as if some foreign object was lodged under her right rib. Strange that despair would choose such a specific place to hide. She'd rub at the spot, wondering why it wasn't on her left, near her heart.

Now the ache was gone, though the memory lingered. It had somehow softened over the last year, and though she missed Ben every bit as much as the first morning she woke after she'd found him in the barn . . . she could now smile at their memories, their time together, and the love they'd shared.

Like the green garden that had replaced the snow outside her window, life had moved on.

She remained on the back porch, thinking of Ben, and Danny, and the boy in the barn. She stood for a long time, watching Danny as he made his way in the moonlight, crossing from her property to his. Long after she could see him, she stood there, until the coolness of the late hour forced her inside.

CHAPTER 7

Emma was standing at the stove frying bacon and scrambling eggs when Joseph knocked on the back door. He came inside when she called out to him, but he stood in the doorway between the mudroom and the kitchen, as if he was unsure what to do next.

Glancing his way, Emma could see he'd attempted to wash, though the water outside must have been quite cold. His hair, several inches too long, was combed down. He'd also put on a different shirt and pants, so he must have had at least two sets. He didn't look particularly healthy—a little too thin and a little too pale. But he didn't appear to be sick either. Mostly, he gave the impression of a lasting misery.

Mary Ann shuffled into the room as Emma carried the plate of bacon to the table. They had spoken earlier about Joseph, when they'd each had their first cup of *kaffi*. She had told Mary Ann about their late-night meeting. Mary Ann approved of Joseph staying and even had some ideas of chores he could do.

"You must be Joseph." She patted the seat beside her. "Sit. Sit and eat. Do you drink *kaffi* or milk?"

"Either is fine." Joseph didn't make eye contact with Emma or Mary Ann. Instead he stared at the table. His stomach growled when Emma set the bacon in front of him, causing *Mamm* to laugh.

"The sound of a growing boy is a blessing indeed. *Ya*, Emma?"

"It is, *Mamm*." She placed *kaffi* and milk in front of him. He reached for the milk and then stopped himself, tucking his hands under the table.

Emma returned with a plate of eggs and biscuits.

They bowed their heads, and Emma silently prayed for Joseph. How long had it been since she'd been so worried about someone else? Someone outside of their family? Yet it seemed God had brought Joseph to them for a reason. After all, he could have stopped at any barn. She prayed for wisdom, for guidance, and that Joseph wouldn't decide to run when he learned what chores he'd be doing.

Mary Ann reached for a hot biscuit, breaking it open and releasing steam and the rich, yeasty smell. "My *dochder* makes the best biscuits around, Joseph. And her pies are *gut* too."

Joseph watched them begin to eat, then hesitantly reached for his glass of milk and downed it in a single long drink. As Mary Ann passed him each plate, he took a minimal amount. Emma could guess easily enough that he wanted more. The child had manners.

"It's only the three of us, Joseph, and I cooked extra for you. Fill your plate."

He wasn't speaking much, but then again, he was completely focused on his food. She let him enjoy the meal, then refilled his glass of milk and cleared her throat.

The massive amount of calories he'd just consumed would be hitting his stomach, so she guessed he'd be less likely to put up too much resistance when he heard their plans for the day.

She thought about offering him some of the lemon cake.

In the end, she decided the extra sugar might push him over. The last thing they wanted was him in the bathroom chucking up his first meal in several days.

"Let's talk about your situation, Joseph."

Mary Ann had moved to her rocker in the corner of the kitchen and was leafing through her Bible. She acted as if she wasn't listening, but Emma knew she'd hear every word they said. And she'd jump in if needed. Bolstered by her presence, Emma ignored the panic on Joseph's face.

"I gather from what you said last night that you're not ready to return home."

"I'm never going back there."

"Never is often longer than we imagine," Mary Ann said.

"It's not something we need to decide now. But there are a few rules you'll need to agree to."

Joseph's glance darted left, then right, but he remained in his seat.

"First, you do the chores I ask of you. There's not a lot of work around here, but there are some regular tasks you can help me with. Once those are done, there are a few things I've put off since my husband passed."

"What if I don't . . . don't do them well enough?"

Joseph was talking to the table, his eyes glued to the spot where his plate had been before Emma set it in the sink.

"Will you do them to the best of your ability?"

"*Ya.*" He raised his eyes to hers, then flicked his gaze toward the back door. "'Course I will."

"Then it will be done well enough."

Joseph shrugged, but Emma thought she detected a small light of hope in his eyes.

"I will not tolerate alcohol or smoking in my barn. Drink too much and you could knock over a lantern. Leave a cigarette smoldering, and we could lose the entire thing. I understand that you're on your *Rumspringa*—"

He flinched at the word.

"A phone, something like that, is your decision to make."

"How would I pay for a phone?" He looked as if Emma had suggested he purchase an *Englisch* car.

She waved away his question. "What I'm trying to say is that I understand the difficulties of your age, but I won't allow the drinking or the smoking. Any sign of that, and you'll have to move on."

Joseph hunched his shoulders and jerked his head up and down at the same time. He resembled a box turtle, which would have been funny if the expression in his eyes hadn't tugged at the heart so fiercely.

"There's only one other thing, and I expect you won't be happy about it. Can't be helped though."

"Why won't I like it?"

"Because it involves our bishop. I gather you'd rather others not know you're here, but I have a responsibility, Joseph."

"What will the bishop do?"

"Simon is a fair man. I expect he'll want to meet with you, and then he'll probably insist on contacting your parents."

"My parents?" Joseph jumped up, and the sound of his chair scraping against the floor echoed across the kitchen. "My parents don't care. They don't want me, they don't miss me, and there's no chance they'd insist I come home."

She doubted that was true, but telling Joseph that would make matters worse. "We'll have to trust that Simon does the right thing, the best thing for everyone involved."

"What if he makes me go back?"

A sigh escaped from deep within her. "No one can make you do anything, Joseph. Unless you've broken the law—"

"I haven't!"

"Then there's no need to worry. You're welcome to stay here, but my responsibility is to notify our bishop and then trust his decision on whether to contact your parents."

Joseph rammed his hands into his pockets. "What chores did you want me to do?"

"Are you *gut* with horses?"

"*Ya.*"

"Then let them into the field and clean out their stalls. Once you're done with that, give them a *gut* brushing and check their hooves. All the supplies, including a hoof pick and conditioner/sealant, are in the barn."

He nodded once, brown hair flopping into his eyes, then turned toward the back door.

"God's mercies are new every morning, child." Mary Ann's voice was as soft as the May breeze coming through the kitchen window.

"I don't know anything about that."

"Perhaps you will learn." Mary Ann reached for his hand, patted it once, and beamed at him.

"We'll have sandwiches for lunch. I'll ring the outside bell when they're ready."

Joseph had no response for either of them. As he clomped through the mudroom and down the back porch steps, Emma watched him from the window.

"What happened to him, *Mamm*? What could cause such bitterness in a fellow his age?"

"Many things are capable of wounding a young man. Maybe the cause isn't as important as the cure."

"And what would that be?"

"What you're doing—a place for him to rest, a full stomach, prayers that he find his way."

Emma hoped her mother-in-law was right. It had been years since she'd had a teenage boy under her roof. If she remembered correctly, it wasn't all pansies and roses.

CHAPTER 8

The rest of the morning passed quickly.

Esther, her youngest, came by with items from the co-op.

Mary Ann had pulled three baskets full of produce from their garden—cabbage, chives, onions, and spinach. Esther had her boys carry into the kitchen what they received in return: milk, eggs, and mangoes. Mangoes!

"Can't say we've received much fruit, other than apples in the fall."

"Paul Byler, you remember him . . ." Esther tucked her blonde curls into her *kapp* as she spoke. Ever since she was a small girl, those curls had fought being corralled. Now Esther was the same height as Emma.

"Sure. He has that furniture shop out in back of his house."

"Right. An *Englischer* stopped by to pick up his order of four rocking chairs yesterday. He was so pleased with the work, he paid in cash and left four crates of mangoes. No idea how he came by the crates of fruit. He did tell Paul that he enjoyed trading, and he was a trucker by profession, so maybe he'd been down south."

"We're happy to have them. They'll work nicely in the sandwich spread I'm making." Emma reached down and caught Daniel and David in a hug. The twins had recently turned eight, and they stood for the affections from their *mammi*, but just barely.

"So where's the boy?"

"Boy?" Emma smiled as she played ignorant.

"You know who I mean, *Mamm*. Do you really think it's wise to let him stay?"

"My, but news travels fast."

"Danny called the bishop, and Verna was in visiting when the call came through."

Emma nodded as if that made sense. "Danny likes the idea of Joseph staying, and so does your *mammi*. Joseph seems harmless enough. Right now, he's cleaning out stalls if you'd like to go meet him."

"Nein." Esther patted her stomach. She was six months along with the next *boppli*. "Stall smells make me feel a little sick."

When they left, Emma spent the next hour giving the bathrooms a good scouring. They were fortunate to have two—one upstairs and one down. She had to remind herself to be grateful as she scrubbed the floors, tubs, and toilets. Her mother had grown up with outhouses. Danny had once mentioned some Amish communities still used them. Was it Wisconsin or Kentucky? It seemed Danny had been to visit districts in over a dozen states. Sometimes the places merged together in her mind, but she loved hearing his stories.

Satisfied with the smell of bleach and the shine of her bathroom faucets, she stored her cleaning supplies beneath the sink and headed to the kitchen. She was half-way through making the sandwich spread—mangoes, onions, green tomatoes, cucumbers, and carrots—when she realized *Mamm* wasn't in her corner rocking chair. She wasn't in the sitting room either. Drying her hands on a dish towel, she looked out the window, and that was when she saw her.

Her heart stopped beating.

Mary Ann was lying between the row of okra and the calico aster plants. Motionless.

Emma must have screamed as she ran down the back porch steps because Joseph appeared at the corner of the barn. One glance and he began to dash toward them. He made it to Mary Ann's side at nearly the same moment Emma did.

"*Mamm*. What happened? Are you—"

"I'm fine."

"You're not fine! Let me help you stand."

With Joseph on one side and Emma on the other, they lifted her from the ground. When had she become so thin? Emma probably could have carried her by herself, except her hands were trembling so badly she would surely have dropped her.

A small groan escaped Mary Ann's lips when she tried to put weight on her right ankle.

"Put your arm around my shoulder, *Mamm*."

"*Danki*."

Joseph's brow was furrowed when he looked at Emma.

The bump on her forehead was beginning to swell, and it was obvious she'd sprained or broken her ankle.

"Help me take her inside."

Mary Ann felt well enough to make a joke about being more trouble than a newborn donkey. Had they ever had a newborn donkey? Emma couldn't remember, but if her *mamm* was joking, perhaps the injuries weren't too severe.

Emma prayed as they helped her into her rocker. *Don't take her now.* That was her prayer, and she would have readily admitted it to anyone who asked. Yes, she realized how selfish her petition was, but she'd had too much grief in her life in the last year. The thought of losing one more person, one more piece of her world, caused tears to splash down her cheeks.

"I'm fine, Emma. I fell is all. Then I couldn't get back up."

"How long were you there?"

Mary Ann had begun to shake, so Emma hurried to the mudroom and pulled her shawl off a hook. "Joseph, fetch her a glass of water, then please bring me the quilt on the back of the couch."

Mary Ann pulled the shawl around her shoulders and patted Emma's hand. "Less than an hour—"

"An hour?" Her heart triple-skipped. What if it had happened in the rain or the cold or the dead of night? The last was a ridiculous worry. Mary Ann didn't putter about after dark.

"Lying on the ground gave me time to study the soil and see how the garden is blossoming. It's coming in *gut*, Emma. Our garden, it's a real blessing."

Emma's tears started falling again. Not because of what had happened or fear for Mary Ann's injury, but simply because she'd glimpsed the future—*Mamm* putting aside this life to follow *Dat* and Ben. Given a choice, Emma knew she would want to pass from this life to the next in the place she loved most, their garden.

"Should I go for Danny? Or your doctor?" Joseph shuffled from one foot to the other.

She'd almost forgotten Joseph was there, waiting, holding the log cabin quilt and wanting to help.

Emma swiped at the tears on her cheeks.

"*Ya.*" Emma accepted the quilt and placed it gently across Mary Ann's lap. "Go next door and ask Danny to call a driver."

"I don't need—"

"Let's allow Doc to decide what you need, *Mamm.*" It could have been the tremor in her voice, or possibly the fear that flooded her eyes, but Mary Ann agreed without any further argument.

Joseph was back by the time Emma had brewed Mary Ann a cup of lemon tea.

"Danny said he'd have someone here soon."

"*Danki.*" Emma reached for his hand as he moved back toward the mudroom. "You were a big help, Joseph. *Gotte* sent you here at exactly the right time."

He said nothing, but his cheeks flushed a deep red. As he walked back outside, she thought he stood a little straighter.

"He's a *gut* boy." *Mamm* had opened her Bible and was thumbing through the Old Testament until her hand rested on the book of Isaiah.

"How do you feel?"

"Fine. My foot, it's old, Emma. Like the rest of me." She cupped her hand around Emma's cheek. "Don't worry, dear. Today isn't the day the Lord will call me home."

Emma pulled out a chair and sank into it.

"My heart stopped when I saw you, saw only your

foot sticking out from the garden row. I was terrified that, that—"

"Don't fear death, dear." *Mamm's* eyes filled with something Emma didn't understand—memories or kindness or maybe hope. "It will be a glorious day when I see Ben and *Dat* and my own parents again. So many of my friends have passed already. It will be a *wunderbaar* day when I see our Lord."

Emma's tears started in earnest then. She knew that what Mary Ann was saying was right, but she couldn't imagine enduring it.

"*Gotte* will give you strength, and He won't leave you alone. You have that promise." Mary Ann tapped the worn pages of her Bible. "You have it right here."

The sound of car tires crunching over gravel drifted through the open kitchen window. How had Danny managed to find someone so quickly? He must have run all the way to the phone shack.

They helped Mary Ann into the car, moving her carefully since her ankle had swollen to twice its normal size. Emma slid in beside her, reminded Joseph he could find lunch fixings in the refrigerator, and thanked Danny. She could tell he wanted to say something. Maybe he wanted to comfort her. But the driver, a sweet neighbor named Marcie, was already pulling away.

CHAPTER 9

Three hours later they drove back down their lane in the breezy May afternoon. Emma saw Bishop Simon's buggy before they'd even reached the house. Had he come to see Mary Ann? Or Joseph?

Marcie insisted on helping them into the house. Emma paid her for the ride, though she seemed embarrassed by that.

"I wouldn't have wanted to load her into a buggy, and you stayed while we found the supplies the doctor had ordered. You've been a real blessing." Emma pushed the money into her hand and reminded her they'd need a ride again the next week, so the doc could check on how *Mamm* was healing.

She could tell Mary Ann was about to fall asleep standing, so she helped her to the downstairs bedroom and lowered the shade to block out the afternoon sunlight.

"I'd rather be upstairs," Mary Ann mumbled as she removed the pins from her *kapp*.

"*Ya*, but the stairs are a bad idea. Doc said so."

Mary Ann's eyes twinkled. "All of this special care. I'm going to be spoiled."

"Rest, please. After dinner I'll bring down whatever you need from your room."

Mary Ann shooed Emma away as she folded back the Lone Star quilt and lay down on the bed.

Emma was washing potatoes in the sink when she looked out the window and saw Bishop Simon walking toward his buggy. She'd forgotten he was visiting! Stepping out onto the back porch, she called out to him. He turned, waved, and then made his way back across the yard.

"I heard about Mary Ann. I didn't want to disturb either of you if you were resting. How is she?"

"*Gut.* Come in. I can make tea or—"

"A glass of water would be fine, and maybe one of your chocolate chip cookies if you have any made."

"I do!" Emma brought the entire cookie jar to the table along with two glasses of water. She thought about resisting, but the day had been too nerve-racking. One cookie could go a long way toward improving her outlook.

"What did Doc Burnham say?"

"He cautioned me to keep an eye on the bump on her head."

"Does she have a concussion?"

"He doesn't think so." Emma pulled the instruction sheet from the stack of supplies they'd purchased while in town. "I'm to watch for balance problems, vomiting, dizziness, or severe mood swings."

"And what of her ankle? The boy told me it was painful for her to stand on."

"Doc x-rayed it. There's no break."

"Praise the Lord."

"He does want her to wear a boot to keep it from twisting again. The sprain could take several weeks to heal, especially for someone her age. And she's to use the cane he gave her several months ago."

Simon reached for another cookie. "Mary Ann has a reputation for being stubborn."

"It's true."

"Do you think she will follow Burnham's instructions?"

"She likes Doc, and she promised to behave herself."

Silence settled over the table as they enjoyed the sugar, chocolate, and touch of cinnamon in the cookies.

When Simon pushed away the jar of cookies, Emma knew he was ready to discuss Joseph. Simon was rather young to be a bishop, having only turned forty a few years before. He was slight of build, with a few strands of gray appearing in his dark beard. His eyes were a deep brown, warm and kind. He was a good leader, and he guided their community with compassion and grace.

"Danny called and told me about the boy. He explained what you learned from him last night."

"And you came to speak with Joseph?"

"I did." Simon hesitated, stroked his beard, and then continued. "I also spoke with the bishop from his district in Goshen. I thought it might be best if I had a little background on the family before I came out to see him."

"You found his family already?"

"Bishop Atlee knew exactly who I was speaking of, even before I'd finished describing the boy."

"So the family did report he was missing?"

"*Nein.*" Simon sat back and studied the kitchen.

It looked the same as any other Amish kitchen, so Emma knew he was trying to separate what he should share and what should remain private. One of the reasons Simon was a good bishop was he kept as much private as possible. No one liked to have their troubles aired in public. Though when a confession was required, it could hardly be avoided.

"The parents didn't report anything, but there's been some trouble with the family before. In fact, in the last year—as the economy has become tighter—it's worsened."

"What sort of trouble?"

Instead of answering, Simon leaned forward. "You're doing a *gut* thing allowing the boy to stay here, Emma. He might not be ready to go home anytime soon."

"Did he tell you that?"

"He didn't tell me much of anything, but I could see that he's comfortable with you. He needs a place to stay, a place where he can work, worship, and find *Gotte*'s plan for his life."

"And he couldn't do that at home?"

"From what Atlee told me, no."

"They didn't . . . they didn't hurt him. Did they? They didn't hit him or—"

"There are many ways of hurting a child that don't involve physical violence. But no. It's not what you're fearing. Joseph's father is apparently a very hard, very strict man."

"He hinted as much."

"Atlee has tried to counsel him, remind him that our

ways are more compassionate. But Joseph's father was raised by very harsh parents, and he thinks it is the only way. Apparently the community knew it would only be a matter of time before the boy left . . . and probably his siblings as well."

"Can't someone step in? Social services or—"

Simon held up his hand, palm out. "I can't share all of the specifics. I can tell you that the family has been thoroughly investigated, and nothing against the law is going on in the home."

"So the other children will stay."

"*Ya*, for now they will." Simon stood. "Should I go down the hall and see Mary Ann?"

"She's resting. Hopefully she's asleep."

"Then tell her I will be praying for her healing, and I'd be happy to stop back in a few days to check on her."

"*Danki*."

Emma walked him to his buggy. Glancing toward the barn, she saw Joseph with one of Ben's horses. He was brushing the gelding with solid, gentle strokes. The horse looked completely satisfied, if a horse could wear such an expression.

"There is one more thing." Simon had already climbed up into his buggy. His eyes had become even more serious than before. "Nancy Schlabach . . ."

Emma might have cringed at her name. Surely nothing had happened to the young woman or her boys.

"We're going to have to move her out of their home until Owen can be treated for his condition. He won't go to any of the facilities we've suggested. Or at least he won't at this point, but it's no longer safe for her or the boys to be there. Another incident and the police will be involved."

"What can I do to help?" The words popped out of her mouth before she'd fully considered them. She already had a crippled mother and a runaway boy under her care.

"I've been looking for a place for them to stay—a safe place within our community." He motioned out the front of his buggy, toward their garden and Danny's pond. "This would be a *gut* place, if you're willing to have them."

Emma swallowed the excuses that threatened to rise to her lips. "Of course."

It would be selfish to talk of any difficulties she might have when that poor woman and her children were in danger.

"The Lord bless you, Emma. You know it is possible that *Gotte* is going to use you, use this place, to care for others."

Emma didn't know what to say, so she remained silent.

"I'll be in touch." And with that, he murmured to his horse.

Emma watched as they made their way down the lane.

Had she just agreed to house a woman and two small children? Had she agreed to care for more if the need arose? Their community didn't have any more problems than other Amish groups, but in her mind's eye, she pictured a long line of folks making their way down the lane and to their front porch.

A feeling of panic bubbled in her stomach, but she pushed it down.

As the Good Book says, "Each day has enough trouble of its own." Certainly that had been true for the past twenty-four hours. No need to borrow problems from the next day when she had quite enough already! But the same Scripture said something about God's provision. Emma walked into the kitchen, picked up Mary Ann's Bible, and paged over to the Gospel of Matthew.

"Do not worry about your life, what you will eat or drink; or about your body, what you will wear. Is not life more than food, and the body more than clothes?" She sank into the chair and continued reading. "Look at the birds of the air; they do not sow or reap or store away in barns, and yet your heavenly Father feeds them. Are you not much more valuable than they?"

For the first time since she'd spied Mary Ann lying on the ground, peace flooded her heart. She didn't know how long it would take Mary Ann to heal. She didn't know what Joseph's problems were. And she couldn't begin to understand what help Nancy and her boys needed.

But God knew.

God knew, and His grace would pull them through.

CHAPTER 10

Danny waited as long as he could to check on Mary Ann the next day. He'd been tempted to stop by in the morning, when he'd taken Shadow on his early morning walk, but he'd resisted. Then as he worked trimming the bushes and flowers bordering his house, he thought about going over. Perhaps they were both resting though, and he didn't want to disturb that. Finally in the afternoon, after he'd rewritten the same page three times, he called it a day and gave in to the desires of his heart.

He didn't want to be a pest, but he needed to assure himself that Mary Ann was healing and that Emma was coping with the latest emergency. She'd appeared quite shaken the day before. Thinking Shadow might be able to bring a smile to her face, Danny called out to him, and the dog obediently fell in step behind him.

The dog's training was coming along well, better than Danny had expected. As they walked toward Emma's, Shadow emitted an occasional whine—no doubt wanting to chase the birds rimming the small pond or take off after the rabbit that hopped across their path. Shadow fairly quivered in anticipation of a good romp, but he stayed at Danny's heel. Perhaps on the way back he'd allow him a good run.

He found Emma and Mary Ann in the garden. No big surprise there. Mary Ann was wearing the big black boot, which stuck out from under her dark-blue dress. She looked good, her color back and her customary smile adorning the wrinkles on her face. She reminded Danny of his own mother, and he understood first-hand how important she was to Emma.

Emma, on the other hand, looked as if she had spent the day chasing after one of her grandchildren.

"I was successful keeping *Mamm* indoors and rest-ing for the morning, but by afternoon she was a force to be reckoned with."

"She does love her garden."

"I can hear you both," Mary Ann called from her bench, where she sat with a shawl around her shoulders. "Surely I can't run into trouble by sitting in the garden. The flowers are beginning to bloom, and I want to enjoy their color and breathe in their scent."

Emma was feeding the roses with the old coffee grounds she kept for just that purpose. Danny knelt beside her, and they worked the old grounds into the dirt with a hand trowel.

"Trying to stick close to Mary Ann?" he asked in a low voice.

"Why do you say that?"

"You've practically dug up that rosebush. I thought the idea was to use the tool thingy to revive it, not kill it."

Danny knew all about gardening, aerating the ground, and applying fertilizer. But he enjoyed the look Emma gave him whenever he played like he didn't.

"I am trying to stay close and keep an eye on her.

Though the bump on her head has gone down nicely, she's still quite wobbly on her feet."

"How's the ankle?"

Emma stole a peek at Mary Ann, then refocused on the rosebush. "The swelling is better, but the bruising is worse. It's a deep purple now. Doc warned us it would be."

They continued in their fertilizing efforts, working side by side in the afternoon sun. Clouds were building in the west, and Danny guessed they'd have rain again before morning. After initially saying hello to Mary Ann and Emma, Shadow had plopped down on his belly, content to lie on the warm ground and occasionally yelp at the butterflies.

"How's our lad?"

"Joseph has been cleaning up Ben's office. Since he insists on sleeping in the barn, he can at least move out of the horse stall."

Danny was about to reply when Joseph walked down the path separating the roses from the vegetables.

"Did I hear a dog?" His question was directed toward Danny and Emma, but his smile was for Shadow. It was the first smile Danny had seen from him, and it made him look his age—a young man who should be enjoying life.

"You did indeed." Danny stood and called to his pup. "Joseph, meet Shadow. Shadow, down."

The smart little pup had been moving toward Joseph at a lopsided gait, but he dropped to the ground at the word *down*.

"How'd you teach him that?" Joseph knelt beside the

dog and rubbed the spot between his ears—black silky fur that was still a bit loose. The dog would grow into his skin in the next few months. He'd be a big one. That was plain to see.

Danny could also see that Joseph was smitten.

"Shadow is a quick learner. Do you like dogs?" Danny stood with his hands in his pockets, beaming at the boy and dog.

"I do."

"Ever have one?"

"*Nein.*" The next words were a whisper. "We weren't allowed."

Danny seemed to consider that for a moment, then nodded his head. "Some Amish don't approve of keeping pets."

"And then there are the puppy mills." Joseph's gaze darkened.

"There are. I saw a few while traveling, but not as many as you might think. Between *Englisch* regulations and pressure from our communities to treat animals with kindness, the mills seem to be disappearing." Danny frowned, remembering the few he had seen, but then that memory was replaced by another. "I also met a lot of Plain families who did have dogs or even cats that they kept as pets. Mostly they stayed outside, of course. Not too many house pets among people like us."

"So you taught him yourself?"

"I did. I can show you how later, if you'd like. It's fairly simple. You have to be consistent, and the occasional treat goes a long way."

"I'd love to learn."

"Excellent! Say, Shadow would probably enjoy a visit to the barn while we're finishing up here."

"Come on, boy."

Shadow trotted at Joseph's heels. The two were gone without another word.

"That was nice of you." Emma scooped more grounds out of the can and worked it around the base of a rosebush that was beginning to blossom pink.

"Seems as if maybe he missed some of the things of a normal childhood." Danny knelt beside her and began weeding.

Emma had shared with him and Mary Ann all that Bishop Simon had told her the day before, all they knew of Joseph's home life, which wasn't much.

"A dog can heal many broken places of the heart."

Emma looked at Danny in surprise and he had the sense she was about to ask how he knew that, but Mary Ann interrupted them.

"I'd like my bench moved."

"Moved? Moved where?"

The wooden bench had sat in the same place for as long as Danny could remember. It had always been at the end of the row of leafy vegetables. The path of hard dirt made a bend in front of her seat. It provided a perfect spot to study the wildflowers to the right, the roses to the left, and the leafy vegetables directly in front. Behind the bench was a large stand of mint, which gave off the loveliest of scents after a rain.

"Perhaps we could move it over between the herbs and the marigolds."

"But, *Mamm*—"

"It's no problem." Danny helped Mary Ann into a standing position.

She clutched his arm with one hand and her cane with the other, balancing precariously on her black boot.

"Emma, why don't you stand here with her while I move the bench?"

The place she had pointed to was a mere three feet away. Emma moved to Mary Ann's side and studied her as Danny picked up the bench, carried it to the new spot, and made certain it was settled firmly.

"Are you feeling confused, *Mamm*? Mood swings? Dizziness? You could have a concussion after all."

Mary Ann looped her left hand through Emma's arm. With her right she tapped the ground with her cane. "Don't worry so, Emma. A change of view is helpful at times."

Change of view? She could throw a pebble from the new spot to the old. Danny helped her to the bench, waiting to make sure she was satisfied with her *new view*.

He had to resist the urge to laugh. Emma looked both concerned and put out at the same time, but she remained the patient daughter-in-law. Wrapping Mary Ann's shawl around her shoulders, she returned to the row of roses and had crouched down to continue her chore when Mary Ann spoke up again.

"We should plant something new there."

"Plant something?" Emma stared around at row after row of garden in bloom.

"I know." *Mamm* clapped her hands. "Transfer a little of the rosemary there. It can grow nice and tall. The tiny lavender blooms will look lovely next to the roses."

Emma stood, dusted the dirt from her fingers, and put her hands on her hips. Watching her made Danny want to pull out a notebook and begin writing about Amish women working hard on a rural farm.

"You want rosemary planted there?"

"*Ya.*"

"And you want it done now?"

"Now would be *gut.*"

Emma was too old to roll her eyes and too well-mannered to stomp her foot. Danny guessed she wanted to do both. Instead she marched over to the small shed where they kept garden tools.

Finding a medium-sized shovel, she backed out of the shed and into Danny. Her face flushed as he stepped back.

"I've got that, if you'll point out which plant is rosemary."

"You know good and well which is rosemary!" When he only smiled, she added, "We have enough to do, and she wants us to transplant perfectly healthy plants!"

Emma took him to the herb area and pointed out a dark-green bush, which had grown knee-high.

"Doesn't look like an herb." This time Danny was serious. He'd never seen such a big rosemary plant.

"They grow large. Some people even use them for landscaping."

"Does it matter which I dig up?"

"I'd take the one to the right side. It will leave a bit of an empty space, but this garden could use more open area."

Emma stifled a yawn. No doubt she'd risen several

times during the night to check on her *mamm*. Danny wanted to tell her to go inside, to rest, but he knew those would be wasted words.

He carried the plant back over to the spot where Mary Ann was waiting. Holding it up, he smiled and asked, "Will this work, Mary Ann?"

"It's perfect. You can leave it here while you dig. Careful with the shovel though. Digging can unbury surprises. A person never knows when he'll hit something hard."

Mary Ann's eyes were wide and focused completely on what Danny was doing. She had the look of a child on Christmas afternoon, when the gift-giving time was about to begin.

Danny pushed the shovel into the rich, dark dirt. Both of their farms had been blessed with good soil. They had very few rocks, and over the years, they'd created pathways for the water to run down each aisle when the rains came.

Placing his foot on top of the shovel, Danny dug up one, two, three shovelfuls of dirt. He glanced at Mary Ann.

"A few more." Now she was leaning forward, hand on her cane and chin on her hand, her eyes locked on Danny and the growing mound of soil.

Danny added a fourth, then fifth shovelful of dirt to the growing mound.

And suddenly his shovel hit something hard, and he heard the sound of metal scraping against metal.

CHAPTER 11

Emma didn't know what to say when Danny stopped, turned, and looked at her. She raised her shoulders up, then down. Perhaps he could dig to the left.

But Mary Ann had other ideas. "Best see what that is." Her eyes twinkled, and Emma suddenly realized her *mamm* knew what was buried.

She stepped forward to help Danny. Together they dug around the object and lifted it from its hiding place. The thing was rectangular in shape, approximately the size of a large book, heavy, and sealed shut with a combination lock.

Danny handed the box to her. She dusted the dirt off and carried it to Mary Ann.

"It's not for me, Emma. It's for you."

"For me?"

"*Ya*. I've been waiting until the time was right."

"And it's right now?"

Mary Ann reached forward and patted her hand. "Open it." She gave Emma the combination. And how had she remembered that for so many years? But then, Mary Ann's mind had always been clear. It was her body that was failing.

Danny had followed Emma over to stand next to her *mamm*. He bumped his shoulder against hers. "*Ya*, open it, Emma. I've seen a lot of things in my travels, but never treasure buried on an Amish farm."

"It's not trea—" The word hung in her throat when she saw what was in the box. She pulled out the clear, weather-proof sack. It looked like a Ziploc bag but was made of a heavier material. What was inside had been wrapped in wax paper, now crinkled and yellow.

Emma sat on the ground at Mary Ann's feet and pulled the large bundle out of the bag, then unwrapped the paper.

"There're hundreds of dollars here."

"Thousands, actually."

"What? How? *Mamm*, where did this come from?"

"Let's have some tea." Mary Ann stood and Danny instantly moved to her side. "Tea and maybe one of your cookies. Then I'll answer all of your questions."

Danny reached for Emma's hand, helping her up off the ground. When their fingers touched, electricity zipped up her arm. Emma felt confused, more confused than she was about the money.

But instead of asking questions, she followed Mary Ann into the house, put the water to boil, and set out tea, cream, sugar, and cookies. Within ten minutes, they were all gathered around the table. Mary Ann sipped her lemon tea, nibbled on a gingersnap, and then began to tell her story.

"You know about the war. You both have heard the old ones talk of it."

Emma glanced at Danny, and they both nodded. War

was not discussed often in their gatherings or their families, but occasionally the topic would come up. When it did, the older folks would describe how they had made it through the years of conscription and service.

Ben's father, Eldon, had been eighty-nine when he died. Emma quickly did the math and realized he was probably eligible for service when he was eighteen, during World War II.

"Eldon had the opportunity to serve with the CPS," Emma said.

"Civilian Public Service." Danny ignored the cookies, something he didn't normally do. His fingers tapped against the kitchen table. No doubt he was wishing for a pen so he could take notes. "Many conscientious objectors ended up working on public service projects— Amish, Mennonite, Quakers, even Methodists."

"We had just married." Mary Ann stared into her tea, a smile forming at the corners of her eyes. "I thought I would die when he packed his bag to leave, but in the end, *Gotte* used that time to bless us. Now I want it to bless you."

"Slow down a minute." Emma reached for the strings of her prayer *kapp* and ran her fingers from top to bottom. The familiar gesture calmed her jumpy nerves. "He worked in the service, versus going to war—"

"Or to jail." Danny's eyebrow arched when she glanced over at him.

"Eldon was assigned to a wildlife camp, tending quail that would later be released in state parks. That was the first year. The second year he worked at a tree farm."

"I didn't think they were paid for their service."

Danny finally reached for a cookie, but he didn't eat it, opting instead to break it into pieces on his plate.

"They weren't. Many families struggled because of this, but Jeremiah, Eldon's father, was always looking for an opportunity to better the farm. During the Great Depression, Jeremiah had planted large fields of mint."

"It was quite the cash crop during the 1930s."

"And continued to be for many years. By the time Eldon had left for the CPS camp, Jeremiah was still making a good profit from the crop. Companies used it to make toothpaste, gum, candy, even food flavoring. We conserved our resources, as everyone did during the war, even though we were doing well with the crops. When Eldon returned from the CPS camp, his father gave him one-third of the profits from those years."

"One-third because—"

"Because there were three brothers. All had served in various camps. Jeremiah thought they could use the money to get started with their families, once they returned."

"So why didn't you use it?"

"Eldon and I didn't need the money to start a home. We stayed here, stayed with his parents. He was the oldest, and it was his responsibility. He told me a few weeks after he returned that he didn't mind serving in the CPS. He missed me and his parents, but he was convinced *Gotte* used that time away from home to mature him. However, he also felt the money from his father was tainted somehow. He was adamant that he didn't want to begin our life together with proceeds made during the war."

"So you buried the money?" The story made no sense to Emma. Who buried money and left it for nearly seventy years?

"*Ya*. We buried it beneath the bench—"

"And near the mint." Danny wore a satisfied expression, as if he'd successfully solved a mystery.

"We didn't want to forget where it was, and we knew that sometimes old people have memory problems."

The clock on the wall ticked as Emma considered all Mary Ann had said. Danny finally began to eat his crumbled gingersnap, then reached for another.

Emma stared at the stack of bills in the box, which now sat in the middle of the kitchen table. "This is a lot of money, *Mamm*. All of it came from a mint crop?"

"*Nein*. You will also find war bonds in the stack."

"War bonds?" She was beginning to feel dizzy.

"Everyone was encouraged to buy war bonds in those days. The local Mennonite community helped us to choose which bonds were not specifically used for war purposes. That way we could help our neighbors but not betray our convictions."

Emma reached forward and flipped through the stack. Finding one of the war bonds, she pulled it out and placed it on the table. "Why didn't you cash them in?"

Mamm smiled and sipped her tea.

Danny offered an explanation. "War bonds were given a ten-year extension, up to forty years."

"Can these still be cashed?"

"Sure. I met a man in Pennsylvania who would take some into his bank once a year. He used it to pay the taxes on his land. A twenty-five-dollar bond issued during World War II is worth approximately one hundred dollars today."

"But these are hundred-dollar bonds—"

"We had no children when Eldon left." *Mamm* stared out the kitchen window. "At first the days seemed so long. Then I began to work in the garden and to sew. I sold the handmade items and canned goods at the local mercantile, and I used the money to buy the bonds."

Emma sipped her tea and tried to process all she was hearing.

"When Eldon returned, we placed the bonds in the box, added Jeremiah's money, and buried it in the garden."

"And you were never tempted to dig it up?"

"*Gotte* has provided all these years." Mamm sat back and sipped her tea.

Emma stared at Danny, but he said nothing, content to smile back at her. This wasn't his family history that had been dug up, but something made her think that it involved him. After all, Mary Ann had chosen to reveal her secret when Danny was present. That couldn't be a coincidence.

Closing her eyes, she pulled in a deep breath. Then she opened her eyes, sat up straighter, and asked the question that had bothered her since Danny's shovel struck metal.

"Why now?"

"I have a feeling you and Danny are going to need it."

Emma nearly choked on the sip of tea she'd taken. "Me and Danny?"

"*Ya.*"

Danny's grin widened and Emma's cheeks warmed to the color of the red roses yet to bloom in the garden.

"*Mamm*, why would we . . . Danny and I aren't . . . That is . . ."

Stuffing an entire gingersnap into his mouth, Danny didn't help her out at all.

"The Lord is calling you, calling both of you." Now Mary Ann leaned forward and pinned Emma and Danny with her gaze. "He's doing something important on this little piece of land, and you two are going to be in charge of it."

"I don't—"

"Can't you see? *Gotte* brought Danny home. He brought Joseph to us. And soon there will be others. The money has been cleansed by nearly seventy years of rain and sunshine. Now it's time for you to use what we have to bless others."

It occurred to Emma at that moment that perhaps Mary Ann did have a concussion, but her eyes were clear and a smile continued to play across her lips. The money on the table was certainly real, though Emma had no idea how much it totaled.

"Don't worry." Mary Ann reached forward and patted her hand.

"But I don't understand what—"

"You don't need to. *Gotte* will provide the answers and the direction you need."

With that, she stood, waving away their offer to help. Leaning on her cane, she stumped down the hall to her new bedroom.

Danny and Emma stared at each other for one minute, then two. Finally he cleared his throat. "She's something else, Mary Ann is."

"I think maybe my *mamm* has misunderstood our relationship."

"Maybe." He smiled down into his mug of hot tea. "And maybe not."

Emma didn't know what to say to that, so she remained silent.

What was the money for?

What were they to do with it?

Had it actually been buried in the garden since the 1940s?

Danny seemed in no hurry to go, and Shadow was still in the barn with Joseph.

Unable to resist, she pulled the bundle toward her and ran her fingers along the time-worn string that bound it.

"Want to help me count?" She suddenly felt emboldened. They had never been poor. Even since Ben had died, they'd been able to meet their financial needs with what was saved.

But this?

With this stack of money they had different options available to them. They *could* use it to help other people. She wondered if Ben had known. What would he have advised her to do? Then she looked up at Danny, and somehow knew he understood what she was thinking.

He reached over and squeezed her hand.

Together, they cut the string surrounding the bills and began to count.

CHAPTER 12

L ater that evening after dinner, Emma carried fresh sheets and blankets out to Joseph.

He'd pulled down an old cot from the attic and set it up in the corner of Ben's office, which was now quite clean. It still smelled of horses and hay and tackle, but the room was warmer than the stall. He wouldn't need a heater, and she was thankful for that. Heaters in barns worried her. On any farm, fire was a constant fear.

She would rather have him in the house, but Joseph seemed to still need his space. Perhaps a little privacy would allow him to work through the things that still haunted him. Perhaps in the barn, among the animals he obviously loved, he could once again find *Gotte*'s *wille* for his life.

Joseph helped her with making his bed. As they worked, he talked about Shadow and Danny and how he'd like to learn to train dogs. Maybe one day, he would have a place where he could raise litters, train them, and then sell the pups to good homes.

It was the most she'd heard him say.

Perhaps the words and dreams that had been bound inside of him were suddenly freed.

The thought made Emma happy. There had been

many days in the last year where she found it was an effort to endure the hours from sunrise to bedtime. Other times the days had merged together, and she found little to look forward to. Seeing Joseph smile made her realize that though her children were grown and living in homes of their own, she could still be a help to others.

Was that what Mary Ann was trying to tell her?

Was that why she'd chosen to reveal the treasure?

Emma had thanked Joseph for his hard work that day and was turning toward the barn door when they both heard the clatter of buggy wheels. Grabbing a large battery flashlight, she and Joseph hurried out into the night at the same moment. The lamplight from the kitchen spilled out across the yard. Emma was able to make out Bishop Simon as he stepped down from his buggy and began to walk toward their door.

"Bishop?" Emma called out as she rushed to meet him. "Is everything all right?"

Joseph was hurrying along beside her. She could feel him tense. Was this about his parents? Were they going to insist he return home?

"I'm sorry to disturb you so late."

"It's no problem. *Was iss letz?*"

"I've brought Nancy and her boys. I'm afraid there's been another . . . incident."

"She's here? Now?"

"*Ya.* Waiting in the buggy."

Emma didn't stay to hear another word. Her pulse had kicked up a notch, and her mind was racing. What had happened to Nancy? Were her boys all right?

Then she walked around to where Nancy waited in the back seat of the buggy with her children. The moment Emma saw her, she knew the details of what had happened weren't important. All that mattered was that they provide this family a safe place to stay.

Nancy's lip was swollen, recently cut open by the looks of it. The black eye Verna had spoken of during sewing circle had turned a deep purple. Nancy's older boy was huddled next to her, his face hidden, pressed into her dress. The youngest was in her arms sound asleep.

"Nancy, *wilkumm*. Let me help you out."

Nancy said nothing, but when she stepped out of the buggy, Emma saw how dangerously thin she had become. The boys wore clean clothes, but when the oldest looked up, the fear in his eyes tugged at her heart.

They moved quickly inside the house. Nancy and her boys sat at the table. Bishop Simon stood at the door, watching the darkness outside. Joseph shifted from one foot to the other, as if unsure whether he should stay.

"Joseph, didn't you offer to help Danny with some home repairs early tomorrow?"

"*Ya*."

"You best go on to bed then. We're fine here."

He glanced from Nancy to the bishop to Emma, and then he shuffled out into the night.

"Let me find you some dinner."

"It's enough for you to let us stay. You don't have to feed us as well." Nancy's voice was strong and her eyes resolute. How did she manage to hold herself together after all she'd endured?

"Of course I'll feed you, and I trust you will accept my hospitality. Now would your boys rather have cold ham or cold chicken?"

"Both, p-p-please." The oldest boy kept his hands folded on top of the table. He was close to five years old, if Emma remembered correctly, and he had his father's blond hair.

"Jacob, Emma might need to save some of that food for—"

"*Nein*. It's leftovers and I already have a casserole put together for tomorrow." She placed the platters of meat on the table and added fresh bread and cheese. It wasn't a perfectly balanced meal, but it would do for an evening snack.

Jacob didn't touch the food. Instead he bowed his head and waited for his *mamm* to indicate it was okay to eat. Her eyes met Emma's, and Emma saw the tears she was valiantly holding back. Nancy touched her son's head and whispered, "Amen."

The boy reached for a piece of fried chicken. When his teeth sank into it, a smile covered his face. "Th-th-this is *gut, Mamm*."

Nancy stared at her son, then looked at Emma. "*Danki*."

"*Gem gschehne*."

In that moment they had more in common than one would have imagined. They were two moms who cared immensely for their children. They were two women whose lives had taken unexpected turns, leaving them alone without their husbands. And they were two members of a community who cared for one another.

Nancy's younger son, Luke, began to fuss, nudging her as if he wanted to nurse.

"You'll be comfortable in the upstairs bedroom, first one to the left. The boys can sleep with you or in the room next door."

Nancy stared at Jacob, uncertainty and worry filling her eyes.

"I'll bring him up when he's done eating."

"All right."

Simon motioned Emma into the mudroom once Nancy had gone. "I have three bags of clothing in my buggy. I'll go and fetch them."

"What of Owen? Will he be looking for his family?"

"*Nein.* He's in town courtesy of the Shipshewana police at the moment."

"The police?"

"Drunk driving."

"Oh my." Emma had heard of folks being arrested for driving an *Englisch* automobile while drinking, but she'd never heard of anyone being arrested while they were driving a buggy!

"Captain Taylor phoned me and asked that I send someone for the horse and buggy, which I've done. They're going to hold him for at least twenty-four hours."

"It was a *gut* time for Nancy and the boys to leave."

"Yes." Simon ran his fingers through his beard. "This is temporary, Emma. I spoke with Owen, and he seems repentant, but I doubt he has the strength to resist his addiction."

"What will you do?"

"Minister to him. Encourage him to seek an intervention at the center in Elkhart or Goshen. After this, I think he will."

"And their farm?"

"Neighbors will care for the animals and his crops. I need you to provide a safe place for them to stay, if you're willing." He hesitated, then continued. "In my opinion, it would be better if Nancy and the boys weren't alone, and Owen will more likely agree to treatment if his family is gone."

"Of course, but I don't know anything about helping an abused woman."

"Love her, Emma. Offer the entire family our Lord's grace and mercy. Feed them. Pray for them. *Gotte* will take care of the rest."

He brought in the bags of clothing, and Emma promised she would take them upstairs. Mary Ann had slept through the entire episode. The less folks tramping up and down the stairs the better.

She tapped softly on her guests' door and then opened it.

Nancy sat in the rocker near the window. Her babe was asleep in her arms. Jacob had carried one of the bags of clothes, which he set down near his mother, kissing her, and then his baby brother, before sitting on the bed.

Emma placed the other two bags underneath the hooks they used for hanging clothes.

Was this all she had left? All she'd brought from her home? But her home was still there. It hadn't blown away in some storm. Perhaps with *Gotte*'s help, Owen would be able to return to it whole and ready to care for his family.

"You're welcome to stay as long as you need."

Nancy nodded and swiped at the tears cascading down her cheeks. Emma's heart broke for her again, so she crossed the room, enfolded Nancy in her arms, and let her cry.

CHAPTER 13

Mary Ann didn't seem a bit surprised to have extra people eating breakfast with them the next morning. As Emma placed raisins and brown sugar on the table, then brought the pot of oatmeal from the stove, she couldn't help smiling. A week before it had been the two of them, but their lives had turned and taken an entirely new direction.

Emma's mind flashed back to the afternoon she had knelt in the garden and swiped her dirty fingers against her clean apron. It had left a brown mark, but one that had washed away after two launderings. In a similar way, Christ washed away their sins. He never failed to offer them another chance.

Joseph was talking to Jacob, telling him about Shadow. Luke lay in a cradle Emma had found in one of the upstairs rooms. Often it had been used for her grandchildren, and she supposed one day it would hold her great-grandchildren. Truly, God had blessed them.

Nancy appeared to have rested, but the bruising around her eye seemed worse in the daylight, and her busted lip looked painful. Emma was certain Mary

Ann would know what herbs they could put on both to soothe the skin.

The morning passed quickly. Nancy washed the clothes that had been in the bags and hung them to dry on the line. It was funny to look outside and see diapers drying in the May sun. Mary Ann baked a cake and fresh bread, while Emma aired and cleaned Jacob's room. By the time Danny and Joseph joined them for lunch, they once again had a full table.

Then there was a commotion at the back door, and Emma's son stepped inside.

Her oldest, Henry was always the first to check on them when anything out of the ordinary was going on. He had turned thirty recently. He was tall, big enough to handle the horses he worked with, and balding slightly. Although he was a farrier in town, they spoke occasionally about him moving back to the farm. They had rented out the fields after Ben had died, but the barn and yard and house were a lot of work for two women living alone.

They weren't alone anymore.

They had an entire family gathered around them now.

"I heard *Mammi* had fallen." He sat beside Jacob as Emma made sure he knew who everyone was. They had two church districts in Shipshe. Henry and his family were members of the district in town. The rest of them belonged to the country district, which Simon oversaw.

"It's true," Mary Ann said. "Tumbled over right outside in the garden. Emma saved me."

"How are you feeling?"

"*Gut!* The Lord is my right hand, Henry."

"And your foot?"

"Sore, but Doc's cane helps."

They spoke of business in town, Danny's pup, and how Joseph and Jacob had searched for worms in the garden.

"Planning on some fishing, are you?" Henry smiled at the boys.

"*Ya*. Emma and *Mamm* say we can . . . can . . . can cook what we catch."

"Hmmm. I have two boys who might enjoy a little fishing. Maybe we can come out Saturday afternoon."

"If we don't ca-catch them all today."

Everyone laughed, everyone except Nancy, who at least managed a smile.

When they were done eating, Emma rose to wash the dishes, but Nancy stayed her hand. "Let me. Please."

"All right. I'll walk Henry outside then."

They were barely out the back door when he started peppering Emma with questions. "Where is the teenager from? How long is he going to stay here? Why didn't you call me about *Mammi*, and what are you going to do about Nancy and her boys?"

Henry had always been her worrier. It wasn't that his faith was weak, but he tended to agonize over whether he was doing enough.

Emma tucked her hand through his arm. "Goshen. I'm not sure. I would have called, but I haven't had time to walk to the phone shack, and I'm not going to do anything. They're just . . . visiting for a while."

Henry grunted. "I'll slow my questions if you'll slow your answers."

"Fair enough."

They'd made it to his buggy, and they both rested their backs against the black side that had warmed in the midday sunlight.

"It's a lot of changes at once."

"*Ya*. Tell me. A week ago, it was only your *mammi* I had to care for. Now, once again, I have a family."

Henry turned and studied her. "It's been hard on you since *Dat* passed."

"All loss is difficult."

"I should have—"

"You've done all you could and should. You're a *gut* son."

Henry smiled ruefully, then turned back to look out over the garden. "The word in town is that you're going to allow people who are in need to stay here."

Emma was a little surprised, since she hadn't quite decided what they were doing herself. But the Amish grapevine worked well, and she admitted to her son that the idea was growing on her.

Then she told him about the money.

Henry let out a long, low whistle and rubbed the top of his head where the hair had disappeared. "Leave it to *Mammi* to keep a secret like that buried."

"I don't know exactly what she wants me to do. She seems to think we should spend it on some kind of ministry here." When Henry didn't comment, she nudged his shoulder. "How do you feel about that? Rightfully the money would go to you and the other *kinner*."

"We're not *kinner*, Mamm. We're adults, and you know that none of us needs the money."

"So you think it's the right thing to do?"

"I think however *Gotte* prompts you is the right thing to do." He turned to her, and Emma was relieved to see the familiar twinkle in his eyes. "'Course we'll inherit this place one day, so any improvements you make will benefit all of us."

"But would you want strangers living on your property?"

"Can't say. I've never thought about it, and these folks aren't actually strangers, except for Joseph, who Danny assures me is harmless."

She wasn't too surprised to hear he'd talked to Danny already. But when had he found the time? Perhaps Danny had managed to slip into town.

"I'm glad Danny lives so close, *Mamm*. He's a *gut* person, and he cares about what happens to you."

Her cheeks warmed, which was probably due to standing in the sun but might have been caused by the idea of Henry blessing her love life.

Did she have a love life?

Did she love Danny Eicher?

The question confused her more than the new group of people who had eaten lunch in her kitchen.

"We all want you to be happy. If you ever decided to remarry, we would understand."

"Marry?" The word caught in her throat, causing her to blush even more.

Henry bent and kissed her cheek, then he climbed into his buggy and promised to come by on Saturday with his wife and children. "I'll even stop by my *bruder*'s and encourage him to come as well."

Emma stood next to the garden, watching him drive away. He was a blessing, all of her children were, and she was grateful to have them close and willing to help.

The rest of the afternoon passed quickly.

Bishop Simon came by, but he stayed less than ten minutes. He told Nancy and Emma that Owen had agreed to go to Goshen.

"While you could go home, I'd feel more comfortable if you'd stay here for at least a week. We can see how Owen is doing and how best to proceed."

"How long will he be there?" Nancy's voice trembled slightly.

"That will depend on him. Technically he could check himself out anytime, which is why I'd rather you stay with Emma. But hopefully he will remain in the facility for the full month."

"Yes. I'll stay." Nancy moved a step closer to Emma.

Emma put her arm around her, glad she had agreed to forgo heading home. Nancy needed time to heal, and the children needed a safe spot. A sanctuary, as Mary Ann had said.

They worked in the garden again that afternoon. Jacob ran up and down the rows, pausing to look at a plant and ask what it was. Luke lay on a blanket next to Mary Ann's bench, staring up at the sky and playing with his toes. While Nancy and Emma sowed beets, lettuce, and radishes, Joseph and Danny built a new trellis to support the tomato plants. The old one had finally crumbled, and at the rate the plants were growing, they'd need the support from the wooden structure soon.

Danny didn't say much, but occasionally Emma

would feel his gaze on her. When she'd turn to look at him, he'd blink once and then return to his work.

She still didn't completely understand why he walked over to help them each afternoon. He'd told her once that it was easier to help with their garden than to grow his own. But he could have purchased what few vegetables one man needed.

He said something to Joseph she couldn't hear, and the boy's laughter mixed with the sound of the afternoon birds searching for worms and insects.

She didn't know when, or if, Joseph would return home. But her heart relished the fact that he no longer looked afraid or anxious.

When they'd finished, Emma invited Danny to dinner, but he declined. He started to say something, then shook his head, reached out and squeezed her arm, and walked away.

Which was strange behavior, even for Danny. It was as if there was something he needed to talk to her about, but he didn't know how. And when had Danny ever been at a loss for words?

Words were his tool and trade.

Emma walked into the house, pulled out the spaghetti casserole, and complimented Nancy's salad. But her thoughts were on the man walking through their garden, back toward his home.

CHAPTER 14

Danny walked back over to Emma's. It was early in the evening, but he worried, nonetheless, that he would be interrupting something.

He knocked on the back door and waited, his hands sweating as if he were a young man calling on a young girl for a date. This was far more serious than that, and he almost laughed at himself.

Emma didn't look surprised when she answered the door. Had some part of her, some part of her heart, been expecting him? Now that he stood on her stoop, hands in his pockets, and the evening breeze stirring the hair at the back of his neck, he wasn't sure what to do.

"Emma."

"Evening, Danny. Did you forget something?" When he didn't immediately answer, she added, "Would you like to come in?"

"*Nein*. I was wondering if you would like to take a walk with me. Maybe through the garden and toward the pond. The weather's *gut* and you wouldn't need more than a shawl."

Emma placed her hand to her throat, then glanced

back toward Mary Ann, who sat in the kitchen sorting beans at the old table. She waved Emma away. "I'm fine. I don't need babysitting."

Emma smiled at her feistiness and asked Danny to wait a minute. Hurrying across the kitchen, she found a dish towel and dried her hands. Then she kissed Mary Ann on the cheek. "I'll be back soon to help you to your bedroom."

"I can walk down the hall fine, Emma. You go and enjoy the stars."

Enjoy the stars.

Those words echoed in Danny's mind as Emma fetched her wrap and joined him outside.

The garden looked like a sacred place in the moonlight.

Emma smiled, then said, "It was a relief to see Jacob's joy as he ran up and down the paths. A young child should have a place to play, a safe place to discover the world."

"A place where healing blooms."

Stopping, Emma placed her hand on his shoulder. "What did you say?"

"Your garden—look at all the abundance and all the blooms, but perhaps its real purpose is to be a place where healing blooms."

"Maybe so." She removed her hand and continued walking.

The light southerly breeze brushed against Danny's skin as they made their way to the bench—Mary Ann's bench.

"How are the boys?"

"*Gut*. Nancy has them all settled in the room next to hers." Emma stared out across her land, toward Danny's pond.

The moonlight bounced off the water, and he found himself thinking of summer. For the first time since Ben's death, Emma seemed to relax completely. Danny thought that perhaps it was because of the idea of summer and warmer days, or possibly the boys upstairs and the one in the barn, or her *grandkinner*. He could picture them all fishing around the banks of the pond, surrounded by marsh marigold, yellow water iris, and brown-eyed Susan grown tall and thick.

Danny reached for her hand and laced his fingers with hers. She wasn't completely caught off guard, but that didn't stop the words he wanted to say from catching in his throat. So instead he raised her hand to his lips and kissed it. Her expression changed again— what seemed to him a river of joy tinged with a little fear.

She said nothing.

Fortunately Danny's tongue wasn't tied. "Do you think we're too old for courting, Emma?"

"Too old? *Nein*." She didn't pull her hand away, but she stared at it in the darkness.

"And are we too old to marry?"

"Danny Eicher! Are you asking me to marry you?" She jumped up from the bench and crossed her arms, but he saw that her hands were shaking. Was she amused or worried?

Danny honestly didn't know. He wasn't that good at understanding women. But he did know that this was the right time to say what was on his heart, what had been there for quite some time.

"If I did ask you, what would your answer be?"

. . .

"You've put the buggy in front of the horse and you know it."

His smile widened as he stood. "I care for you, Emma. You know I always have, since we were youngsters . . ."

"We were children, who had no idea what twists and turns life would take. You left, set off traveling, and I—I stayed here and raised a family."

Danny didn't answer.

Emma realized in that moment that Danny had learned some important lessons while he'd moved about. He'd learned that life wasn't a race, and he could afford to take his time. He'd learned where his home was. And he'd learned how to listen.

She walked to Mary Ann's rosebushes. The buds nearest her showed a hint of yellow. In another week or so the rose hedge would be a dazzling display of yellow, white, pink, and red, and the scent would be heavenly.

Danny stepped behind her. He didn't push, didn't say anything else. Instead he stood close and waited as she studied the roses.

"I loved Ben."

"I know you did."

"And I miss him still."

"I expect you always will. I miss him too. He was my *freind*, and I'm glad the Lord saw fit to bring me home before his passing. I'm glad we had those few months to become reacquainted again."

Turning, she nearly bumped into Danny, who had moved closer. He didn't back up, but put his hands on Emma's arms to steady her.

Slowly, he lowered his head and brushed his lips against hers. She let go then—of all her doubts and fears and regrets. She closed her eyes and allowed hope to seep into the empty places of her heart.

Clasping her hand, Danny turned them, and they began walking toward the pond.

"We could build the *Wilkumm Haus* there, on the southeast side of the pond."

"You've already named it?"

"With a porch across the front and side, so the folks can look out on the garden—"

"Or the pond," she whispered, catching his vision.

"It will be a *gut* place for those in need to come. A quiet place, and a haven of safety."

She stopped suddenly. "Is that why? Is the house why you're asking me to marry you? Because we can build it, we can help those in our community without—"

His lips brushed hers again. Then he tugged on her hand, pulling her toward the pond. "I asked you because of what's in my heart, Emma. What has always been in my heart. It seems *Gotte* had a plan for you and me, one where we care for each other and offer grace to those who need it most."

She shook her head in the darkness. How could God's plan include Ben's passing?

"He would want you to be happy. You know that Ben

would. And you would have wanted the same for him if you had gone first. It's not *gut* to be alone, and you do care for me. Don't you, Emma?"

"*Ya.*"

"Ben would want this, and your *mamm* wants us to use the money."

"Your land—"

"And your money—"

"It will take six months, maybe longer." Emma thought of Nancy and the boys and Joseph.

"To build the *haus*? *Nein.* The bishop has hinted around, promising me we would have help for whatever we decide to do. The families here know such a home would be a blessing to our community. Certainly we would be done before the heat of summer, before your *grandkinner* start appearing for their summer stays."

How had he known about their family plans? Perhaps he guessed. Perhaps she'd mentioned it and he remembered.

Emma knew then that Danny was someone who paid attention. Maybe it was a habit born in his writing and carried over into his personal life.

Her biggest worry about creating a safe place, a haven, tripped away into the night. She hadn't wanted to push her own children, or their children, out while she was helping others.

"If we wed, we'd live in my house?"

"I'll live wherever you want, Emma."

"But what of your house?"

"Young Moses Byler is marrying in a few months. He'd be happy to rent it while he works my land. Once he saves up a little, we can decide whether to offer it to him for purchase."

"Perfect." The word was as sweet as a lemon drop on her tongue. "It all sounds . . . perfect."

"Life is rarely that."

"But—"

"But it would be close, and what isn't perfect, we'll work on together."

From the direction of the barn, she heard Ben's horse whinny. The sound was like a blessing sweeping through the night. Sweeping over her heart.

They'd reached the pond and Shadow had joined them. He licked Emma's hand once, then pounced into the weeds in search of night critters.

Emma turned and studied Danny in the moonlight. The quiet, steady look in his eyes convinced her of what she was feeling, of all he promised, and of what God intended.

"Yes."

He seemed about to let out a holler. His eyes crinkled with the smile that spread across his face. He kissed her again, softly, tenderly, and then they turned and walked back toward her house, Shadow trotting by their side.

"You'll still help with the garden, right?"

"*Ya.*"

"Because you do seem to enjoy it, appearing every afternoon as you have."

"The hours weeding and trimming have been the highlight of my day, Emma. But I would have appeared in the barn if you were cleaning stalls. Each day I would wait as long as I could, and then when I could wait no longer, I'd come to see you. The time I spent here in your garden has been precious to me."

"We'll have plenty more."

"*Ya. Gotte* willing, we will."

With her free hand, she brushed the butterfly weed as they walked by, sending up a sweet, fragrant odor.

A place of healing, that was what *Mamm* had called it.

A place where healing blooms, that was what Danny had said.

Both seemed good descriptions to Emma. Sometime in the past year her heart had healed.

She thought of Joseph, sleeping in the barn. Perhaps he would grow comfortable enough with them to share his past. Perhaps with time and guidance and hard work, he would heal as well.

Then there were her guests, Nancy and the boys upstairs.

She heard Luke's cry through the upstairs window, and saw the shadow of Nancy moving to pick him up, then sitting in the rocker. It was the same rocker she'd used to comfort many a child.

Together, they made an odd sort of family, but perhaps it was a family God could use. One God could bless, and one that would endure through the seasons.

Perhaps together they could create a place where healing blooms.

Discussion Questions

1. Emma is struggling to find purpose for her life. She's content, but she also feels an emptiness because she's not needed in the way she once was. How do the people in her life convince her otherwise? What does Scripture say about our service to the Lord? (Read Colossians 3:23.)

2. We never learn the details of Joseph's history with his family. The author purposely left this out so that you could envision people in your community who need help. The bishop does make it plain that Joseph has not been physically abused. What specific things can we do to help those around us who are experiencing a harsh home life?

3. Mary Ann has kept her secret buried in the garden for many years until she felt the time was right to reveal the box. What are some reasons that we keep secrets, and how do we know the right time to reveal them?

4. At the beginning of the story, Emma suspects she is too old for romantic love. Read I Corinthians 13:4–18. What does the Bible say about love?

5. Gardens are a place of healing for many of us. Discuss the gardens in your life (past and present) and why they have been special to you.

ACKNOWLEDGMENTS

This book is dedicated to my husband's Uncle Joe. Though he is now legally blind, he still keeps a garden. He's the person to see when I need a cutting or have questions about why something isn't flourishing. His garden is a thing of beauty, and he is an inspiration to me.

Thanks also to my prereaders: Donna, Dorsey, and Kristy. You girls know I love you. Becky Philpott is a joy to work with and a fabulous editor. I'd also like to once again thank Mary Sue Seymour, who is a wonderful agent and a good friend.

I enjoyed this return visit to northern Indiana. If you're in the area, I encourage you to visit the quilt gardens in Middlebury, Goshen, Nappanee, Elkhart, and Shipshewana.

And finally . . . "always giving thanks to God the Father for everything, in the name of our Lord Jesus Christ" (Ephesians 5:20).

Blessings,
Vannetta

About the Authors

AMY CLIPSTON is the award-winning and bestselling author of the Amish Heirloom series and the Kauffman Amish Bakery series. She has sold more than one million books. Her novels have hit multiple bestseller lists including CBD, CBA, and ECPA. Amy holds a degree in communications from Virginia Wesleyan College and works full-time for the City of Charlotte, NC. Amy lives in North Carolina with her husband, mom, two sons, and three spoiled rotten cats.

Visit her online at amyclipston.com
Facebook: AmyClipstonBooks
Twitter: @AmyClipston
Instagram: amy_clipston

. . .

BETH WISEMAN is the award-winning and bestselling author of the Daughters of the Promise, Land of Canaan, and Amish Secrets series. While she is best known for her Amish novels, Beth has also written contemporary novels including *Need You Now*, *The House that Love Built*, and *The Promise*.

· · ·

VANNETTA CHAPMAN is author of the bestselling novel *A Simple Amish Christmas*. She has published over one hundred articles in Christian family magazines and received over two dozen awards from Romance Writers of America chapter groups. In 2012 she was awarded a Carol Award for *Falling to Pieces*. She discovered her love for the Amish while researching her grandfather's birthplace of Albion, Pennsylvania.

Visit Vannetta's website: www.vannettachapman.com
Twitter: @VannettaChapman
Facebook: VannettaChapmanBooks

Enjoy Amy Clipston's Amish Heirloom series!

Available in print and e-book.

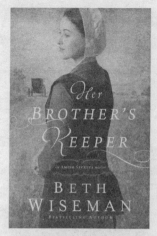